The Loudest Silence

New Edition

~ The Loudest Silence ~

The Loudest Silence

New Edition

by
Kai

Guaranteed Paper Publishing, Inc.

12138 Central Avenue
Suite #542
Mitchellville, MD 20721

The Loudest Silence – New Edition
Copyright © 2012 Guaranteed Paper Publishing, Inc.

ISBN 13: 978-0615737584
ISBN 10: 0615737587

The text of this book is set in Garamond and Garamond BE SwashItalic.

Printed in the United States of America

www.guaranteedpaperpublishing.com

~ New Edition ~

~ The Loudest Silence ~

Dedication

The things which hurt, teach
Love has hurt me deeply; she has been my most
perfect teacher

This book is dedicated to Love

For making the tumble so smooth
The fall so deep
The thrill so endless
The realization so stunning, but
The lesson so sharp
The pain so paralyzing
The recovery so unforeseen
The aftertaste so bittersweet
The next tumble, even deeper
The next thrill—even more delicious…

Thank you, Love, for teaching me
For hurting me so completely and restoring me so
thoroughly
For insuring that you always find me
And allow me to reside in you again

Acknowledgements

Special thanks to:

My beautiful children, I love you with every breath that I take. You already know that. Never give up on your dreams and on the special gifts God has deposited in each of you. We are spending your childhood nurturing your gifts, it will be up to you to protect and cherish them, and not abandon your calling. I pray you have the courage that it takes to stay true to yourself.

Tim, for always encouraging me and finding beauty in the invaluable gems that others overlook.

Cawana, for taking this journey back to publishing with me. I cannot express how much strength is gained from just having a sound listening ear. I am grateful.

Tea and Mirna, I can never thank you enough. To read this manuscript over and over, and tighten it more and more —it's an unbelievable task.

Darlene, for so bravely fighting for your idea of life and love. I get my strength from you. To a lifetime of no regrets. Our debts have already been paid by generations of women, this lifetime is ours to achieve.

Fellow authors and *bookstores* for your support of all my previous works written under numerous pen names and the acceptance you have shown me—my cup runneth over.

Finally, and most importantly, there are no words for the awe and humility that God's grace inspires within me. Knowing deep in my heart that He loves me; nothing and no one can keep me from Him.

…then you start dressing, and you start leaving, and I
start crying, and I start screaming, the heavy breathing,
but what's the reason.

…tired of letting passive aggression, control my mind,
capture my soul, okay, you're right, just let it go…

~ Nikki Minaj, Right Thru Me~

Prologue

"So this is how you are now, huh?" Sophie's voice was raspy. Cold.

Lani shifted uneasily in her chair and glanced just over her mother's head at the snack machines lining the wall. She could never meet Sophie's eyes, could never cope with the tiny reflection of herself in those steel gray pupils.

"I'm no different." Lani ran her hand along her arm, trying to ignore the goose bumps forming under her fingertips.

"Shit. You some kind of different." Sophie glanced around the room as she leaned forward on the wooden table. Her calloused hands made Lani want to cringe. She fought the urge to look at her own manicured hands. The softness of her hands, of her life, as compared to the struggle Sophie faced daily wasn't fair. But, it wasn't her fault.

"Look, Ma, I'm not going to stay long." Lani rested her fingers on the wooden table, and then snatched them up. The table looked filthy.

"You not gonna stay long?" Sophie shook her head, her long hair brushed back into a braided ponytail. The question in her voice was harsh. "Why the hell did you waste a visit if you wasn't gonna stay no time?"

Lani shrugged. "My visiting you is a waste, huh? Wish I had known that before now, I could have saved myself the trip."

"Lani, come the fuck on." Sophie slapped the table and pushed her thin body back in her seat. The sudden motion caught the attention of the prison guard at the front of the room. She raised her head. Sophie pursed her lips together and gave a subtle nod to indicate that she was under control. The guard rolled her eyes and looked away.

Sophie spoke through barely parted lips. "I only get two visits a week. You know that—shit I been locked up in this bitch since you was in grade school. You don't never come up here to see me. Then you finally show up and say you ain't staying long, looking pitiful. If you leave early, I don't get that time back. That only leaves me with one visit for the rest of the week."

"Ma—"

Sophie rolled her eyes as she continued. "Why you ain't bring Dee? Or my grandbabies? Since you ain't got shit to say, my daughter and her children woulda kept me company."

"Dee's your only daughter, huh?" The practiced properness of Lani's voice disappeared, her street accent returned. "You always poppin' that shit about 'your daughter Dee.' Like I don't exist. Like Dee don't carry no fault. Then you can't figure out why I don't bother to visit your ass."

The smile on Sophie's face gleamed like platinum. "Oh, so there is some color left in you, huh? I thought that bourgie ass college of yours had turned you completely stale."

"What do you want from me?" Lani's voice was soft again, strained against the lump forming in her throat.

"I want you to remember who you really are." Sophie drummed her nails against the table, her eyes scanning the room. "You see her...?"

Lani blinked, shocked by the shift in conversation. "Who?"

"Damn, don't turn your head." Sophie sighed as if Lani were the biggest idiot alive. "See the chick sitting there holding that baby girl's hand?"

Lani's eyes scanned the visiting room without moving her neck. "The one with the short red hair?"

Sophie nodded.

Lani observed the young woman about her age, who sat in the "inmate" chair three visiting tables over from them. Each table contained four seats, one for the inmate, three for the visitors. The "inmate chair" at the perfectly square table, was facing the armed guard. The prisoner Sophie referred to held onto the hand of a tall thin man who was holding a toddler. Her other hand was in the baby girl's hand. "Yeah, I see her."

"That's the one that went on the murdering spree a few years ago. You remember?"

"Hell no." Lani could care less. She averted her gaze and glanced back at the machines.

13

"You remember ...," the gossip was good to Sophie and she watched Lani's face as she spoke, searching for a hint of interest, "...the one that got stomped out at a summer cookout by some females over her man. Spent the summer hunting down each and every last one of them."

"Damn." Lani was impressed, even though she didn't want to be. "How many?"

"She got four of them before they finally caught her. Only caught a charge for one of them, I think. She's a conniving bitch." Sophie's voice held admiration.

"Who is he?" Lani glanced back, noticing how pretty the inmate's daughter was.

"That's the dude she killed all them females over."

Lani's stomach fell. "Stop playing." Lani snorted. "Why the hell would she even let him visit her?"

"Oh, they still together." Sophie shrugged like it wasn't anything out of the ordinary. "That's *her* man, didn't she make it clear?" Sophie laughed. "They transferred her here after she had the baby."

"A damn waste." Lani sat back with a frown and adjusted her sweater.

"You judging?" Just like that, Sophie was back to angry.

"I'm not Dee, Ma; I don't want to know the jailhouse gossip. I don't want to bump into people on the streets and have them remember me from visiting Sophie in the clink. I ain't tryin' to know her or her damn people or who had a baby from who that's got them locked up. I don't give a damn."

14

Sophie's shoulders sank. A couple of minutes lapsed while she looked at Lani and Lani watched the clock on the wall. "Why are you here?" Sophie said; she finally looked tired.

"I'm getting married. I thought you should know."

"Thoughtful, I guess." The sarcasm was heavy.

They sat in silence and listened to the never ending sound of popcorn popping in the microwave. The smell made Lani's stomach lurch.

"You marrying *him*?"

"Terrence, Ma. His name is Terrence."

"I know his fucking name." Sophie shook her head. "Why?"

"What kind of question is that? What do you mean, 'why'?"

"Why? You see what a man can do to you, Lani. You know how low they can make you go. Why in the hell would you marry this fool? Dee says he don't respect you or us."

"Who is us?"

"The family."

Lani shook her head. "Dee's word ain't gospel, Ma. And what is there to respect?"

"What?" Sophie shook her head. "Lani, that's not you." Sophie's voice didn't have an edge to it.

Lani looked up in surprise. Their eyes met. For the first time in years, Lani didn't look away.

Sophie pressed forward. "That's not the man for you. You are a jewel, baby girl. You need a man that respects that, not one that thinks you are lucky to have him."

"He doesn't think ..."

"No, Lani, hear me out. If he wants to marry you, then why isn't he here with you? Why haven't I met him at all? Are you embarrassed of me, or he don't want to come here?"

Lani didn't answer. The truth was a little of both, but she refused to admit that to Sophie.

"Dee said you come to the family stuff all alone, that he doesn't come to nothing. And, when he does come, Dee says he just sits there looking at ya'll like you're filthy. She says the rude bastard won't even eat the food she cooks."

"Dee says this and Dee says that ..."

Sophie covered Lani's hand in her own. Lani started to rip her hand away, her mother's touch felt foreign to her. She had avoided it for years. But Sophie held on. "Lani, listen, you can't erase who you are. And you shouldn't want to. You are perfect, baby girl, just the way you are. Who am I, what I have done, I had to do. I fought for my children—"

"No," Lani interrupted, "you didn't fight for us. You lost us. So busy being in the streets that your bullshit ruined it for all of us."

Sophie repeated herself with her eyes closed, her chin set with determination. "I fought for *you*. For my children's safety. And I don't have to apologize for that. You don't have to apologize for me, you or us. Don't marry a man who can't see you for who you are."

16

"He loves me." Lani hated that the weak admission had escaped her lips, that she somehow felt privileged that someone of Terrence Hall's caliber could love her. She had never said it out loud before, had never realized how it sounded from the tips of her lips.

"Baby girl, his love is irrelevant. Do you love you? Huh?"

Lani pulled her hands back and folded them neatly in her lap. She dropped her focus to the wooden table. Lani took a breath and repeated the words just as she had practiced them on the long drive from Virginia. "I'm marrying him. I just thought you should know."

"Well, you're not asking for my opinion and obviously don't give a damn about my blessing—"

"It's not like I have a father for that, do I?" Lani's sharp voice raked across the space between them. "So no, it's my decision—I am not asking for your opinion or your blessing."

"Then there is nothing left to say." Sophie nodded at the guard and waited for her escort to lead her from the table. She drummed her fingers on the table as she glanced around the room again.

"I guess there isn't," Lani said softly, the words muttered more for her benefit than Sophie's.

It took time for the guard to make her way to the table. Her obvious irritation at being beckoned by an inmate added to Lani's feeling of helplessness. Lani hated this place—hated the smell and the feel of it. The tears that Lani held back for years tumbled down her face. Sophie owed her more. She owed her a smile, a word of congratulations. She owed her a look of awe for having wiped away the stain of being an inmate's daughter who had transformed into someone worth being married by a person as elite as Terrence, as fine as Terrence, as sought after as Terrence. Sophie owed her some acknowledgement for having made something of herself despite Sophie having all but fucked up their lives.

Sophie owed her more.

"I swear to God …," Lani couldn't stop the thought as it took verbal form. "…I hate you." The whispered words passed Lani's lips on a breath, sounding more like a quiet hiss than weighted words of spite.

Sophie's eyes raked over Lani. She didn't even blink as the guard with the loaded shotgun stood in front her, ready to lead her from the room.

"That might be. It's no surprise to me." Sophie stood up and shrugged. "But you are me, whether you want to be or not. So the real question, Miss Wannabe Bourgie, is how long are you gonna hate yourself?"

Lani sat alone at the table, folded her arms across her chest and watched her mother walk with a slight limp until she passed through the heavy bars outlining her captivity. Sophie never bothered to look back.

Chapter One

"Wake up, baby." Terrence's warm breath brushed against Lani's neck.

Lani's dream drifted away as Terrence's hand pressed against her hip and his fingertips groped the softness of her bottom. She didn't want to wake up. In fact, annoyance danced around the edges of her brain like soft mist. Was it selfish to be tired of her husband? Tired of him yanking her out of much needed rest to satisfy his own needs? Even if it was selfish, Lani didn't care. In fact, it was her turn to be selfish; she deserved the bitter indulgence every now and then. After all, she just wanted to sleep.

Lani moaned softly in disgust as she rolled away. Maybe *he'll get the hint*, she thought. He didn't. The pressure of Terrence's hand increased, roaming her body with a slow intensity with his fingers splayed wide open. Somehow, he managed to turn her from her side to flat on her back, the palm of his hands pressing the soft bump of her belly as his fingertips grazing her nipples. Lani cracked her eyes. Terrence was staring at her, the look of raw hunger beamed from his light brown eyes with fierce intensity.

She fought the urge to roll her eyes and push him away.

Terrence smiled the smile of anticipation, of dirty dancing and intimate adult play. Lani pressed her lips together, fighting the frown that was taking over her lips. How could she make it clear to him that she didn't want to be bothered? She looked away from the devious smile, from the moist tongue that licked his round lips just before he planted them along the upper curve of her rib cage.

Lani's eyes glanced at the old fashioned alarm clock resting on her night stand. *3 am? He is waking me up at 3 am?* She squirmed under the pressure of his hands and the tickle of his tongue. Why couldn't he have started this sooner? Or better yet, waited until later? Lani had to work. She had to be up by 5:30 am to beat rush hour traffic and get to the office. As the Director of Human Resources, Lani didn't tolerate lateness and she had to set the example of being punctual. But, Terrence only thought about himself, only reached out to her when his urge overtook him. It was apparent to Lani that her needs were the last thing on Terrence's mind.

"Where have you been?" The words tumbled from Lani's lips, bouncing off the top of his curly hair as his mouth tongue stroked Lani's breast. Instead of answering, he sent a warm stream of air across her sensitive mound. A sharp jolt of sensitivity shot through her body and she whimpered as her back arched and her mouth fell open. Just like that, the anger at being awakened was fading as his touch overwhelmed her. Despite wanting resistance, Lani was slipping into the mindless comfort of erogenous pleasure.

Hello no. She wasn't giving in this easy.

"Terrence," Lani pushed him away. "Terrence, where have you been?"

"Downstairs." She could barely hear the words, spoken through teeth that clenched the side of her neck, as he nestled his body against hers and tenderly sucked the skin. Terrence ignored her push and raised himself up on his elbows—his broad chest hovered just inches over hers and his pelvis pressed against her. Terrence could work her into frenzy and cause her to explode just by playing with her breasts. Unfortunately, he knew it. "Where else would I be?" he breathed.

Lani opened her mouth to respond, but her thought was lost to the sudden explosion of feeling as he switched gears, caressing the back of her thigh while licking the curve of her hip. There was only one place he could be going when his mouth was this close to her explosive zone and, despite her frustration, just the anticipation of what was to come wiped her mind clear of all thoughts.

For several minutes she was lost in euphoria, as his tongue tickled her upper thigh and traced a hot path down her inner thigh to the back of her knee. He bit the back of her knee. Lani whimpered in delight. His thick fingers were back, resurfacing from the haze of sensation, massaging her inner petals.

"Look at me, baby." The command was quiet. But Terrence was in control now and Lani knew it. She hated that he had this power over her and abused it. He played her body like a fine instrument, stroking her into his unique tune, causing her to crescendo at his mere will.

Lani closed her eyes.

"Look at me."

She felt his thick erection pushing against her, sliding along her river. Lani clenched her eyes closed.

"I can make you look," Terrence was enjoying himself. "You know I know how." He still had her leg up in the air, was still massaging the back of her thigh while her ankle rested against his shoulder. "Lani..." He pushed; the gentle pressure forced his wide head into her tender space.

Lani's eyes flew wide open, her lips parted. Her hands grabbed his hips and pulled him into her.

They both groaned. For a second, they both closed their eyes.

Lani bit her lip. Terrence stroked slowly, his groans echoing across the room. Lani arched her back.

Terrence pulled out and kissed her ankle. "That's just a preview."

Pulling out was a mistake. Disappointment flooded Lani's mind and recalled her original thoughts of annoyance.

Selfish, Terrence, always so selfish. "Why?" Lani placed both hands around his perfect face and stared into his eyes.

"I want to feel you all night."

"No." Lani lowered her leg. Terrence caught her leg with one hand and lifted both her legs up to his shoulders. He smiled again, she didn't. "No, why were you still downstairs at 3 in the morning, Terrence?"

"Fell asleep." Terrence's fingers crept down the back of both her thighs and he kissed the inside of her knee. Terrence slowly slid two fingers into the folds of her love, lightly tickling her swollen button. She knew he sensed her hesitancy and wanted to quickly get her to the point of no return, where talk ended and deep lovemaking ensued.

But Lani couldn't let it go. She couldn't release herself when the deep seeded doubt tickled her mind. She wanted to say something, release the words that held captive her annoyance. But she couldn't do that either. His passion felt too intense as he submerged his long mass between the soft folds of her inner sanctum, lightly rubbing her tender inner lips.

Her complaints left, vanished as her back arched again in response to Terrence's unique rhythm and her neck curved to the heat of his tongue. While Terrence thrust into her, sparks shot up Lani's spine.

Lani couldn't stop him; she couldn't stop herself. Terrence was her man. Her husband. The sole target of her genuine attraction and never-ending desire. Disgust drowned her thoughts. This was the problem. She couldn't control herself with him. She couldn't find the power to leave him. *But I need to leave him.* The thought tore through their passion, ripping across Lani's mind like a jolt of electricity.

She wanted to fight this; she wanted him to tell the truth. Terrence needed to answer her question, to put into words the unspoken truth. Then they could stop the silly charade of marriage. Although pleasure made her shriek in unison to Terrence's every move, her anger never faded, it just rested on pause until their lovemaking was complete. Her issues remained unresolved, piling up into a huge mountain of pain and unforgiveness. And that mountain was beginning to topple, threatening to drown Lani.

"You feel so soft." Terrence pushed deeper, lifting her hips high. Consciousness disappeared. Lani rode the delectable wave of euphoria, diving deeply into orgasms pit, holding her breath as her body began to hum.

"Nothing can separate us." Terrence said. "Do you hear me? Nothing and no one." He stared into her eyes. Terrence paused, withdrawing the full length of him that had been submerged into his wife. "Lani, I love you."

The second withdrawal ended the seduction. The words were the catalyst that brought Lani's reality back into the haze of the night and destroyed their perfect distraction of lovemaking.

"Where were you, Terrence?" Lani pushed herself up and shifted her hips, closing her legs. "You weren't asleep." Terrence tried to re-submerge into his wife but she shifted again.

"I could have sworn I heard you talking," Lani pushed.

He stared at her, the genuine look of want dissipated. "Don't ruin this." Terrence's voice was tight. Annoyed.

A knife of anger tore through Lani. Anytime she questioned him, he denied the obvious truth.

"Ruin what Terrence? You getting your man?"

Terrence rocked back on his knees. He had the nerve to look insulted. He stared at her. Then a slow, sad smile crossed his face, as if she were pathetic. "Why did you have to go there?" he said.

"For the same reason you would wake me up at 3am to climb on top of me."

"So, now I can't get none?" Terrence said.

"Damn." Lani pushed herself to the other side of the bed. "Get off of me."

She pulled herself closer to the headboard as Terrence shook his head. The judgmental turn of his mouth pissed her off. She was not pathetic, nor was she the one causing problems.

"You don't touch me any other time. Nothing. No hug, no kiss. Nothing for weeks. Then you talk to Kenya until three in the morning and you want to come to me and release your sex."

Terrence's eyes widened in horror. "What the hell are you trying to say?"

His beautiful almond colored face contained an expression of disgust Lani had never seen before. To be fair, it was a statement she had never uttered before, although she had wanted to a hundred other times. Tonight was different. Here she lay, exhausted, turned on and throbbing, frustrated and anxious. The filter that sometimes guided her tongue had loosened again; it had been failing her lately. They argued more and more. But tonight she could care less about guarding her mouth and protecting his feelings.

"It is what it is," Lani said. She shifted, pulling her silk nightie back over her breasts, tugging the straps onto her shoulders.

"No." Terrence said. "You tell me what it is." He moved back from her and narrowed his eyes, as if daring her to give voice to the unspoken angst between them.

"I already said."

"Are you implying that I am sexing my sister? That I want to have sex with my sister?" The words seeped out of Terrence, as if simply saying them was a sin.

Lani sighed. She turned away from him and tucked her pillow under her head. "She is not your gotdamn sister. If she were, she would tell you to get your ass off the phone late at night and go spend time with your wife."

"She is a sister." Terrence's low voice sounded like thunder. "Kenya has always been a sister to me."

"Fuck Kenya!" Lani screamed and sat straight up, her fist banged against the headboard.

"What is wrong with you?" Terrence's fury filled the room. He jumped away from her. "What the hell are you screaming for?"

"You! You are what's wrong with me. 'Kenya wants this' and 'Kenya said that.' I don't want to hear her damn name anymore."

"So now I can't talk to my sister on the phone in my own gotdamn house."

"You are really going to sit there and fight with me over Kenya," Lani said. "You really don't see a problem with that."

Terrence sighed. He rubbed his large hand through the low sponge of curls. "Lani, I don't understand you. I never …"

Lani didn't want to hear it. Terrence never listened to her anyway, that much was obvious. She jumped out of the bed and tried to wrap the sheet around her waist, feeling the blood rushing to her head and filling her lungs. Lani had to leave the room. But she couldn't breathe. Lani paused, placed her hand on her chest to calm her emotions. This was how she felt in the last few months. The pressure seemed insurmountable and only a few words set her off, making her unable to cope. Terrence was killing her. Slowly, he was breaking down all of the barriers that held her in place that solidified her and made her golden.

"What the hell are you doing?" Terrence's voice broke into her mind as she tugged madly at the sheet caught on the bedpost and tore it.

Lani refused to respond. He walked to her side of the bed, hesitated and then stood in front of her as she turned in a circle trying to wrap the damn sheet around her body without falling. *Why can't I lay my head on his chest and lean into him for comfort? Why won't he listen to me, or even try to hear me?* There was a time when he did. Back when he loved her. She didn't believe that he still did.

How could she make him see that things between them were wrong, unfair and uneven? How did she let him know that she always felt sad and miserable, that his loyalty to Kenya confused her? Didn't she mean more than crawling in the bed and releasing himself into her? Was that all she was, while Kenya remained his backbone. Lani tugged again.

"Kenya ... damnit, Lani, what are you doing?"

The verbal slip stopped her; it extinguished the whirlwind of thoughts and the fog of confusion. *What the hell* am *I doing?* The question rebounded through her soul.

An answer exploded within her. "I am putting your shit out," Lani answered, her voice calm and serene. She dropped the sheet, but she tripped over it as she headed to his closet.

"Lani, come on. Calm down, I simply got your names confused. Because you just mentioned her and..."

Lani refused to answer as she neatly removed piles of clothes from the closet and laid them on the hallway floor.

"... Lani, come on. You're making a big deal outta—"

"No," Lani interrupted. "I am tired. I am tired of this."

"Then take your tired self to bed." Terrence chuckled as he tried to take the clothes out of her hand. "Stop throwing my stuff on the floor."

Lani released the clothes and stared at him. When the tears escaped the thin bravado she had in place, they poured from her eyes. She turned and left the room, seeking refuge in the guest bedroom.

Chapter Two

They hadn't spoken to each other in two days. Terrence watched Lani move around the bedroom, her eyes scanning the room as she checked for her wallet, searched for her car keys and rubbed lotion on her hands. Lani's face looked uncomfortable and pinched. The tension stuffing the room felt awkward as Lani looked at everything in sight, except him. Terrence sighed. These childish games that they so often played were whittling away at his patience like a mouse nibbling at cardboard. He was sick of it.

"Lani." He took a step toward her, his hand outstretched. Someone had to be the more mature one. And Terrence needed her today. The want for her quiet smile tore at his heart. There was no need to face the hostile world alone—that was why he had gotten married. Had he known it was going to be this ... he would have rethought his options. "Lani, enough already."

Lani turned her back and grabbed her pocket book.

Terrence shook his head. This is what she did— start an argument about nothing, get mad when it didn't work out the way she wanted, and then spend days pretending he wasn't there. So childish. Terrence headed to the bathroom and closed the door. Within the quiet sanctuary, he observed himself in the vanity mirror. It was time for a haircut; his soft hair grew quickly. He needed to shave, but could get away with the stubble for the day. There was no question, he was a handsome brother. The ladies never let him forget.

There wasn't a day that went by when some sexy woman didn't catch and hold his eye, or linger nearby too long, letting him know he could have whatever he wanted, whenever he wanted.

But he didn't want them. Terrence had his fill when he was younger and bouncing from woman to woman was as simple as changing underwear. That was for when he was childish. When he became a man, he wanted a woman to be the wind beneath his wings. And the only woman he longed for was Lani. His wife. His sweetheart. His sexy queen. When she wasn't pouting, arguing, ignoring and acting like a spoiled brat.

Terrence finished the Windsor knot on his striped Donald Trump tie and stepped back to appraise his ensemble. *Six feet of male perfection at her disposal and my wife wants to argue about nothing.* The thought made him shake his head. He stepped back into the bedroom and watched Lani's hips as she walked in a brown tight fitted skirt, her lean legs accented by sling back pumps.

"What time will you be home?" Terrence refused to let her walk around sulking another day. She was going to acknowledge him.

Lani shrugged, still refusing to look up.

"Lani, you hear me talking to you."

"I'll get home when I get home." Sarcasm dripped from her lips like word saliva.

"Damnit, Lani, how long is this going to go on?" As soon as the words were uttered, Terrence regretted them. He didn't want to beg her to talk to him. The question was a capitulation, a sign of weakness. Why was he groveling for Lani's attention anyway? He shouldn't have to. He didn't have to.

"You don't even get the point, do you?" Lani finally looked at him.

"Obviously not."

"All you think about is you."

Terrence rubbed his hand through his hair. Lani sounded like a broken record, one that he should consider throwing out. "If all I thought about was me, then I wouldn't have come to bed at all. I came to bed to be with you."

"It's not about that, Terrence."

"Then what the fuck is it about?" Terrence raised his voice and his arms.

Lani squared back, hand on one hip. "You are not going to yell at me. I know that much. I'll be damned if you stand up in here yelling at me—"

"I'm not yelling!" His explosive shout drowned out Lani's statement.

"Conversation over." Lani pushed past Terrence into the hallway. She kept talking as she walked away. "Make sure you move your things into the other bedroom so my mornings aren't interrupted by this bullshit."

"Maybe you should move your things to your special little room, and then I won't be in your way."

Terrence muttered, referring to Lani's small private office downstairs, which was her personal 'femme fatale' space.

"Whatever," she said, flinging the word over her shoulder.

He watched her run down the main staircase.

"I know one thing, tonight is the night we go through those bills." Terrence spat the words out. "You need to have yourself here."

She ignored him as her heels clicked across the marble foyer. Terrence held his breath as she slammed the front door.

Terrence wondered what would happen if he left her. If he took one of his coworkers up on their constant offers. If he couldn't get some from Lani and had to deal with all the anxiety, then he might as well sample some other honey.

No. That's not who he wanted to be. He had sworn himself to Lani, no matter what. And when things were good, they were damn good. Just a look, a whisper, a light laugh and he and Lani would lose themselves in each other for days at a time.

But it had been a longtime since that had happened. The constant uneasiness in his home was bothering him. Terrence needed a release, some type of escape.

He grabbed his suit jacket and briefcase and headed out the front door. The silver Infiniti gleamed at him and he smiled. She was a beauty. Terrence climbed into the car's smooth leather seat, slid the key into the ignition and pushed the button to start the car.

His cell phone rang. Terrence glanced at the time. Without looking at the caller ID, he answered.

"What up, Kenya?"

"Nothing. I fell asleep last night. Sorry."

"Whatever. You snored in my ear."

"No, I didn't," she laughed. "But thanks for staying up with me."

"Yeah yeah yeah. You know I'm looking out for you."

"I just couldn't sleep," Kenya continued. "And I didn't want to wake up Christopher."

"Or little Christopher," Terrence continued, speeding onto the 395 N into Washington, D.C. He was late to work. Not that it mattered, he was in charge of his schedule, but he liked to get to the office early to plan out his day. He was building a good career as the Marketing Vice President for Trianger Corporation. There was an ad campaign to pitch, an account to sew up. Today was a day for greatness, not lateness.

"Or little Christopher." Kenya paused. "So what are you doing today?"

"Same thing I do every day, baby girl. Trying to—"

"Take over the world," Kenya interrupted him, laughing. "Well, I'll talk to you tonight, after you are a day closer to that mission."

"Naw, check in at lunch," Terrence said. "In fact, I'll call you."

"Whatever. I won't hold my breath."

"See there. That's how you treat the brother that suffered for you, staying up all times of night and then having to pay for it." The statement was a direct reference to Lani. Kenya's silence verified that she got the hint, knew that he and Lani had another argument. He wondered whether she would say something. She never did.

"You're right," Kenya continued, her voice smooth as whipped butter. "I am sure I will wind up paying you back some way or another. But call me at lunch, Ok?"

Terrence nodded. Kenya didn't take the bait. He wondered when she would notice the strain her friendship had on his life. But then again, it wasn't her fault. Lani needed to grow up and understand the meaning of lifelong friendship.

"All right, babe." Terrence closed the cell phone and dropped it into his lap as he dodged in and out of traffic. Some small part of him, deep in the recesses of his brain, wondered how he could have such an easy conversation with Kenya after having days of hell with his wife. Wasn't it proof that Lani didn't really appreciate him? Not like Kenya, anyway.

Terrence turned on the radio station, hoping to catch Steve Harvey analyzing the Strawberry letter. Better to listen and laugh at the fools who sent in their problems then to think about his own.

***

Leaning over the table, Terrence picked up another statement. Argument or not, the bills had to get paid.

"It's not an issue of blame," Terrence muttered, his eyes scanning the bill. "You can't just run up the American Express. It has to be paid monthly."

"Don't you think I know that?" Lani sighed. "Who pays it every month? Damn sure not you."

Terrence bit his tongue. That was a low blow, a never ending reminder that she now made more money than him. "Lani, just stop using the American Express."

"You are not going to tell me how to use my money."

"Your money? Is that right?" Terrence stared at her. "When it was my money, I had no problem sharing it and you had no problem spending it. But now, it's your money."

"What do you want me to do, Terrence? Earn the money, but then turn it over to you to regulate how I spend it?"

"If you're going to waste money while we are trying to get out of the hole, then yes."

"How is buying clothes for myself a waste? And I didn't bust my ass to get to this level in life to have to answer to you."

Lani and Terrence stared at each other. Terrence slowly smoothed the wrinkles out of the folded paper and placed it on the table. "Two thousand four hundred and nineteen dollars this month on American Express. American Express, Lani. And you don't have one thing to show for it. A waste."

He saw her jaw flexing as she squinted at him. Terrence didn't care. It was time she dealt with reality.

It was their money, not hers, and she was wasting it. Without warning, the large mahogany chair flipped back as Lani jumped out of the seat. The chair banged so loud against the hardwood floor that Terrence thought it cracked.

"What the hell is wrong with you?" Terrence stared up at her for a second, wondering whether he should stand too. He studied the scowl on her face, her lips tight and eyebrows arched. Her eyes were so dark that they seemed empty. *Funny, I never noticed that until now.*

"I told you, I will get what I need to get." Lani's lip curled as she spoke in a low voice. It was a new approach. *Better than her shouting,* Terrence decided. And it displayed that inner ugliness that resided in her, which he sometimes forgot was there. It was still there, despite how he had tried to change her. Better her. It was good for him to remember.

She placed one hand on her hip. "You are not going to blame me for the current financial mess, since you quit your job without notice last year." She leaned over the table and lifted a pile of bills. "This is not all my fault. I carried us while you searched for yourself. Or did you forget?"

Lani slammed the papers on the table, the rush of air disrupting the mountain of papers that rested in front of Terrence.

He watched a few float to the floor. "Whatever, Lani. I am not doing this with you tonight." Terrence folded his arms and leaned back in the chair. "I'm working now. I'm making good money again. How many times can you throw that shit in my face? You need to grow up and sit down. I want to get through this."

"Grow up?" Her tone was sharp.

Terrence felt his heart stop. The words felt like bullets coming from her. *Damn. Here we go.*

"I know you, of all people, didn't just tell me to grow up. You're right. I should have grown up and realized what a selfish ass you can be."

At first Terrence stared at her, wondering why he didn't just leave her. It would be so easy. Everyone who knew them would understand. Then Terrence stared at the table, focused on blocking her verbal tirade. *I don't have to deal with this. I don't. I'm a good man. And I am sick of this.*

Lost in thought, he finally looked up when he noticed the silence. She was gone. *Peace. At last.* He hadn't heard anything she said. He knew that if he ignored her she would go away. She always did.

"Damn bitch." Regret filled him as the words tumbled from his tongue. *What kind of man calls his own wife a bitch?* Shaking his head, he leaned down, picked up more papers, straightened the table and returned the chair. He refused to get sucked into this anger game with her. *Always some drama with her immature ass.*

Leaning over the table, he picked up another bill. It was easier to balance the budget without her. Terrence plugged away for a few minutes, but, disgusted at their financial state, he gave up and stretched his legs instead.

Hunger tapped at him. Lani hadn't bothered to cook. Again. Terrence wondered into the mammoth kitchen and opened the cabinets one by one. Somewhere upstairs a door slammed and then he heard stomping, followed by the sound of furniture dragging across the floor.

$865,000 for a house that she tears up every time she has a tantrum. Why in the hell is she moving furniture?

The sudden urge to run upstairs, pick her up, and throw her out invaded him. Terrence placed his hands flat on the marble countertop and bowed his head. He had to calm down. He had to stop thinking about Lani. He took three deep breaths while he stared at the back staircase and convinced himself not to act on impulse.

Terrence grabbed a bag of chips and some soda. He trudged into the two story family room, with its cathedral ceilings and balcony overlooking the upstairs hallway. Each step felt heavy and obligated. He sat the goods on the large wooden coffee table and then sank back into the soft brown leather. This was his furniture, paid in full. It felt good to be in his space without interruption, without all the tension. If Terrence could, he would stretch out and sleep right there. He twisted the soda open, leaned his head back, and let the cool liquid pour down his throat. Peace, if only for a little while.

Out of the corner of his eye, a flash of brown startled him. He jerked his head up, just in time to see a brown missile flying through the air. Terrence jerked back, covering his head with his arms. Soda spilled all over him and the couch. The brown bomb exploded on the floor, an inch from where his ankle had been. Shaving cream, aftershave, razor, cotton balls, and nail clippers lay across the floor. His toiletry kit.

What the...? Terrence bit his lip and clenched his fists. He wanted to scream, but refused to give her the satisfaction. How far was she willing to push?

"Keep your shit in your room." Lani's voice sounded calm. Satisfied. It infuriated him. He didn't look up. She turned on her heel and stomped back into the master suite.

Terrence put the soda bottle down. His movements were slow and deliberate, fighting the sea storm brewing inside of him. He rubbed his face with the palm of his hands. Between stretched fingers he eyed the liquid that oozed over the floor.

Be cool, man. Just be cool.

Terrence stripped off his wet shirt and wiped the soda off the couch. Sliding over to a dry spot, he leaned back and pressed the remote. Finding a show, he became absorbed. The stomps and door slams faded to oblivion.

A couple of hours later, he tore himself from his television trance. The house was quiet. Finally. Terrence drifted to the guest suite, his new residence. He threw his stained shirt on the floor and stared at himself in the wall mirror. It was time to get back in shape. He wanted to tighten up his abs and make sure his six-pack showed. Summer was coming and he wanted to look right. The women would surely notice. Kenya came to mind. Speaker phone, instant direct dial. Instead of hearing a ring, Kenya's voice filled the room. Terrence felt himself relax.

"I was just calling you," answered Kenya.

"What's up?"

"You tell me." Terrence could hear the smile in Kenya's voice.

"Absolutely nada," Terrence heard muffled moans floating through his house, then a soft cry. Let Lani cry. Her ass deserved whatever she was feeling.

"Hold on," Kenya whispered. There was a deliberate pause. A different cry filled the line—loud and frustrated. "I woke the baby. Let me go check, so I can try to put him right back to sleep."

"Yeah, alright." He felt disappointed, then confused at the emotion. He was a married man and she was simply a friend. Why should he care that she had to get off the phone? He shouldn't. He didn't.

"Oh yeah," Kenya's breathing was uneven as he listened to her move with the phone. "Christopher said to tell you that the game is on for this weekend. Ya'll want the tickets?"

"Uhm, yeah." *Hell no.* The last thing he wanted to do was go to a three hour game with Lani. "Tell him we'll be there."

"All right, I'll talk to you later." Kenya hesitated. "Wait a minute. Are you ok?"

This was why Lani couldn't stand Kenya and complained that she was in their business. She was in tune with him more than Lani ever could be.

"Of course. You better go handle that crying baby."

"You sure?"

"I'll call tomorrow. Promise." Terrence made his voice sound light.

"Yeah. Do that." Her voice sounded tight, suspecting. But she didn't ask.

After they hung up Terrence laid there an extra second. The truth was that he didn't want to put the phone down. Light breathing filled his ear, followed by muffled air. The phone clicked and then he heard silence.

Terrence felt his stomach drop. *Come on, I know she wasn't listening with the mute button pressed.*

A few seconds later the sound of Lani's sobs drifted through the air.

Chapter Three

Terrence lay on the sleigh bed with his arms stretched out. He didn't know what to do. Lani's sobs drifted through the house, sounding so weak and frail. Something in him wanted to reach out to comfort her, assure his wife that he only loved her.

But it had been so long ago when that was true. Now, saying it would just be smearing words across vast emptiness. Yeah, he loved her, in an obligatory sort of way. She was his wife and he had a responsibility to her; Terrence knew that even when he didn't want to acknowledge it. But her tears did not stir up any genuine emotion, only a desire to do what was right, be what was right. He was tired of operating by this silent code of conduct.

Her sobs subsided, replaced by muffled crying until she finally fell silent. But the silence grew thick with tension and blame carried through the air. He could sense it. *She is expecting me to explain myself. I won't.*

Terrence waited. Listened to the silence and waited. He recalled his conversation with Kenya, easy and relaxed. He enjoyed her company. But, it wasn't exclusive to Kenya. He enjoyed black women who weren't stock full of cynicism, critical at every turn.

Kenya's childhood had been easier than Lani's, but so what? Lani needed to get over it.

The silence became deafening, roaring with animosity. Terrence leapt off the bed; he wasn't going to stay up the entire night, sleeping with one eye open to avoid an Al Green moment. Lani might go too far. It was time to make his escape.

He slid into large sweat pants and threw a T-shirt over his narrow frame. Terrence scanned the room for his keys while he stepped into his sneakers. For the life of him, he couldn't remember where he had put them. Maybe they were downstairs in the kitchen. He rounded the corner of the suite and headed for the stairs. Lani stood just outside of the door. Terrence almost walked right into her. Terrence stumbled. His heart felt like it was kicking in his rib cage. It shocked him that she was just standing there, lingering so near without being detected. Terrence thought he knew her sounds and could tell her location in the house at any given moment.

They stared at each other in silence. Terrence straightened his back. He coughed. Lani squinted. She appeared so small and helpless now. He didn't want to, but his eyes surveyed the sexy landscape of her body, admiring the crème lingerie and the matching robe that hung open. Her long hair was parted at the center and pulled back into a ponytail. She was still beautiful. Terrence couldn't deny it.

But he knew he had better harden his heart. He wasn't going down that easy. No telling what she would open her mouth and say, insults could pour from her like liquid hate. The sexy lingerie thing had tripped him up before and led to more heartache than he'd ever imagined possible.

"Where are you going?" she whispered, her voice trembling.

Those timid words brought understanding. Terrence fought the urge to snort. So a call to Kenya and Lani thought he was going to get his freak on. *So this is what it takes for her to expose some weakness, to be human, instead of a damned superwoman, ruling every aspect of our lives.*

"I need some air," Terrence fidgeted.

"Can we talk?" Her voice trembled.

Terrence didn't want to talk; he had done enough talking, begging, and pleading to last a lifetime. He felt like a punk, always running around trying to please her. The more sacrifices he made, the more she took. And what did he get in return? A cooked dinner, a kind word? No. Just more complaints, more insults.

He recalled years of reaching to hug her while she pulled away. Trying to kiss her while she protested. The truth was she should be worried about him cheating, since she never wanted to give him any. Sex was just another chore, something she rolled over and submitted to, which made him feel dirty and unwanted. Like taking something and violating her. He would lay in the dark, trying to purge the feeling of an unwanted aggressor and he began to hate her because of it.

"Naw, I don't want to talk." Terrence moved toward the back staircase.

"Please, please!" Lani shrieked as she rushed forward to block the steps.

"Lani, don't." He pushed past her and trotted down the stairs.

"What is wrong? Why ... what is happening? Do you hate me?"

The sincerity in Lani's voice scared him. It was a side she never revealed. Not hardcore street girl Lani. Terrence recalled how much he initially loved her spark. But he had grown up around southern girls, who liked to tease their men with flirtatious smiles and loving tones, not bark commands at them like trained puppies. That was not Lani.

"Lani, I am not doing this with you tonight. I said that before."

"Terrence, please." She followed him down the stairs. "Please, talk to me."

His eyes darted around the family room. *Where are those damn keys?* He wasn't going to look at her or acknowledge her. He was leaving.

"You are driving me crazy!" Her screams echoed through the large house. "Look at me. Why won't you even look at me?"

The keys were on the mantel. He just had to get to the mantel and then make his way out of the house. The woman had clearly lost her mind, screaming like a maniac.

"Terrence, what are you doing to me?" Lani sobbed, falling to her knees. "Don't you feel anything for me? Anything? I just don't ...," the words faded as she collapsed into gut wrenching moans, slumping into the side of the couch.

It occurred to him that she might do something crazy. The last thing he wanted was the house to burn down, or her to try some suicide. She was clearly losing her mind and he didn't know what to do. *If I stay, she might hurt me instead. Nope, I better leave.* She was only acting out because she was jealous of Kenya anyway. She would get over it. He made his way to the back door.

"Terrence." Lani's voice sounded husky.

His name rolled off her tongue, the way she used to say it with love on her heart. Way back in the day, during undergrad, after they made love and she would rub oil on his scalp and softly call his name. Over and over again. He stopped, stood still and waited for what seemed an eternity.

"Terrence, don't you still love me?"

"Lani, I can't do this anymore."

Terrence walked out the garage door without looking back.

Chapter Four

Kenya sat there holding the phone and staring off into space. She was Terrence's friend, after all. Hadn't that always been clear? She held no obligation to Lani; the lines were drawn long ago. Kenya remembered when Lani's name first invaded her sphere, tapping through her social networking and invading her territory without proper notice. And she had always thought Lani was tacky, at best.

To this day, Kenya still didn't understand how such a hood rat had lured her friend. Terrence was the golden one; the man to land. In college, many girls befriended Kenya just to get next to Terrence. She hated to admit that their "relationship" alone catapulted her into the "somebody" category. He made her popular. It was simple popularity based on a friendship formed by proximity. Fair or not, Kenya took advantage of it.

It must have been ordained, or written in the stars that she and Terrence would forever be in each other's lives. They had grown up the only two black kids in their exclusive Potomac, MD community. Back then, anyway. Black folks were doing well now and there were more families in the exclusive suburb now. But she and Terrence hadn't experienced that luxury—she was always aware that her hair didn't swing around like the little white girls, that her darker skin separated her, somehow, from the others. To preserve her sense of heritage, her parents had formed a bond with Terrence's family—a tight unit to protect them from alienation. They kept them together in every way. School, social clubs, tennis, gymnastics. Church. In every childhood memory, Terrence lingered somewhere in the background. He was home.

The three of them, both mothers and Kenya, imagined wedding bells years ago. Of course Kenya and Terrence should end up together, who else would be a perfect fit? Kenya had never questioned it. When they were both accepted to the "Home by the Sea," Kenya believed that their fate was carved into stone. During high school and even the first year of college, they both dated other people and played in the real world. But in the back of her mind, she and Terrence were reserved for one another, once playtime was over.

Kenya would never forget the day everything changed. Terrence came by the dorm to pick her up. His eyes glowed, despite having bags around them. He hadn't slept. He claimed that he needed to talk. It was their junior year in college. Kenya hadn't seen him that often lately; she was so busy with her social life and commitments. But his sudden intensity surprised her.

"What's up?" she asked, hugging him and gently caressing his cheek with the back of her hand.

Terrence stared at her and remained silent for a moment. When he finally spoke his voice cracked. "I don't know, really. What do you know about Lani?"

Her heart skipped a bit, like it always did when he mentioned other girls. She bit her tongue and put on her nonchalant face. *I just have to bide my time*, she reminded herself.

"Not much." Kenya didn't gossip. She found it distasteful.

"I ... I can't get enough," he continued, a dam of emotion breaking as he waved his arms wildly in the air. "I think she is so damn fine."

Kenya just nodded, taking a stab in the heart with each word. "Does she know?" Kenya tried to ignore the awkward pause.

"I just spent the weekend with her. I am sure she knows," he chuckled, and Kenya shifted, feeling uncomfortable. It was the chuckle that let her know they had made love during the weekend. While she had gone to the salon, studied in the library and attended a stupid Student Union meeting, Terrence had been making love to Lani. Kenya fought back the urge to vomit.

"I needed to tell you. Best friends keep it real, right? I don't want many people knowing, other guys will try to get with her and my exes might give her a hard time, you know?"

Yeah, she knew. His ass was just that fine. Other females would torture Lani if they knew. Lani did not have the social clout to be with Terrence on any level. Deep seeded hate surged through Kenya at that moment. He was protecting Lani. Guarding her. Lani didn't deserve him. She had no idea what being with Terrence would mean, what dues had already been paid to love Terrence for a lifetime. Kenya bit her tongue and kept her turmoil to herself.

But that had been years ago. Even now, Lani endured none stop speculation and rudeness. Kenya didn't participate in it, not directly. She didn't want anything repeated to Lani that would force Terrence to make a choice or push her away.

Yet, here she sat, cradling the telephone and contemplating Terrence's latest request. Terrence, once again, consumed her thoughts. She had married an acceptable man. After Terrence made Lani his queen, Kenya found Christopher, someone who possessed all the required credentials to justify his marriage to a legitimate Black American Princess. And Kenya loved Christopher in a slow easy way. But her heart still raced at the thought of Terrence. In the deepest recesses of her mind, during moments of heartbreaking honesty, she still believed him to be hers. But she accepted her fate and sealed the deal when she gave birth to little Christopher. Her family was formed and settled into a suburban existence that felt comfortable. Despite her love for Terrence, she would never do anything to ruin little Christopher's world.

"Can't you meet me, just for a few minutes? I need to talk," Terrence had whispered into the phone, oblivious that it was the dead of night and she had a young baby. Oblivious to the fact that her husband would hit the roof at the thought of her leaving the house to be with Terrence, again.

Damn him for calling and rocking my world. Kenya would do anything Terrence asked and he knew it. She didn't owe Lani a damn thing and she wouldn't think about Christopher, not yet. Kenya reasoned that she was just going to meet a friend; there was nothing wrong with that.

She slowly returned the telephone to the narrow base. Getting dressed,

Kenya glanced at the small newborn resting in the cradle, his tiny hands drawn together in tight fists. *Nothing to ruin his world ... remember, nothing to ruin his world.* Kenya walked out of the bedroom, refusing to look at her own reflection in the full-length mirror.

Chapter Five

Christopher leaned over the edge of the kitchen island as he prepared a late night snack. The sports analysts were going to preview this week's college games and Christopher didn't want to miss a moment. He wondered whether Kenya was hungry because she hadn't eaten anything earlier. He had noticed that she seemed consumed with losing the baby fat, but he still wanted her healthy. Starvation wasn't going to help, especially while she was nursing.

Christopher thought that Kenya made too much of an issue about the extra pounds she was carrying. Kenya had been gorgeous when she was pregnant. Her smooth complexion had a natural glow and her hair had grown thick and healthy. To him, she had always been beautiful, a classic beauty like the women found in Essence magazine. Everything about Kenya always felt classic, simple haircut, basic colors and simple jewelry. Simple yet elegant, that was his Kenya.

And Christopher had enjoyed every single second of her pregnancy, from her plump waist to her expanded breasts. He touched her all the time, amazed by how curvy and round she felt and how much it stimulated him, made him want to make love to her. Much more than ever before. He had marveled daily that his seed grew inside the remarkable woman he had been blessed to marry.

The thought of Kenya, his son, their small home and his comfortable life, pleased him. Christopher started humming Usher's "There Goes My Baby." No regrets, that's what his father had told him. Live life with no regrets. Christopher was managing to do just that, despite life's disappointments. Every now and then he imagined himself holding a football, running into the end zone before thousands of adoring fans. Truth be told, Christopher had never thought he could recover from the sudden end to his football career. There had been nothing that mattered more. Without football, he had felt vacant.

Now, ten years later, life was more than he ever thought it could be. UVA had been good to him; he completed his degree and used his contacts to stay in the field. Now he was a sports trainer working with professional athletes and area athletic wear companies. One of the few that were able to still be involved with the sport, but not jaded by it. He was still able to be a fan without carrying the pressure of publicity on his shoulders.

There was nothing in his life to complain about.

The soft ring of Kenya's cell phone distracted Christopher. He listened. She answered. *Probably Terrence*, Christopher thought, shaking his head. The boy hung onto Kenya like Little Christopher. Christopher didn't mind, he had no reason to. Who was he to come between lifelong friends? When they first met, he most certainly kept an eye on Terrence. Kenya was worth sizing up and destroying the competition, if need be. But Terrence wasn't interested in anything but that hot *senorita* he married. Lani was *bad*, in that way only men understood. She oozed sexuality. The kind of woman a man could date and enjoy his every fantasy with, but definitely didn't tie down as his woman. Who would want to be with the finest woman in the room? Who wanted to deal with the pressure of making sure that she didn't respond to the constant barrage of attempts to claim her?

It was the kind of thing that made Christopher remain at ease around Terrence. Terrence's decision making was suspect. Close to a million dollars on a house when he and his wife barely brought in two hundred thousand dollars annually? Christopher shook his head. When their mansion was being built he had to lend Terrence money to cover unexpected expenses, just so he wouldn't lose face in front of Lani. Both Terrence and Lani drove high maintenance cars and wore designer labels, but Christopher was willing to bet money that they didn't have a penny saved.

Christopher chuckled a little. His family lived in a smaller house, but he was setting his wife and son up for life. With smart investments and frugal spending, Kenya would never want for anything. He was going to take care of his baby; she was the crown jewel of his throne.

He liked Terrence, foolish though he was. He watched Kenya talk to him, counsel him, and understood that she cared about her friend. He figured she knew Terrence was childish, but he never discussed it with her. Christopher hoped Terrence didn't bring Lani to the football game, though. Lately, Lani just sat around moping. She and Kenya had given up trying to be friends a long time ago, so it always turned into a three way party, with Lani keeping to herself. Terrence never even tried to include her. Christopher thought about helping her fit in, but then decided to keep out of it; she was another man's wife, and, fine as she was, he didn't want to get involved.

He sliced the chicken salad sandwich in half and poured some chips onto the large platter. He had used his sister Jackie's recipe for the homemade chicken salad. Smiling, he slid the spoon in his mouth, pleased with another culinary masterpiece. This recipe was going in his list of favorites, there was no doubt.

Kenya rushed past him in a jogging suit, heading toward the door.

Terrence swallowed the mouthful of food. "What's up?" She never just up and left. Something bad must have happened.

"Got to get some formula," Kenya mumbled, throwing her purse over her shoulder.

"What? You're breastfeeding." He cut the second sandwich in half. "You want lettuce and tomato?"

"No, I'll be right back."

"Can't it wait until tomorrow?" Christopher put his knife down.

"No, I want to start supplementing. I have to get little Christopher weaned before I go back to work."

Christopher looked down at his plate. He had been meaning to talk to her about that. There was no need for her to go back to work; she could focus on raising little Christopher. He wasn't turning over his tiny baby to a stranger. Not yet, anyway. But, he would hold off on that discussion until later.

"It's late; not safe for you to be running around by yourself."

"I'll be alright. Promise. Just want some fresh air."

Christopher paused, surveying her. Terrence had his wife upset. Must have been him on the cell. No telling what he had done now. Christopher wasn't going to add to her stress.

"Alright, baby, be careful." He took a couple of steps forward to give her their standard departing forehead kiss, but she disappeared into the garage before he made it to the back door.

Chapter Six

What am I doing? Sitting in this car in the middle of the parking lot. Looking like a woman trying to creep. *Damn, Terrence, where are you?* Kenya turned off the engine, biting on her thumb nail. This was crazy. How far was she willing to go? She had nothing to worry about. She was only here to talk, anyway. She thought of the beautiful baby sleeping in the cradle and her gentle husband bopping around the kitchen island, humming to himself. Kenya was a lucky woman and she wasn't going to ruin it.

Terrence's silver Infiniti turned slowly into the parking lot and Kenya's heart did the same little jump it always gave at the sight of him. He pulled up next to her. She tried to look annoyed. It didn't work. He rolled down the window. Low cut thick curls revealed cinnamon brown skin, flawlessly spread over his angular face.

Kenya bit her lip.

She hadn't seen him since just after the baby had been born, and had been was so caught up in little Christopher that she had almost forgotten the effect he had on her. The sight of him took every woman's breath away. He seemed so smooth and masculine in the expensive car, making Christopher seem frumpy and cheap in comparison. Christopher's mid size car didn't compare.

Stop it. Kenya shook her head; a small taste of guilt skirted the edges of her mouth. Christopher could have this, or any other top of the line car, but he made a choice to sacrifice for her and their family. Still, in the presence of masculine beauty, logic faded and Kenya found all reason disappearing.

The perfect face broke into an easy smile. "What's up, girl?"

Kenya smiled, despite herself. "What's up with you is the question, right?"

Terrence nodded and Kenya heard his doors unlock. "Get in, I'll drive."

Kenya did as she was instructed and didn't ask where they were going. She leaned her head back on the head rest and allowed herself to sink into the soft interior, Kenya inhaled deeply. She loved the way he smelled. Terrence put his hand on her knee. "Thanks for coming out. Was Christopher pissed?"

"No," she paused, to emphasize the point. "But he will be if he ever finds out."

Terrence glanced at her for a moment, curiosity evident in his eyes. Then he nodded and pulled off. They rode in silence. Kenya felt keenly aware of the time. She only had another ten minutes before her cell would ring. Christopher kept watch on the time when she was out. He hated for her to be out late at night by herself. Sometimes his caring was suffocating.

"How long will we be?" Kenya's voice was soft.

Terrence shrugged.

Kenya shifted in the seat and turned toward him. She needed an answer. "Terrence," she began, but fell silent when she noticed the strain in his eyes. His forehead was creased and his smooth jaw line flexed over and over again. That's when she noticed the raggedy t-shirt and jogging pants.

Kenya reached out. She rested her hand on his forearm. The light touch seemed to startle him. He jumped a little, glanced at her and sighed. With the deep exhale he seemed to relax.

"Where are you?" Kenya touched his forehead.

"My mind is overflowing. I'm thinking crazy shit."

Kenya sat in silence. Her bag vibrated. *Christopher.* She ignored the buzzing and pushed the bag from her lap to the floor. Terrence breathed. Kenya smelled mint on his breath. She wondered what his mouth tasted like. He pulled the car over to the side of the street. Not sure what she had been expecting, Kenya felt her heart fall a little bit. She had definitely hoped for something more than the side of the road.

"I am leaving Lani." He turned off the engine.

"What?"

"There is no reason to stay. I've thought about it, over and over. For what? It's just nonstop bullshit. Hell, I mean..."

A glimmer of hope stirred deep within Kenya. Startled, she became embarrassed. She didn't think of herself as the type of person who waited in the wings until an opportunity presented itself, but, damn, look at this man. His mouth moving, hands clenched, body solid and masculine. Did she stand a chance? She noticed he had stop talking and was waiting for her response.

"What did you say?"

"You know Lani. You know what I am up against. What do you think?"

Kenya swallowed. Here was the opportunity. Damn being the good girl and the righteous woman, that's how she missed him the first time. Could she have him now? She lowered her head. She was going to say it. *Leave that tacky little hood rat.* It was long overdue. She should have said it years ago.

The words were just about to tumble from her tongue when her bag vibrated again, rubbing against her ankle. The sudden movement shocked her. It jump started her mind. The phone buzzed angrily and she could hear it in her soul. Kenya's mind's eye saw Christopher, frantic on the other end, wondering why she didn't answer. She knew that he was pacing and glancing at the clock. What about Christopher, her life, little Christopher? Little Christopher. Her pulse quickened. The tiny baby whose entire stability rested on her and Christopher. Kenya and Christopher. The family unit.

"I think you should go home to your wife, Terrence."

The words were thick, forced out past her screaming heart, which ached at the denial of this second opportunity. But she would not do anything to ruin little Christopher's world.

Chapter Seven

Christopher sat still on the couch and stared at the television, his eyes unseeing. His cell phone lay on the coffee table next to the half eaten sandwich. He knew Kenya was alright. She had to be. Still, why wasn't she picking up the phone?

He stood up, sat down and then stood up again. Another girl—young, thin and adorable—filled his mind. Christopher grabbed his head, kneeled forward. He wasn't going to think about her. Hadn't thought about her in years. But fear always brought him back to that place in time.

Her round big black eyes always smiled at him. She wore her hair in a short cropped cut, Halle Berry style. All the girls had chopped their hair off after seeing Halle sport the look, but his girl was one of the few that could wear it well.

"Alayna." Her name eased past his lips, seeped out of him like a gentle breeze. He rarely spoke her name out loud—he tried to keep her so close to his essence that he didn't want any part of her, of her memory, to escape him. She was the first one. His first real one. It was love, deeper that anything he had ever felt—even even now if he wanted to be real. Kenya was his life, but it was more practical, more careful, thought out

61

and planned. Kenya was a decision. With Alayna, he had no choice.

She was intoxicating. He remembered how he stared at her like a lost puppy when he spotted her at cheerleading tryouts, while he ran laps around the track. When she smiled he tripped all over himself. A goofy freshman. Alayna had laughed, keeping her eyes on him, and the laugh caused chills to ripple up and down his spine. The sound made him want to hear her for the rest of his life.

Within a week, she was his. They were a couple the entire first semester. As the freshman football superstar, he had girls coming at him from every direction, but he didn't cheat. Actually he never even considered it. Only the sight of Alayna could make his heart stop. And their lovemaking so deep and intimate that it initially scared him. But then he became addicted to it. To her. They were one.

Christopher remembered how, after the holiday break, he had begged her not to ride with a couple of other cheerleaders to a school party. It was late and they had all been drinking. He knew they weren't going to be careful driving his girl and that they couldn't know that her life was worth more to him than the air he breathed. Christopher had begged her, but he had still been young. A boy trying to be a man, Christopher had let his pride get in the way. Instead of telling her about his reliable instinct, about his deep seeded fear that something bad was on the horizon, he argued—issued ultimatums and threats, taunting her so she would stay. Instead, Alayna had walked. It was the only time she ever looked at him with hurt in her eyes before quietly closing the door.

Christopher never saw her again. The funeral was closed casket. No one knew what happened. No survivors, just a demolished vehicle and three young undergraduate girls' dead, without explanation.

Christopher picked up the cell phone again. He didn't want to go hard, but if Kenya forced him, he would call On Star. He was giving her ass another ten minutes. She hadn't seen his possessive side, he had tried to control it, but she was making him relive events that were hidden in his core. The mother of his child should know better than run out in the middle of the damn night anyway.

The phone rang and rang until he threw it across the room against the fireplace. Headlights at the end of the driveway flooded the room for a second before pulling into the drive. *Thank God.* He stood still, trying to regain his composure. He was overreacting and he knew it. Christopher walked to the front door, intent on escorting his queen into their home.

Christopher swung the door opened and spotted the silver BMW. Definitely not Kenya. The driver's door opened and a woman climbed out of the car. Her movements were slow. Wary. She wore a crème hooded cape, the hood hanging so low that he could barely make out her face. Christopher moved further onto the wrap-around porch, closer to the drive.

The car chime rang, its annoying bell warned that the door was open. He could hear the automated voice, instructing her that the door was ajar. Christopher squinted, wondering who she was. In a swift motion the woman swiftly pulled back the hood, running both manicured hands over her hair.

Lani.

"I'm sorry to bother you Chris, I really am." Her voice was soft and ... sad. Lani was the only person who called him Chris. He decided long ago that she was too sexy to correct. "I know y'all have a sleeping baby and all. I, I was just wondering whether you and Kenya have seen Terrence or know where he is at."

Her hands trembled as they fidgeted: pulling at the cape, then running over her head again, tapping the top of the car, clenched together. What had this fool Terrence done now?

"No, but do you want to come in for a moment? I haven't talked to him, maybe Kenya has."

Lani nodded and walked around the car, leaving it running with the door wide open. He ushered her inside and sat her in the family room. After giving her something to drink, Christopher doubled back outside to turn off the car, retrieve the keys and shut the door. *Suburbs or not, you can't tempt folks with an empty BMW, engine running with the door wide open. That damn Terrence has her acting frantic.*

Christopher eased back into the house. "You want something to eat?" he asked, knowing she would decline.

"No, no thank you," Lani nursed the drink. "Do you think Kenya will mind coming down this late, with the baby and all?"

Kenya. The site of Lani had made him forget that Kenya wasn't here. His pulse began to race and his head started pounding. The earlier call to her cell. Kenya running out of the house. Here he was worried sick and his wife had run out into the middle of the night after Terrence. The knowledge shook him and he stumbled to the loveseat and tumbled into it, the wind knocked out of him.

"What's wrong?"

"Kenya. I think she's with Terrence." Christopher avoided Lani's eyes.

Chapter Eight

This is turning into one helluva night. Lani watched Christopher fold his body into the love seat, the awkward motion stunned her. Christopher was always so calculated and planned, to see a sudden loss of control from him was unusual. This is what Lani loved about Terrence and made her hate him too. Only Terrence could make big ass Christopher fold up. *As usual, when Terrence has a damn temper tantrum, he has to wreck everyone else's life.*

Kenya. Of all people. Lani couldn't believe that Terrence had called a woman with a newborn baby to ease his troubles. The most obvious woman, at that. Even she hadn't thought he would be so bold.

Lani wrecked her brain to remember what had started the arguing between her and Terrence. Tonight, anyway. There was always an argument, a different point of view, a correction. Never support, never understanding, never encouragement. Never. Then, any reaction to the criticism followed by silence. Dry, cracking, brittle silence.

Lani didn't know which was worse, the arguing or the silence. Definitely the silence. She couldn't take it, but it was her fault for marrying his pretty bourgie ass. His family never talked about anything real. Every gathering was just a room full of uppity black folks who didn't like each other but sat around exchanging false niceties while judging each other. Everyone knew everyone. From the same church, sorority, fraternity, same social clubs, same circle of undergrads. Same same same. The only time anything changed and they were in agreement was when it came to judging her. The common theme: Lani wasn't good enough for their precious Terrence.

Not that she gave a damn. Lani had more culture, experience and life than all of them put together. They could all kiss her natural black ass, as far as she was concerned. She would go hard, Bonnie and Clyde hard, for her man. But Terrence had stopped protecting her a long time ago. While he forced her to attend every function imaginable, he disappeared when they arrived, leaving her in the corner to fend for herself.

First, Terrence ignored the way his people treated Lani, then he smirked and quietly joined in the snubs and inside jokes. Somewhere along the way, he had left her team and left her by herself.

Lani had to admit that she missed when it happened. Somehow she didn't notice the slight shift in his body language or the judgment in his eyes. But recently, she could identify it. He stopped veiling the angst and held his contempt for her in a bold manner for everyone to see. Proof was his interactions with Kenya; he would sit on the phone chit chatting with another man's wife for hours, after having barely spoken to his own wife for weeks.

But Lani still loved Terrence. She had signed on for life. Her family didn't like him either. They talked about real problems, discussed life decisions, mistakes, who did what and why. Normally, her family got all in the other folks business. But they were good people. There was always a get together for any imaginable occasion and they had a good time. Her family, which consisted of drunken uncles and cussing aunts, her sister and beautiful nieces. They loved her. But Terrence always sat among them like he was afraid of getting dirty, brushing off sofas before he sat down and examining the silverware before he ate. The family picked up on that real quick. And Lani couldn't be herself when he was there; she didn't double-dutch with her nieces, didn't play pinnacle or spades with her aunts. Instead she politely smiled and tried to keep the peace. Eventually, she stopped inviting Terrence and it worked out best for everyone else. Her uncle's would smile when they saw that she was alone, making jokes about her 'tight ass' husband. Her sister would breathe in relief, glad that she wouldn't have to have another word battle with Terrence. Only Lani felt disappointed that she had married a man who would never be a part of her real family.

Maybe the disdain fell into place when she started earning more money than Terrence. No, he enjoyed spending more than she did. Could it have been the constant flirting by other men? At first he was proud to have landed her. Then possessive. Now, it empowered him to put her down, make her feel less. Did he think that made him more?

Lani shifted in her seat, her eyes locked on Christopher. She wasn't leaving. She wanted to know just how long this idiot with a brand new baby was going to run around playing aid to Terrence. *What a fool.* Kenya didn't have a shot at taking Terrence from her, which was one thing Lani never worried about.

Kenya couldn't talk about sex; much less take it to the level that Terrence needed for satisfaction. Even if she tried, Terrence would tire of her easy.

But doubt sprinkled Lani's thoughts. She knew that there was more to it than sex. Terrence had never had to make his wife his friend because Kenya had the role filled. Lani desperately sought friendship with Terrence, a loving partnership, but he had the role filled by an outside source. Sometimes, Lani felt like the other woman, with Terrence laying in her bed and making love all night long, then waking up to call Kenya and discuss his day. There was no real need for conversation between her and her husband. She gave up trying, succumbed to her frustration. And Terrence responded with the wall of silence, which he resorted to so easily, separating her from the only man she loved. She knew that Terrence loved Kenya as a friend, but sometimes wondered if he wanted to take it farther.

I wonder how Chris deals with this, knowing his wife is head over heels for Terrence. Obviously, he wasn't taking it that well. Lani fought the urge to snicker. *Serves his conceited self right. Always preaching to folks, telling people right from wrong, but never noticed his wife drooling after my husband.* Regret followed the thought, slapping against Lani's conscious. Christopher hadn't done anything wrong. In fact, he was the type of man she should have married, could have married, had she not been blinded by Terrence.

Lani observed him, not bothering to be discreet. His large frame seemed so comfortable; Lani could tuck her body against his and feel immediate comfort. He had rugged features that were accented by smooth brown skin. Her eyes panned down to his legs, where his hands rested. Solid thighs and huge hands. A man. Nothing pretty about him. No competition. A real man. Lani always liked Christopher and didn't argue about visiting them. She knew she would be excluded, as usual, but Christopher was the one who reached out and made simple gestures to include her. Everyone loved him because of the sports thing so he didn't have to kiss bourgie ass to be accepted. While his wife was ogling Terrence, he would bring Lani a drink or wipe off the seat before she sat. She appreciated it.

"Chris, can you call her?" Lani made the suggestion with caution, trying to snap him out of embarrassment.

"I've been calling her." Her effort had failed— from the odd jut of his chin, Lani could tell he was past embarrassment. "She isn't answering."

Lani stared at him. She couldn't help it. When he glanced up at her she knew she should look away, let the man have his emotion in peace. But she couldn't. He seemed so open, so vulnerable, that she became fascinated. Never before had she realized that he was so sincere.

He grinned a little, a cover to mask the pain. "Any other suggestions?"

She shook her head no and patted the couch next to her. If she was going to wait, at least she could feel the warmth of a special person, of a man that had real emotion. She wasn't going to seduce him, or anything. She just wanted to be nearer, to feel the comfort of his strong body while she waited and found out how her life was going to play out.

Christopher gave her a puzzled look, questioning.

Lani shook her head a little, and then grinned. A telling grin to let him down with no hard feelings. *No, I am not trying to do you. Interesting that you went there.*

She patted the couch again and tilted her head. Emotion got the best of her: Confusion, sadness, regret and despair etched itself into the depths of her spirit. Christopher moved, from the love seat to the couch, sitting close to Lani but not touching. She handed him the remote control that had been left on the cushion, and leaned back into the sofa while he found something for them to watch.

After a few minutes, Lani leaned on his shoulder and he wrapped an arm around her. They waited, two betrayed spouses, comforting each other in silence.

Chapter Nine

"It's me. Pick up. Are ya 'll there …?" A pause. A muffled sound. A deep sigh. "… Damn. Call me back. Please."

The voice sounded panicked and raspy, whispered tightly into the headset. Dee listened to the message a fifteenth time. Her baby sister hadn't sounded that shaken in a long time. What could possibly have her that upset? Dee pressed redial again, trying frantically to reach Lani. Four rings and then voicemail. Dee slammed the receiver into the telephone. Why the hell wasn't Lani answering?

Dee pressed play on the old answering machine, repeating the message again. Dee had heard that desperation before, knew it well. It was the indefinite sound of fear, which kicked in right before a woman reached breakpoint; just before she abandoned all reason and bottomed out. And it was always caused by one thing—chasing after some damn man.

Only Terrence could make Lani leave this crazy message, knowing it was going to scare Dee half to death. Dee's husband Ricky sat at the table and shuffled the salt and pepper shakers. One flew off the table and broke her concentration. Dee whipped around toward the sound, finally noticed Ricky and exhaled. She had thought one of her daughters was awake. *Can't let the baby girls hear Lani's voice. Not that desperate sound. Can't let them know what men will do to them, yet.*

"Dee, what you wanna do?" Ricky neatly positioned the shakers as he waited for an answer.

She shrugged, her mind jumbled. Everyone knew that Dee tended to overreact and cause chaos. Maybe Lani didn't need her just yet. Terrence knew that an ass whipping was guaranteed if she and Ricky showed up in the middle of the night. But she didn't want to mess Lani up. What if Lani had done something, trying to get Terrence's attention, and gotten in trouble that Terrence didn't know about? If Dee just showed up, Terrence would be suspicious, on to Lani. She needed to protect her baby sister, but didn't want to make things worse.

"We can go now, you know. Reedi said she would watch the girls. I ain't scheduled to work tomorrow. Quick trip down, find out what's up and come right back."

"Let me try to call her again."

Dee knew that Lani was unhappily married. She had tried to tell her that Terrence wasn't a knight in shining armor. That boy couldn't keep himself from drowning in a tub of water. He was useless. Pretty as hell, but she never liked pretty men. She liked her men solid, steady, secure.

But Lani couldn't be figured out. It seemed like she should have had enough drama to last a life time, the way Sophie brought random pretty ass men home. Lani had seemed the most shaken by the men in the

73

next room—laughing loudly, then grunting and then snoring, their repugnant sounds seeping through the paper thin walls.

The thought brought back memories that Dee didn't want to entertain. She shook her head. She and Lani spent nights alone in the tiny apartment above the liquor store. They were scared to death from the moment their mother stumbled out into the night with her girlfriends, until the thin door finally creaked, announcing her arrival. But when her mother would finally show up reeking of liquor, she always dragged some stranger into their small space. Sexing in the apartment with the girls crouched in their room, hidden under the bed sheets, desperately hoping that the strange man would leave afterward, instead of peeping in their room while their mother was passed out. A couple of times, they weren't so lucky.

Dee never let them touch Lani, though. Lani was the gorgeous one, the one they always went to first. She looked just like their mother. But Dee protected her, jumping her little self out the bed with her knife in hand. She couldn't remember when she had started sleeping with a knife in her bed; all she knew is that there was no memory of not having one. The first man had laughed and tried to knock her out of the way. She plunged the knife right into his leg, just like her aunties had taught her. The family knew they weren't being taking care of, but wasn't much they could do then. So they taught Dee how to protect herself and take care of Lani. And she did it. She would always do it.

That one had glared at her and called her a little bitch. Dee had angled the knife as if she were confident in using it again. He gritted his teeth at her, like the predator he was, and left the room. The other one she had bargained with—she tolerated him as long as he left Lani alone. But when he closed his eyes, the knife found its way to his chin. Before he left, he slapped the shit out of her, knocking her small body into the wall. But he left. And that was all that mattered.

Dee glanced at her watch. It was a six hour drive to Lani's house. She would have to go by Smoke's house first, though, to get some heat. Maybe she should bring Smoke and Stink on the road with her. The options twirled through her mind. No. This high falutin' college boy wasn't going to require all of that. Her cousins would stomp Terrence just for having to drive six hours to check on Lani.

Lani was the star of the family. The one who made it. All of their cousins would volunteer to ride down to Maryland and rearrange the life of any man who crossed her. The family treated her like gold, because she still loved them and kept it real. Despite the man she married, Lani had never changed. But she married a brother who didn't understand them and never even tried to. Terrence would come to parties dusting off furniture before he sat down and rinsing off silverware before using it. Like they were dirty. When Dee tried to serve him dinner, he eyed the collard greens and pig tails with disgust all over his face. And when her uncles got to drinking, Terrence would always find a reason to leave, pulling Lani away from the card game or Double Dutch with the girls, making an early exit.

Dee decided she wouldn't even show the gun, or tell Ricky she had it. But she would carry it, just in case. She stored it at Smoke's to keep it out of her house; away from her girls. Hopefully, they would never have to know about being raw.

Ricky stood up. The decision had been made. Dee was amazed how he could read her body language and understand her so easily. While Ricky went to their bedroom to change clothes, Dee made one last call to Lani's cell.

"Please, please let her be alright." Her silent prayer seemed unlikely.

The phone clicked on the fourth ring, but a long pause, not a voice, filled the line. Dee held her breath. If Terrence answered instead of Lani, she would know Lani was in trouble, possibly in danger.

"Hello," Lani whispered into the receiver, her voice thick from sleep.

Chapter Ten

Terrence and Kenya sat in silence. He wasn't sure what to say, or why Kenya seemed so strange tonight. Distant. More reserved than usual. She hadn't lost the baby fat yet and her round face and curvaceous body surprised him. She was such a stickler about her appearance, always exercising and dieting. In Terrence's opinion, Kenya had always been too skinny. Not enough curves. He could never tell her his opinion, though, would keep it to himself that her rounder, healthier frame was more appealing.

She had told him to go back to Lani. Judgmental. That was her tone. Even and judgmental. It pissed him off. She didn't even like Lani; he knew it when he first asked her opinion years ago. Her voice had been the same even tone, just like tonight, and the distant eyes. Kenya was always so formal and always so official. Just like his mother. Everything had a code, a level of appropriateness and a certain way of behaving. The right clothing, the tasteful jewelry. The correct forks and required attendance to unnecessary social events. Their plastic smiles covered forked tongues and hardened souls. They practiced double speak—a cynical code designed only for those in the know.

Maybe he was close with Kenya because she felt so much like his mother and all the people he had grown up with. But he also wanted to escape that life. Terrence longed for the freedom to be casual and reject the social bullshit. Maybe his kids would have a choice and be allowed the opportunity to decide whether they wanted to participate in the black bourgeoisie society or play it cool. No doubt, Kenya already had little Christopher's Jack and Jill application completed and already had him wait listed for the appropriate independent private school. Little Christopher's life would be all beige and crème, just like Terrence's had been.

Until he met Lani. She was color to him. Her laugh felt like light rain on his ears and her smile was like a flavored kiss on the tip of his tongue. Excitement. That's what Lani was, she caused a euphoric intensity to surge through him—it was an indescribable feeling. He remembered how the world seemed more colorful in her presence, as if he were noticing it for the first time.

But, that was then. Now was now. The world was back to crème and beige, back to safe and secure

"I'm not going back." Terrence looked straight ahead.

"You have to, Terrence. That is how it is. You don't just up and leave your wife. It's not right."

Right, correct. Is that really all that matters to you? Terrence looked at his fingers to avoid her eyes. "Kenya, I'm not happy. I need to spend some time alone … to regroup."

"Happy?" Kenya snorted. "Since when was this about being happy?"

They stared at each other in awkward silence. It had never occurred to Terrence that Kenya might not be happy. She and Christopher were the perfect couple.

"What do you mean? You're happy with Christopher. Ya'll fell in love and it has been all good since, right?"

Kenya shifted in the seat, facing Terrence. "No Terrence, I am married to Christopher. I love him. I did not fall in love with him. We got along, he was a good companion … I married him."

She bit her lip. Terrence couldn't help but press the issue. It was rare for Kenya to open up and, for some reason, he felt fascinated.

"So what are you saying, you aren't in love him?"

"Terrence, we are not children. Wake the fuck up, this is real life!" Kenya clenched her fists. Terrence grabbed one of her hands.

"Talk to me, damnit. Tell me what's up. I am always honest with you but you never tell me what's really going on. What are you talking about?"

"No." Kenya snatched her hand away. "I am not going to talk about Christopher. This is about you and Lani."

"No, this is about me. I need to know … why are we doing this? Why should I stay when she is crazy? Why are you married if you didn't fall head over heels?"

"Terrence, you wouldn't understand."

"Tell me."

"Listen, I had feelings for someone else. Always have. So I wasn't in love with Christopher. But I did love him ... do ... I do love him. He's a good man." She shrugged. "It's that simple."

"Who? Who is this other person? Tell me."

Kenya's eyes filled with tears and she stared at him silently. He pulled at her hand again and this time she didn't fight.

Terrence didn't get it at first. Anger pounded at the walls of his chest. How had someone hurt his sister without punishment? It had to be someone he probably knew. His mind flipped through the handful of men he knew about in her life prior to Christopher. None of them would dare cross him or devastate her.

Realization sprinkled across his mind when he pulled her in for a hug. It spread, developing into a blanket of understanding as her body melted into his. Terrence finally understood. Kenya had never hugged him completely before, not without the appropriate space between them. The pieces fell into place.

"I didn't know," he whispered in her ear.

"Would it have mattered if you did?" Kenya's fingertips rested on the edge of his T-shirt, barely touching his neck.

No, it wouldn't have. His focus had been on finding 'different' and Kenya was the purest definition of 'same.' But same felt comfortable now, steady and sure. It made a difference, now.

"I'm sorry, for being so ... stupid." Terrence wiped the tears from her cheek.

She pulled back, embarrassment scattered across her face. She looked beautiful tonight. So earthy and freshly clean—the exact opposite of Lani. Terrence ran his hand across her cheek again.

Kenya caught his hand with hers and planted a gentle kiss on his palm. The softness of her lips made his heart stop and heat surged through his body. She held his hand more firm and kissed it again. Terrence's mind went blank as all reserve faded. He leaned toward her, desperate to taste her lips.

She did not stop him.

Chapter Eleven

Christopher felt nothing. Numb—that's what it was. A solid numbness that crept up his arm and landed on his chest. At first he thought it was the pressure of Lani leaning against him. The warmth of her body should have occupied his mind and kept him alert. On any other night it would have. But tonight, it was just another bizarre incident piled on top of the others.

He shifted her, leaning her back against the couch. Christopher needed his blood to flow through his limbs; maybe it would release the numb feeling. If he could, he would just shift her to the other side or let her lay in his lap. But one was impossible and the other inappropriate, so he leaned her against the sofa and covered her with the soft cloak.

Then Christopher sat … waiting. Waiting for the blood to return to his limbs; waiting to feel a release from the pounding void within his chest. But the release never came. Instead, without Lani touching him, the numbness spread quicker. It felt like it covered his entire chest and spread down both arms.

Heart attack! I must be having a damn heart attack.

That would explain it. He rose slowly, hoping to make it alive to the cell phone thrown haphazardly across the room. Fear caused his mind to go blank. The numbness and possible heart attack dominated his thoughts as he pushed through an invisible sea of pressure to get to the cell phone. But, there was something else. Something he was supposed to think about, something that wasn't quite right. Christopher just couldn't remember what.

Reaching for the phone, he surveyed the room. Lani was asleep on his couch. By only a miracle, little Christopher was sound asleep in his crib. What was it that was just beyond Christopher's grasp? What was the elusive thought that clawed at his psyche? He lifted the phone and leaned against the mantle as he replaced the battery and back panel.

I hope I don't scare Lani when I wake her to go to the hospital. I have to tell Kenya to make sure Lani...

Kenya.

It all returned to him then, the weight and numbness digging into his soul. Terrence, Kenya, Lani and him. Four characters in some weird drama, playing out his worst nightmare. Kenya still hadn't returned. In fact, she hadn't even bothered to call. Terrence's wife dozed on the couch; her facial expression pained, yet, Terrence was nowhere to be found.

Anger capsized inside of Christopher. He tried to silence the groan of anger's pressure and calm himself.

Kenya couldn't be with Terrence. She would never do that.

What was he thinking? What would Kenya want with Terrence when she had him? The realization swept through him like fresh sea foam, cooling him. Kenya had never given him pause before; she had never been caught in so much as a white lie.

Alright, think. Where would Kenya have gone?

He called her parents. No answer.

They must be asleep, so she's not there.

She didn't have any girlfriends that she would visit so late.

An accident. She must have had an accident.

That made the most sense. This entire night was some sort of punishment for poor Alayna. Karma was revisiting upon him the hell he had suffered for arguing with her so many years ago and forcing her to take a stand against him. A stand that cost her life. *Of course.* His mouth went dry while he raced around the house. He had to go look for her. But maybe he should call the police. Where would he tell them to go?

TouchOn. The car tracking service that he subscribed to was also in Kenya's car. This would be easy. He would find the location of the car and could find out whether Kenya had contacted them and was in danger. He frantically fumbled with the phone. It took a few seconds to locate the help line, but it was posted on the refrigerator.

In the midst of panic, Christopher noticed that the operator was kind. She took the information and placed him on hold. His mind wondered to the infant laying upstairs. What would become of his son if something happened to Kenya? What if the life they had planned evaporated just like that, transformed into spiritual residue by life's anguish. His karma might be his baby boy's demise.

"Sir?"

"Yes. I'm still here."

"We have found the location of the vehicle, sir. The vehicle is intact, there does not appear to have been an accident."

Thank God. Christopher held the received to his head for a moment as relief flushed through him.

"The doors are now unlocked. Please hold while I try to contact the driver."

Another pause. Christopher waited to hear his queen's voice on the line. The thin nasal sound of the operator disappointed him.

"I'm sorry sir. The vehicle seems to be vacant. Do you want me to contact the local authorities?"

Hell yeah! His first reaction lunged from his throat, threatening to push past his lips. Something in the deepest recesses of his mind told him "*no.*" The deep instinct that had carried him this far in life whispered for him to be still for a second and think this out. Kenya hadn't been in a car accident. The vehicle was fine. Panic tried to overtake him: *maybe she was abducted!* But his internal alarm didn't sense that. No, now that the obvious was out of the way, he was dealing with something different, something more sinister. It was possible that Kenya was with Terrence after all.

"No, ma'am, thank you. If you could just give me the location of the car that would be fine."

The operator hesitated. "Yes sir. I need to confirm that you are an authorized subscriber to give you that information."

"Not a problem..."

Christopher went through the motions, verifying his information and writing down the location of the car. The grocery store parking lot. She had gone where she said she was going. Terrence must have met her there.

Christopher called his brother.

"What's up, Baby Brah? Why the hell you calling me in the middle of the night?" Darryl's words were stretched over a tremendous yawn.

"Why are you answering the phone like that? Damn Darryl."

"What's wrong?" Darryl's voice changed, alerted by the tension in Christopher's voice.

"Nothing's wrong. I just needed a favor." Christopher was changing his mind about involving Darryl. The situation was bad enough without having to admit it to his eldest brother.

A moment of silence. "Name it."

"I would do it myself, but I got my son and…"

"Boy, stop playing with me. What you need me to do?" Christopher could hear Darryl moving around, already putting on clothes.

"Kenya went to the grocery store. She hasn't come back—"

"What!" Christopher heard the phone drop and then Darryl's voice filled the line again. "Christopher! Why didn't you call the police?"

"I think she is alright. Terrence's wife is here. Can't find him either. I just want to check … you know, check if—"

"Oh shit." Understanding rode on the space between the words.

Christopher breathed; glad he wasn't going to have to put his suspicion into words.

"You're probably overreacting." Darryl's voice was light. Nonjudgmental.

"Probably."

"Kenya just had a baby, too? You know how emotional women get."

"I guess."

"Where I am going?"

Christopher gave his brother the location. He hung up the phone with deliberate effort, he was tempted to stay on the phone the entire time and live vicariously through Darryl. Instead, he collected the small remaining fragments of his pride and sat down on the edge of the chaise lounge, opposite Lani's sleeping frame.

He watched Lani sleep for the entire 20 minutes it took Darryl to locate the car and call back. Christopher studied how her chest rose, how her eyelids fluttered. There was no way to hide his curiosity—how had Terrence gotten so lucky?

"You sure she is alright, Christopher? No one is here."

"I don't know. I think so, though. Anyone at the grocery store?"

"The store you named, it closed a year ago. She didn't go to the store here."

"So the car isn't there?"

"Naw, I didn't mean it like that. The car is here; she isn't and neither is a grocery store."

Christopher remained silent, his teeth grinding together as he processed the news.

"Hold on a second…" Christopher could hear Darryl shifting in his car, "… the parking lot security is riding around. Let me catch them…"

"Wait, you have to ask them—"

The phone disconnected.

Christopher sat back down, his eyes back on Lani. *Too much. This is all too much.*

The phone vibrated.

Christopher clicked it open and Darryl picked up right where he left off. "I talked to the parking lot security." The words dragged out, as if Darryl was trying to pull them back even as he said them.

"And…"

"I don't think you need to call the police."

"What did he say?"

"She." Darryl waited a moment.

"Huh?"

"The parking lot attendant. She was a she. She said the driver parked the car and climbed into a silver car with another man. She said she noticed because it was closing time for the other stores and that's when they pay attention to who is leaving."

There it was. Kenya was definitely with Terrence.

"Uhm, one more thing." Darryl coughed. It sounded fake.

Christopher rubbed his forehead. "What?"

Darryl chuckled, but there was no humor in his voice. "The parking lot attendant ... she called the tow company, since the car was here for more than two hours."

The pressure in Christopher's chest turned into fire. A deep searing burn tore through his body. Kenya was making a fool of him. She was running after an idiotic man, leaving him, their home and their child. Alayna was in his thoughts; his damned wife had made her memory return.

Like a deep rumble of thunder, the words escaped Christopher's clenched jaw. "Come get me."

"Baby Brah, I'm already on my way."

Chapter Twelve

Lani felt the slight vibrating of the cell phone on her hip. She patted the seat around her, although her eyes remained closed. Sleep transformed into reality and the fabric upon which she was sitting felt foreign and stiff. She couldn't remember any item in her house that felt or smelled the same.

Where am I? With a jolt she remembered the house, her and Christopher, sitting in silence. *Where is Chris?* Her cape was spread around her instead of on the chair where she left it. Digging in the side pocket, she rushed to answer the phone, hoping Terrence had returned to his senses.

Finally. "Hello?"

"Lani, I've been calling your ass all night. Where are you? Is everything all right? That message you left … I don't know what to do!"

Lani gasped, she had completely forgotten that she called Dee.

"I'm alright. I promise. Terrence walked out. Said he was leaving me. I panicked and called, but you weren't there. I went looking for him."

"What? He's leaving?" The loud smack or her lips conveyed her doubt. "Whatever, that fool ain't going nowhere. Where did you find him?"

"I still haven't," whispered Lani. She looked around again. *Where is Chris?* "I came over his friend's house."

"What friend? Not that girl … Kenyatta?"

"Kenya. Yep, I'm here now. She is out with him somewhere. I'm waiting."

"What!" The scream was so sharp that Lani moved the phone from her head. "I'm on my way."

Lani's heart pounded in her chest. She couldn't control the situation once Dee was here. "No, no. Not yet. Let me find out what's going on first."

Christopher entered the room with a blue tooth in his ear. He wore a crazed expression, clearly stressed out. He spoke in low tones with a set of car keys in one hand and a flashlight in the other.

"Look, Dee, don't come yet. I'll call back alright?"

"Call me as soon as you know something. I am getting stuff ready to come down." Dee stated.

"No, Dee, you and Ricky go to bed. I'll call in the morning. And don't go by Smoke's place either."

Lani ended the call and then glanced at the phone. Terrence hadn't called. In the past two hours, he had not called once.

"Yeah, now? All right, I'm coming out," Christopher said into the headset.

Maybe something was wrong, something had happened. Was he on the phone with Kenya?

Christopher ended the call, turning to face Lani. "I didn't want to wake you. I can't keep waiting. Will you listen for the baby? He's in our room. If he wakes up, just change him and give him a bottle. I left one on the counter." Then, without giving her a chance to respond, Christopher moved toward the door.

"Wait," Lani stood. "Have you heard anything? Where are you going?"

"I'm going to get my damn car." Christopher met Lani's eyes and the determination in them caught her by surprise. "I called TouchOn. My brother is going to take me. I'll be back in ten minutes."

She nodded, but when he was out of sight Lani grimaced. It was obvious that Christopher was not playing around. *What is Kenya thinking?* She went to the window and watched him step off the porch and jog to the waiting car. Then Lani called Terrence. Once again, he did not answer.

***

Lani floated through the empty house. It was a nice place, very cozy. Their different personalities were evident in the furnishings, Kenya's areas were plain but expensive and Christopher's space was practical and cozy. The maid was pretty good too, Lani decided. There was no way Kenya knew how to keep a house this clean.

Lani climbed the steps slowly, barely breathing. She just wanted to see the baby, to get a glimpse at new life in its purest form. Cracking the door to the bedroom, she could just make out the small bundle in the cradle, his thumb jammed in his mouth. His expression changed when the hallway light tumbled across his face and the muscles relaxed in his tiny brown face.

Oh my God, he is beautiful.

She hadn't really looked at the newborn the last time they visited. It was a trained skill, to visit other people and their babies and maintain a neutral stance. To contain the longing and pure agony that swallowed Lani whole at the site of other small blessings, given to everyone but her. Lani had run out of stores to avoid breaking down and she purposely sat in the balcony at church, so high that most parents wouldn't bother with climbing all those steps with their little ones.

Lani didn't dare touch little Christopher, or move too close. She prayed he wouldn't wake up; the thought of handling him terrified her. *Am I cursed?* She shook her head; she would not go there tonight. She had enough to worry about. But the doubt still lingered, it was always a palpable presence.

Her first child would have been seven by now. That was before she and Terrence had finished college and there was no way they could play off the pregnancy.

"I won't have a bastard child." That's what Terrence had said when she pressed and pressed and fought for the life of the baby. A bastard child. The words still scratched at her soul. What about all the love, desire and whispers of forever? What happened to him telling her he wanted her pregnant, he wanted to see his seed grown in her. It became apparent that those were words without meaning. The truth, from his tongue, was that a child by her out of wedlock would be a bastard. A bastard. Lani remembered falling silent and staring straight ahead while she listened to the sound of her heart shattering. It produced an actual sound.

In a daze, Lani had climbed out of Terrence's bed that morning, pulled on her clothes, and walked. She didn't know where she was going. But she walked. He swore later that he drove along side her, trying to convince her to get in the car, come out of the rain. She never saw him, didn't even hear him.

Dee came to the campus the next morning and drove her to the clinic. It was taken care of, quick and efficiently. Dee paid for it. But to this day, she could envision the baby boy's face, what he looked like, how he would grow. She knew in her spirit that it was a boy. She swore she would never again talk to Terrence.

But over time, she couldn't fight him off. Terrence followed her around, showered her with gifts and promises and open displays of affection. He created a public campaign for her forgiveness. She had never had anyone work so hard for her or pay her so much attention. Over time she could stand the sight of him again, smile as he sung to her while she walked to class or played the saxophone outside her classroom window. When the professor slammed the window shut and demanded she go out and put an end to the interruption, Lani didn't return. She took Terrence by the hand and led him inside the building, down to the basement hallway. They made intimate love on the steps, unfazed by the sounds of students stomping around in the hallway above them. She was his queen again.

The second one was after graduation. Both had completed their internships and Terrence's position with the marketing firm was a guarantee. They were impressed with his credentials and intelligence, and thought a young handsome bachelor could only be more incentive to the clients. Marriage wasn't an option. Not yet. Lani had to consider their lives, their future, Terrence had argued. How would the child live, who would support it? She hadn't wanted to do it again, but this time he was with her. He took her and waited with her. This time, Terrence paid.

When she walked through the exit doors, he had inhaled quickly, surprised by how ashen and frail she looked. Terrence stayed with her for two days, nursing her to health. She smiled and encouraged him, whispered how happy she was that he stayed with her. And when he finally left to go to work on Monday morning, Lani cried the entire day, howls and screams of utter pain and disappointment blending with the noisy television. A part of her soul was fading and she knew it couldn't be restored.

Last year, Lani didn't even tell him about the third one. Not initially. They were married and life was smooth. She knew the answer would be no, it always had been. So, she just did it. This one, she paid for herself. In cash. She steeled herself against the pain, the hurt, the eternal doubt. Lani refused to envision this one, to imagine her playing with her siblings in heaven.

But when she returned and Terrence saw her, he instantly knew. He had become angry, yelling and crying. It was his child, too. Why hadn't she asked his opinion? How could she do this without his input? The more Lani had tried to explain, the larger the knot in her throat had become. She had to scream to release it, to keep from choking on all that pain. Her scream rattled in her throat, scratched the calm of their home, and ripped the soul of their marriage. Terrence's head jerked back, his eyes wide with distaste. He stared at her; judgment was etched into the smooth lines of his forehead. And Terrence responded with silence. Dead and cruel silence.

It didn't matter. Her babies were gone, forever gone. And she couldn't bring them back. Was Terrence worth it?

Little Christopher made sucking noises, squirming just a bit. Lani snapped back to reality, stepped back and closed the door. She headed for the family room.

Sitting on the couch, Lani made another attempt to call Terrence. She wanted to laugh when he didn't answer. Neither Terrence nor Kenya knew who they were playing with. The call went directly to phone mail. His phone was off.

That was his last chance.

With a new vengeance set in her heart, Lani went into the bathroom to freshen up. She heard Christopher pull the car into the wide driveway, past her car and into the garage. She listened as the garage door lowered. Checking her reflection in the mirror, Lani unbuttoned a few of the buttons on her blouse. *Terrence has no idea how far I will go.*

Lani moved slowly back into the family room, listening for Christopher. Keys dropped onto the kitchen counter and he made his way into the room, a beer in each hand. As he handed her the beer, his eyes scanned her shirt and then met her eyes, questioning. He sat down across from her in the loveseat.

"I'm sure there is nothing to worry about. Kenya is just probably trying to talk some sense into Terrence. Did ya'll have an argument?"

She nodded, her eyes locked on him as she took a swig from the beer.

Christopher pushed out more fake words. "Terrence will come around."

"I'm not worried about that," she said, her voice husky and confident. "It's more a question of will I want him, now."

Christopher chuckled, a dry, painful sound. "Yeah, I know what you mean."

"So, you think Kenya is just with him to help him, huh?" There was cynicism in Lani's voice and she didn't try to cover it.

He took a long drink from the bottle, but kept his eyes on Lani.

Obviously you don't think that or you wouldn't have gone to get that car. Don't try to cover for her. "So, you're cool with that, huh?" Lani pressed. "It's alright for her to comfort him?"

"Hell no!"

"You've never wondered how far their friendship would go?" Lani squinted and watched Christopher closely.

He sat there staring at her. Lani knew he wasn't going to answer that question. What man would? But she wanted to see his reaction, and now she had her answer. The confusion, doubt and disbelief had all flashed in his eyes before he could contain it. That was what she wanted to know. That was what she would use to her advantage.

Chapter Thirteen

Lani's presence had kept him calm before. Christopher had wanted to ease her pain and console her at first. Now she sat in front of him, her blouse unbuttoned to the top of a lace bra, a cold beer in hand and her legs uncrossed. He could have her. Her eyes told him and her body confirmed it. Truth be told, he had wanted her for years.

But trying to contain his anger was taking all the control Christopher had. If he took Lani up on her unspoken offer, it would be angry, frustrated sex. It would be an attack on Terrence, an attempt to soil his precious wife. It would be a message to Kenya, too, an event to break her heart. Christopher would have some measure of temporary relief in invoking his anger and wrath in a palpable way against Kenya and Terrence, in a way that couldn't be denied.

The only one that it would not be about is Lani. Christopher would not have her in that way. He had always liked her and her body wasn't going to be the sacrificial lamb. He slowly placed the beer bottle on the coffee table. Lani had asked him a question, but he didn't really hear her. Her mouth was moving, but he was thinking about preserving her and himself. They were going to stand on their high convictions tonight.

Kenya and Terrence were not going to be given an opportunity to twist there indiscretions into victimization. Only they would be in the wrong.

Christopher stood up and walked toward Lani. Her eyes sparkled a bit, but beside that her expression did not change. She was clearly a woman used to having her way with men. He sat on the couch next to her, removed the beer bottle from her grasp. Holding her face in his hands, he kissed her tenderly on the forehead, then the nose. Lani yielded, eyes closed, lips slightly parted. He kissed her once on the lips.

Lani opened her eyes and he gazed into them. He wanted her to understand this decision, to know that he was not rejecting her, but was protecting her. He buttoned her blouse with careful deliberation, while he held her gaze. He picked up the cloak and stood, guiding her with one hand to stand also. He wrapped the cloak around her and held her close.

She began to cry, softly, grasping him.

"Go home, Lani." He spoke the words into her ear, still holding her close. "Go home and wait."

She nodded.

He led Lani to the car and leaned across her body. Lani didn't move out of his way, and the back of his hand brushed against her breast as he placed her keys in the ignition. He kissed her on the forehead then, after a great pause, on her lips, again. Lani held onto him, her palms against his chest, her lips clinging to him. Christopher wanted to pull her back out of the car and taste every inch of her. But he didn't. He stared into her eyes, kissed her fingertips and then placed her hands on the steering wheel. Christopher stood at the edge of the driveway and watched her drive away into the night.

Chapter Fourteen

Kenya was fighting herself; she had to keep her head above water. Her mind was foggy with the realization that she finally had Terrence. It was finally happening. The kisses that she had dreamt of her entire life were finally happening. An intense heat surged through her torso, landing squarely between her thighs. She moaned, lost in the kiss. Mouth open and back arched, her body throbbed for Terrence in a way she hadn't felt before. Terrence's hands rested on her. Their angle felt uncomfortable, the car wasn't designed for front seat making out, but Kenya didn't care. Terrence stared in her eyes, questioning. She didn't need to answer. She had given him permission to touch her body years ago.

Terrence's hands ran the length of her torso, pressing gently pockets of flesh, kneading away any tension. They continued to kiss. Kenya had not felt this on fire before. Ever. Kenya lightly placed her hands on Terrence's chest and then slid them down, her hands blazing a slow trail. Her hands searched for the waist of his sweat pants, caressing the hairs that lay against his ridged stomach. Kenya sighed when her fingers plunged a little deeper and she pulled the pants away from his waist.

Terrence jerked away from the kiss and grabbed her hands. His hands were clenched in a fist around hers. "No Kenya," Terrence patted her hands. "You don't want to take it there."

Kenya removed her hand from his and headed back toward his waist. She inhaled and sighed at his scent. Kenya had past the point of no return long ago. There was no stopping now. "Yes, I do."

"No." Terrence sounded firmer this time. He grabbed her hands and placed them back in her lap. "I don't want to take it there."

Kenya opened her eyes.

Terrence ran one hand back and forth over his hair. The silence felt like dead weight on Kenya's chest. The heat in her body evaporated, morphing into painful embarrassment. "You don't want me." She said it matter of factly, vocalizing the belief she had always carried. "Even now, when you can have all of me, you don't want me."

Terrence gazed at her in silence for a moment. "Kenya, I just found out five minutes ago that you had feelings for me. You sound like we have been doing this for years or something."

"We have. I have. I mean, what's wrong with me?"

Terrence glanced out the window. "I really don't know what you're talking about."

"Me. Why didn't you choose me?" Kenya heard her voice shaking.

"Choose you? What the hell are you talking about? We weren't like that. You were my best friend, my sister. I mean, you think it would have been alright for me to hit on my sister?"

Even though she suspected it, having her worst fear confirmed took Kenya's breath away. "So you never even thought about it?"

Terrence shifted and leaned back in his seat. The honest answer was 'no,' but he wouldn't say it. "Kenya, I can't do this right now. I … I don't know what I should say. I don't want to hurt your feelings. I love you, you know that. I didn't know."

"Well, now you do," Kenya heard her voice, her unsteady pitch rose and cracked. "What is the problem now?"

Terrence glanced at her like she had two heads. "Well, for one thing, you're married. No, that's reason one, two and three." His voice was tight. "Reason four is my newborn godson. Reason five, I'm married…"

Kenya stared at her lap. *Be calm. Do not cry. Keep yourself together.*

Terrence continued, both hands running through the soft hair, over and over. "…I mean, where would this go? I got enough on my mind with Lani. I can't even entertain this shit right now. Not with you."

Not with me. Kenya knew she was behaving irrationally and that Terrence probably didn't understand most of what she said. Confusion and disappointment twisted her mind and she gave up and stopped trying to explain. "Terrence, take me back to my car."

***

Terrence felt helpless. There was no other way to describe it. He stared at his hands gripping the steering wheel. Silence had settled like a heavy blanket suffocating them both. He didn't really have anything to say. When he glanced at Kenya, he noticed she just sat there with her arms folded and her chin squared as she stared out of the window. For a second Terrence started to speak, to say anything to lighten the mood, but the words evaporated on his lips. Kenya was ignoring him anyway, so his words probably wouldn't make a difference. She had already dismissed his apologies, waved them off with a hand to his face while she stared out of the window. It annoyed him. She annoyed him.

What am I apologizing for, anyway? Fighting the urge to speak, Terrence decided that he didn't want to hear his voice rumbling through the cold car. *Why the hell would she lay this on me, anyway? Why? Your best friend says he's leaving his wife and you hit on him? What type of shit is that?*

It was unbelievable, actually. What did it say about Kenya? *What type of person hits on her best friend? Isn't that like trying to get with your brother? Some ole incestuous stuff. What about her husband? Baby?* What is she thinking? Kenya had always been special because she was the only girl in his world who never tried to get with him. All the women chasing him could be annoying; actually, the nonstop flirting eventually turned into nothing more than a challenge. Every woman had a different angle on it, a different way to get at him. Kenya represented a reprieve, the only one that hadn't given in to it, had looked past his face to learn his person. He thought she saw him for who he was, not that superficial nonsense. But here she was, pulling the same old shit as every other woman. Disappointment blocked his tongue and his mind. It was true that he had kissed back, but only after she put it out there. Confusion had blocked his mind and allowed him to get lost in the physical representation of love and care. But then she tried to get in his pants, treating him like a sexual object. Just like the others.

Loneliness overwhelmed his heart. Suddenly, his world felt so much smaller and closed in. There had been one other girl, actually, who hadn't chased him or obsessed over his physical without even knowing him. Lani. And he missed her. Terrence wondered what Lani was doing right now. *Probably asleep. Downstairs on the couch waiting for me.* The thought of her waiting for him in the white lingerie ignited a fire in the pit of his chest, giving him clarity. He was going home. Returning to his real base. With Lani on his mind, Terrence turned into the plaza parking lot and slid into a spot. He stared straight ahead as he waited for Kenya to exit. They had nothing else to say to each other.

"My car?" Kenya screeched as she waved her arms in the air. "Where is my car?"

***

This was the last thing Terrence wanted deal with. How was he going to explain bringing Christopher's wife home in the middle of the night without a car? And why had Kenya lied to Christopher in the first place? Now Terrence watched her walking around the lot in a blank daze. Now that he thought about it, what had she been planning that she couldn't tell her husband where she was going? This wasn't the first time he had contacted her in the middle of the night needing help and seeking advice. If Kenya had innocent intentions, then she would have told Christopher exactly what was going on. He'd heard it all before anyway. Terrence didn't feel comfortable showing up at Christopher's house with Kenya now, not under these circumstances.

"Terrence, my car has been stolen." Her composure had disappeared, she was terrified. "I know." Terrence climbed out of his car. "Let me think."

"Shit!" Kenya screamed, her voice reverberating through the empty lot. "What am I going to do?" She began hyperventilating. "Wait." She bent over and tried to catch her breath. "What should I do?"

Terrence had never seen Kenya become unglued before. He watched, fascinated for a fraction of a second. It seemed as if a shell had cracked open, and an entirely different person stepped through. This person felt real, her frantic energy resonated as he wondered about Kenya.

She began dry heaving through gut wrenching sobs. "I can't go home. What would Christopher say? What should I do?"

Terrence moved forward and rubbed her back, bending over. "Calm down, Kay Kay." The nickname he hadn't used since middle school slid from his heart. "Just calm down. Then we can figure this out."

Kenya sunk to the pavement. "Christopher. What about Christopher?"

"Listen, I'm going to take you to your parents. It's the only way. Tell Christopher you decided to go by there and fell asleep without realizing it. When you woke up the car was stolen from their yard."

Kenya whimpered; her eyes wide and her fingertips pressed against her cheek, playing it out in her head. She nodded at Terrence with wide helpless eyes. His heart softened.

"Alright." Kenya's acquiescence was quiet.

Terrence bent down and helped her stand. She moved slowly, as if her bones were arthritic. Terrence guided her back to the car, opened the car door, ushered her inside and fastened the seat belt. The need to console her caused him to rub her back. "Kenya, we didn't do anything wrong. It will be alright."

"Yeah," She nodded. "I know."

"Calm down, baby. Just calm down." Terrence grabbed her hand and held it on the short ride to her parents' house. When he pulled into the yard, she took out her key chain. Terrence had forgotten she kept a spare key, just in case. This was even better, he wouldn't even have to face her parents or wait for them to open the door. He went over the plan: "Remember, you brought something from the store to your parents. Fell asleep talking to them. Woke up and the car was gone. Clean and simple."

"Clean and simple." Her simplicity reminded him of a child; fear lingered but the confident stature returning.

"Alright. Good night." Terrence smiled at her and let go of her hand.

"Goodbye, Terrence."

He watched her enter the house and then peeled off into the night. He was ready to go home.

Chapter Fifteen

The house was dark when Terrence pulled into the driveway. He climbed out of his car and glanced at the front of his house in admiration. Terrence loved this house, loved what he had accomplished. His heart skipped a beat as he glanced around the landscaping in pride. What had he been thinking—walking away from his house? Even for just a few hours; this was his home and he wasn't leaving it. Sensor lights lining the brick pavement flicked on as he moved toward the house and climbed onto the brick steps.

Flavored air wafted into his nostrils when he opened the ornate wooden door with the gold plated glass. The house was dark. Terrence smiled. Lani always turned off all the lights when she was upset. *She probably wants me to break my toe, stumbling around in the dark.* He chuckled to himself as he flicked on the hallway light. The soft glow filled the foyer. That was why he loved her, the fight in her made the challenge worth it.

Home. Terrence loved the smell and feel of home.

Terrence climbed the main steps and crossed the bridge to the guest suite. He planned to wash the entire night off, find his bride when he was fresh and clean, and make love to her all over their beautiful home. Terrence imagined Lani naked on the carpet in the hallway, running her hands through his hair. He didn't care what it took—he was going to make that image come true tonight.

Kenya's break down reminded him of the life he escaped—the plastic women with their perfect etiquette and cold souls. Lani was real. He was confident that their marital problems could be resolved. It was time to lose himself completely in his wife. He could even forgive her crucial mistake; the one that had turned his heart to stone. *My son.* He knew it would have been a boy. But he wasn't going to think about that now.

Terrence showered, washing carefully to erase all memory of Kenya and the forbidden kisses. He grabbed a towel after he finished showering and wrapped it loosely around his waist. Wet, he set off to find Lani, walking directly to the master suite.

Lani sat on the bed fully dressed. The white lingerie was gone. So was the look of love. Her eyes were cold and fierce, stopping him in his tracks. Next to her was a duffle bag filled with clothes.

He raised his eyebrows; the unspoken question hovered between them

She rolled her eyes; the answer in the turn of her nose and the rigidness of her spine.

Lani was leaving.

Terrence had to steady himself to keep from staggering. He never thought she would leave him. Never. It had never even occurred to him.

"Oh. You found your way back, huh?" Lani was the first to speak, although she didn't bother to look up.

She was baiting him and he wasn't going to fall for it. He wasn't going to respond to the anger in her voice.

"Baby. Baby, I'm sorry." Terrence moved forward. She would relent eventually. She always did. He just had to wait her out. "I was out of my mind and I know it. I'm sorry."

He leaned forward to touch her and she snatched away from him, standing suddenly.

"You're sorry?" Lani smiled a thin twisted grin that scared him. She looked deranged.

"Come here. Please." He moved forward again and attempted to hug her. "I need you Lani, please. Let me hold you, baby."

Lani jerked away again. The towel fell from his body, leaving him nude; arms opened wide, pleading for his wife. He didn't budge. He wanted her to understand his sincerity.

"Lani, we just had an argument. It's over. Come here."

She looked up and down his body, her eyes resting below his waist. He knew he could get her interested fairly easily. She stepped forward, stopping an inch from him. *Yeah, come to daddy...*

"Obviously," Lani paused and examined the hardened mass that stared straight at her. "Kenya wasn't enough for you tonight." She smiled again. "Or maybe she really couldn't handle you, huh?"

Terrence stood there, speechless. What should he say? Did she know for a fact he had been with Kenya or was she guessing? If she knew, what had she actually seen? Kenya's name from Lani's mouth felt like cold water being splashed across the back of his thighs.

"Yeah, that's what I thought." Lani's voice was riddled with tense satisfaction as she watched his resolve shrivel and retreat.

***

When Lani left Christopher, his gentleness lingered on her skin like morning dew. She recalled the kiss that had stolen her breath, it felt so kind and sincere. But one look in his eyes and she knew that the night was over. For a second, burning shame surged through her body, but his eyes held no judgment and his gentleness restored her comfort level. Christopher's decision protected her, stopped her from retaliating against Terrence with her body.

Lani had driven to her large home and sat in the driveway, contemplating her options. Eventually, she entered the house and loneliness stretched before her like a chasm as she climbed the wide staircase and began packing and folding clothes. She wasn't staying, that much was certain. In fact, Lani felt relief that the house remained empty. She needed the time to think.

While she finished packing, the front door opened. Terrence's light voice carried up the staircase, as he hummed to himself. *This mutha ... after all the friction he caused he has the nerve to come in here humming?*

Lani had almost given herself away in grief, the man who caused all the trouble was humming like he had a secret. The sound of his obnoxious hum grated against her nerves, restructuring her confusion to a solid wall of anger. The cold hard steel spread through her like molten rock. A familiar place. Lani could raise hell while angry; she could tear the entire house down if she had to. Even Terrence knew better than to mess with her once he registered her anger. She calmly sat in the middle of the bed, reliving that night and the past year, waiting for her husband.

When she heard the shower, her worse fears were confirmed. Instinctively, she reached for the nearest vase. She would smash it into the shower. *No. Calm down.* This was not about getting his attention. She just wanted to cause him mental pain and anguish. Give him a taste of her pain.

Lost in her thoughts, she didn't notice him filling the doorway with his long frame, the towel wrapped loosely around his fit body. *Damn, he is fine. But that means nothing right now.* She tore her eyes from his body, noticing the shadow of a grin lurking just underneath his eyes. He had said something, but she missed it, staring at his body. *Focus girl.*

"What?"

Lani knew he was naked on purpose, and she would only lose if she engaged on these terms. She wasn't going to be fooled by Terrence. Determined not to listen, she shoved a few more items in the bag, moving swiftly. He muttered her name with his "desire" voice; the one she thought only belonged to her. *Although, Kenya probably heard it tonight.* Her stomach lurched. She would surely beat Kenya's ass the next time the opportunity arose. *Trust.* But, Terrence would pay a different way.

Lani argued with Terrence with useless words until the towel fell off. Here her man stood, in all his glory, and all Lani could see was another man's wife, on her knees, savoring enjoying what rightfully belonged to her. She unleashed her most deadly weapon, her tongue, to put him in his place. Dethroned his masculine call. Then she swung the heavy bag over her shoulder and marched out of the room.

"You see how you act!" He followed her. "Where do you think you're going?"

This punk ... runs whenever we have problems, but follows me now? "Don't try to flip this, Terrence. Even you don't have that much game."

"Flip what? What are you talking about?" Terrence screamed at Lani's back from the bridge and leaned over the bridge as she descended the stairs.

If he really wanted me, he would have followed me down.

"Where the hell are you going in the middle of the night? What, you think I am going to do—get jealous and react? You runnin' out in the middle of the night, chasing some dude."

"I'm chasing some dude? After you were just with that bitch? Are you crazy?"

"I wasn't with any—"

"Terrence, save it." Lani stopped in the foyer and glared up at him. "I don't want to hear anymore. I don't care anymore."

"What do you expect me to do, Lani? Kiss your ass just because you're throwing out accusations and having a damn tantrum."

Lani took a step toward the door. "I don't give a damn what you do, Terrence. That's the part of this you seem to be missing."

"Yes, you do. You care. Don't front like you don't."

"Are you serious, right now?" Lani shook her head.

"Now, we're children, right? This is some tit for tat bullshit. No, you ain't going no damn where." Terrence headed down the stairs. "You're staying in this house."

Lani swung the front door open, pressing the car alarm. She turned slowly and faced Terrence, looking up at his naked body coming down the stairs.

"I'm leaving, Terrence. You gonna deny you were with Kenya, but I know better."

"What do you know?" He was screaming now, standing only a few steps from the top of the stairs. "What do you know; when I am telling you I was not with Kenya." He was silent for a second as he took deep exaggerated breaths, showing that he was trying to contain himself.

Lani sighed. "Whatever, Terrence. All the drama? Really?"

Terrence stepped down another stair. "Come back up here. Please. I want to talk to you. Let me make things right."

Lani stepped back into the doorframe and swung the bag over her head, so that it lay diagonal across her chest. Squaring her shoulders, and slowing her tongue to speak clearly, she made her final plea.

115

"Last chance, Terrence. Tell the truth. Where were you?"

"I told you...," with forced calm straining his voice, "...I stopped by Christopher's to talk to them. Then I rolled out. Parked and thought about you. Came home. Come up here, baby."

Lani took one step out of the door, with her hand on the doorknob. She wanted to get as far out as she could.

"Terrence," Lani continued with a roll of her eyes. "You weren't at Christopher's tonight. And you weren't parked by yourself. Where do you think I was, while you were hugged up all under that man's wife?"

The foyer fell silent. Terrence's face registered guilt. She stood still, waiting for him to work through the information and arrive at the only logical conclusion. His brow furrowed and he locked eyes with her; the unspoken question lay between them.

Lani cocked her head to the side, raised one eyebrow and shrugged. "Don't worry, baby, I didn't do nothing you didn't do, right?"

He continued to stare.

She smirked.

Terrence let out a guttural roar.

Lani jumped back onto the brick landing and slammed the door. She could hear his feet pounding down the staircase. She ran full speed to her car and locked the door. He reached the car as she was pulling out of the yard, slamming both hands on the hood of the departing vehicle.

"Stop the car! Stop the car, damnit!"

Lani shifted out of reverse, jerking the car into drive. Her eyes were set; she would run him over if she had to. He slapped the hood one last time. Lani sped off into the night, while Terrence ran behind her, chasing the car, naked and exposed.

Chapter Sixteen

"Fuck!" Terrence breathed heavily as he walked back to the empty house and his bare foot scraped a shard of glass. It wasn't until he reached down to brush off the glass that he realized he was butt naked. Homeowner or not, his black behind was going to end up in jail if he didn't get back into the house. He ran to the bushes that lined the sidewalk and crept along them until he reached his driveway. Now, the same sensor lights that had brought him calm before annoyed him as they highlighted his return home. He dashed for the door, while rage twisted in his gut. *That bitch.* He'd always known Christopher wanted her; hell, any man who met her did. But the thought that Christopher would violate Terrence and help himself to his wife infuriated him. An image of them together tore through Terrence like lightning.

I am going to kill him. Period. Burn his house down. Terrence threw on fresh sweats and a T-shirt and bounded down the staircase. Stepping out the door, a small voice whispered in his ear through the bombarding of pain. "*Go after your wife.*"

"Fuck her!" Terrence shouted to himself. He had only left for a few hours and she was off screwing some other woman's husband. That's all it took? She was that much of a tramp? And Kenya's husband at that? Terrence's mother had put up with way more stuff from his pops, and she hadn't dared make the move Lani just made. If Lani was that easily unfaithful, then she wasn't worth it to begin with. No, Terrence was about to give Christopher a beat down; plain and simple.

The voice in his head wouldn't stop as he climbed into his car. *"Go after your wife."*

Terrence slumped down in the car seat. He couldn't believe that Lani and Christopher would do this to him. His wife? His godson's father? Terrence felt paralyzed. They were all traitors. First, Kenya was kissing all over him, her hands reaching down his pants. Then Lani and Christopher were waiting together at his house, getting their freak on in revenge.

All three of them were full of shit.

Wait a minute. Panic replaced anger as logic replaced emotion. *If Lani was with Christopher, then Christopher knew the entire situation and probably put together that Kenya was with him.* Terrence felt his gut drop. *What if Christopher had searched for his wife? What if he had been able to find the car, to know that she had left it and went with someone else?*

For the first time, Terrence really thought about it. What would Christopher had said or thought if Lani went to him and he discovered that Kenya had left her vehicle and "met" with him. It was all so obvious. When he and Kenya had returned to the parking lot, there hadn't been any broken glass or any sign of distress. The car had been taken, not stolen. Taken by Christopher. There was no doubt.

"Shit!" He had to warn Kenya, to let her know that Christopher knew the truth. Their stupid lie wouldn't work. Then again, he needed to check, to verify that Christopher knew the truth and had the car. What about Lani? Where was she going? Terrence didn't know what to do.

***

In the end, the decision was simpler than he had realized. He could always get Lani back; there was no rush in chasing her. He had to know whether Christopher had Kenya's car. The knowledge would change everything.

Terrence parked three blocks away and approached Christopher's home from their neighbor's yard. He climbed over the low brick wall that divided all the homes. He wasn't going to step foot on Christopher's property. Gone was Terrence's righteous indignation against Lani and Christopher. If Christopher had the car, then he had drawn a line in the sand. Terrence wasn't stupid, and he definitely had no intention on confronting a man who looked for his wife while she was with another man, and then retrieved his vehicle and left her stranded. Leaving Kenya without transportation was a clear message.

The lights in Christopher's house were on. Terrence could see right into the kitchen. Christopher was talking on the telephone and tucking a blanket around the car seat containing the baby. *Where is he going?* Terrence crept further up the neighbor's yard until he was opposite Christopher's garage. He groaned as his eyes confirmed what his heart already knew. Kenya's car was stationed in its normal port.

Christopher stepped into the garage, and loaded the car seat into his car, parked next to Kenya's. For an insane second, Terrence wanted to make everything right. He stood straight up, determined to talk man to man with Christopher. But the impossibility of that hit him in the next second. How would he explain being covered in grass and morning dew, his car parked four blocks away while he spied on the man, after having been with his wife through the night? Plus, Terrence still didn't want to think about Christopher alone with Lani. Kenya's car in the garage confirmed his worst nightmare. Of course, Christopher had taken revenge and soiled his wife. It was a fact he would have to swallow. There was really nothing he could do right now. He waited, sitting against the brick wall, until Christopher pulled out of the driveway. Then he slowly climbed back through the various yards to his car.

In the car, Terrence stared into the night. What had he done? He had left, for a couple of hours, and now everything had changed. No one was in their home or their right place. Confusion had replaced stability. Terrence ached for the comfort of home. Not his house, but home. His wife.

He called Lani over and over again, but she refused to answer. His call went to voice mail on the first or second ring. *God, please don't let her go to New York.* There was no controlling the situation once she got around that wild family of hers. Things would surely get out of hand if she told Dee that he had even walked out. But he knew that's where Lani was headed. The empty feeling inside of him grew and, with tears in his eyes, he relented. He had no choice but to follow his wife.

121

The purr of his engine did nothing to calm him. Kenya's scent still lingered in the car. He had to call her, now, while driving after Lani, and warn her that Christopher had the car. A small part of him didn't want to. *Let her suffer, her double dealing caused all this.* But he had to warn her on the basis of their lifelong friendship. He called her cell phone. No answer.

Terrence drove in silence for a few minutes. He called Lani again. No answer.

He went back and forth, calling both for several minutes. "Pick up the phone, damnit!" Terrence's voice rumbled through the car. He had never had a hard time reaching both of them before —someone was always there at his beck and call. One of his women—wife or sister.

"Alright, you don't have to yell."

Terrence went mute. He had forgotten whose number he had dialed.

"Hello?" The lighter voice was tense and stressed out. It was Kenya.

"Yeah," Terrence breathed. Kenya's voice was thick, but he knew she hadn't been asleep. "Listen Lani and Christopher know we were together. I don't know how. Your car is at home so don't lie when you finally talk to him. Just tell him you met me at your parents."

"What! That doesn't make sense. Why would I meet you there?"

Terrence sighed. Of course it didn't make sense. None of it made any sense. He pressed forward. "Listen. Tell him you were trying to talk me into going home with Lani. Uh, I took you to your parents and you fell asleep."

"Now coming here makes me look guilty, either way. Oh God, my baby. I left my baby."

"Alright, try this..." the phone beeped. Terrence checked the Caller ID. It was Lani. "Uhm, Kenya, you have to hold on."

"What! You can't put me on—"

Terrence clicked over, cutting Kenya off. "Where are you?" His voice was deep, angry.

"Why do you keep calling me, you cheating bastard? Stop calling this phone." Lani sniffed. Terrence felt a small thrill pass through him that she sounded so upset. She was still his.

"I didn't cheat, Lani. I swear." The statement was met with silence. At least she wasn't screaming. "Where are you?"

More silence. It was obvious that she was beyond angry. "Lani, baby, let me meet you. I understand about you and Christopher. I'm not mad at you, I swear."

"You understand? You're not mad at me? What did you just say to me?"

Terrance knew he had said the wrong then, but the words were out there and he couldn't pull them back.

"Fuck you, Terrence."

"Promise me. Please, promise you will." More silence, but he could tell she smiled, despite herself. He knew her well, had trained her body to respond to him, even when her mind didn't want to.

"95 North. Near Wilmington."

Delaware? She had made it to Delaware already? "Get off at the nearest hotel. I'll meet you there."

"No." Lani didn't hesitate. Terrence hated when she said 'no.' "I am going home."

"Aw baby, don't do this. Stop at a hotel, just to get some rest. Don't keep driving tired, you've been up all night. Just stay by that plaza, where we always stop for gas. There's a couple of decent hotels over there. Are you near there?"

Her pause felt like hours. "I'll be there in a few minutes."

"By the Wal-mart?"

"Yes, Terrence, I know where we stop for gas."

"I'm going to drive up and I'll call when I get to that area. If you don't want to see me tonight, then I'll get a separate room. Okay?" There was no way that Terrence was sleeping in a separate bed. He would be inside of his wife before it was all said and done. Of that, he was confident.

"Alright." Lani sounded weak. Guilt flooded his mind. "I love you, baby."

She didn't respond.

He tried again. "I'll call you when I get there."

"Alright," Lani said again and hung up.

Terrence lowered the phone and offered up a prayer of thanks. She would wait for him in Delaware. If he could just keep her from New York and Dee then he had a chance. He rode in silence for five minutes, thinking about the best way to approach Lani.

A nagging feeling crept at him. What was he forgetting?

It wasn't until he turned on the radio that Kenya returned to the fringes of his thoughts. Fumbling with the phone, he flipped it back open and called Kenya.

Her voice sounded foreign. "I can't believe you put me on hold, you self centered asshole."

Chapter Seventeen

Kenya stared at the tiny phone in her hand. Had Terrence really just put her on hold? In the middle of telling her that her life was completely ruined, he had put her hold. For Lani. "For his wife," she said out loud, her voice echoing off the walls in the guestroom, located in the mammoth basement of her parent's house.

What had she been thinking? She laid the phone on the bed, moving in slow motion. Here she had been, hoping, praying and dreaming about a man for years, only to find out that he had never given the idea of her much thought. She lay across the bed and mulled over the dull feeling of rejection. It occurred to her that she hadn't experienced it before. Kenya had always been so careful, always mindful to present herself just right and only allow the proper boy to pursue her. Now, her careful, planned life was upside down because of Terrence, and Lani was still on the forefront of his mind.

The phone rang again. She started not to answer it; how much more could she take tonight? But Terrence owed her, he was the cause of the problem, he had better find a way to fix it.

"I can't believe you put me on hold, you self centered asshole."

"What? Self centered? What did I do to you that was self centered? My damn wife was on the phone."

Kenya wanted to jump through the phone, wrap her small hands around his neck and throttle him. "Yeah, the wife you just left a few hours ago."

"No, you got it twisted—the wife that was, is and always will be mine." His voice was irritated, nasty. She had never heard this tone. Terrence had never used it with her or anybody else that she could recall. "So hell yeah, I put your ass on hold for my wife."

"Who the fuck do you think you're talking to?" Only the knowledge that her parents were asleep two levels above kept her from screaming. "I risked everything, everything for your ass. And this is how you are? You put me on hold and then talk to me like I'm trash?"

A heavy screeching sound filled the phone. For a dreadful moment, Kenya expected to hear a collision. Then she realized that she had just heard Terrence slam the brakes, bringing his car to an immediate halt.

"*You* risked everything? What? Hell no. Shit, you put everything at risk. Who the hell told you to lie to your husband? And why? Why didn't you just tell him what was up? Because your ass wanted to creep; not because you were risking shit for me."

"No Terrence, you can believe what you want to flatter yourself." Embarrassment made Kenya's face hot, she was glad that she was alone in this moment, hidden from eyes that would see the secrets of her soul etched across the pain in her face. "What was I supposed to say? 'By the way, Christopher, I'm going out in the middle of the night to meet Terrence?'"

"Hell yeah, that's exactly what you should have said. Or better yet, 'Terrence, I don't feel like coming out, you come over here.' Here's another one for you, why not tell Christopher that I am losing it and let him come talk to me, man to man." Terrence was screaming into her ear.

She swallowed. "Stop yelling at me."

Terrence ignored her quiet request. "It's time to be honest. This is your shit, coming on to a married man when he's at his lowest. You're so damn righteous and sanctimonious all the damn time, but I try to confide and there you go—down my pants."

"I didn't come on to you, Terrence." Her voice was low, quiet and shaky.

"Bull shit. I fell for it, for a minute. But then you tried to molest me and shit. Knowing we are both married. Now you going to sit here and talk about you risked some shit?"

Kenya remained silent.

"You were the one plotting, Kenya," Terrence hadn't taken a breath; his words were coming out in short puffs. "Now this shit has blown up in both our faces. Talking about what you risked; hell, where do you think Lani was while you were trying to fish for gold."

"Why would I care?"

"Of course, you wouldn't care. Because you don't think past what you want. But *my* wife sat with *your* husband waiting for me. So don't tell me what you risked..."

Kenya's ears went numb. *What? Lani had been with Christopher? Alone?* She couldn't speak, not that Terrence would have given her a chance. He was on a roll.

"...shit, I trusted you. Now, Lani is sure we fucked and Christopher obviously thinks so, too. Who knows what they did in response? But, I tell you what else. Whatever they did, that man had enough spite in his heart to get his ass up in the middle of the night and take your car. He left you without transportation." Terrence dragged out those last five words. "You need to think on that, instead of coming at me with that self pity bullshit."

Kenya remained silent.

Terrence breathed.

The silence seemed to last forever. Terrence finally spoke with a soft voice, an obvious attempt to regroup. "We need to come up with a cover before we both get busted over some shit that I didn't even do."

There was no cover good enough to undo the wrong that had been done.

Kenya lowered the phone, oblivious to the tears streaming down her face. What had she done? She thought of her beautiful baby boy and began to sob.

***

"When did you get here?" The gentle sound of motherly love and warmth filled the wide guest bedroom. Startled, Kenya jumped further back on the bed. Kenya's mother, Connie, stood in the doorway, her short stout frame leaning on a bat.

"Ma, you scared me."

Connie sighed with a wide smile. "I heard something, and you know your father. James sent me down here in the middle of the night to face the burglars." Connie stepped into the room.

"You can't creep up on folks like that, you scared me," Kenya tried to smile, but she didn't have it in her.

"Hmph. A grown married woman in my basement without her family … just before dawn? Am I the one who should be scared?"

Kenya's head drooped, the blanket of despair draped around her. Thank God her father hadn't come down here. What would she have said? What should she say now?

"Kenya, what is going on?" Connie pressed her lips together as she sat on the bench at the foot of the bed.

Kenya wondered what her mother would think about her racing out in the middle of the night. The situation was so pathetic that it was almost laughable. Terrence had cussed her out. Christopher had taken her car. She missed her baby boy, who would have accompanied her in the bed by now. She was the better woman, the one who was trained to be a queen. Yet, the men around her were turning on her, taking the side of the simple tramp that didn't deserve any of it.

She exhaled deeply and then allowed the story to tumble out to Connie. One thing about her mother—

she didn't hold grudges against anyone, didn't judge people for their faults and she was the master secret keeper. Kenya told it all, grateful that Connie listened carefully, without any judgmental grunts or moans. This was why Connie's friends were always at their house, looking to Connie for comfort. When she finished, exhausted by the mere thought of how foolish she looked, her mother held her for a few minutes, rocking, like when she was a child.

"I'm going to lose everything ..." Kenya's mind focused on Christopher for the first time, "... and over what? I don't know why I acted the way I did. Why did I lie?"

Connie peeled Kenya from her small frame and disappeared into the hallway. She returned a few minutes later, a box of tissue in hand. Partially closing the door to block the sound of their voices, but leaving it ajar enough to still hear anyone that might approach in the hall, she handed Kenya the tissue.

"I had to check in with your dad, let him know that I was still alive. Obviously, he wasn't too concerned."

Kenya smiled as she wiped her face with the small tissue. Somehow, Connie always made everything alright. That comment alone had returned Kenya to some level of normalcy.

"Now listen, little girl." The matronly woman disappeared; Connie wore a stern expression with hands on her hips and her eyebrow raised. Kenya's stomach dropped as she watched the tiny woman in front of her transform into the powerful force Kenya had always known. Apparently, she wasn't going to the same 'listen without advising' treatment that Connie's friends received. "You don't ever expose your life, lifestyle, family and least of all your husband to someone else's bullshit."

Kenya's mouth flew open. Connie never cussed.

"That was your first mistake. Your reasons are irrelevant, for now. There are ground rules to marriage, which are formed from steel. You don't bend them, you don't break them. That man is paying the bills, feeding and clothing you and providing for your family—your future. You don't run out in the middle of the night to anybody else, for anybody else. Period."

"I didn't think ..."

"Doesn't matter. This is real life, now. No kid's games."

Kenya's neck burned in shame.

Connie sat next to Kenya on the bed and patted her knee. Her voice sounded tired. "You have got to let go of this idea of you and Terrence. You don't want to trade places with Lani, trust me honey. Plus, no one man is easier than the other; they all have something about them that we have to tolerate. Some bullshit or another."

Kenya nodded. She saw that now.

Connie ignored her, the lessons flowing from her now. "And another thing, I don't like how ya'll treat Lani. None of you. I watched how rude you were at your last cookout. How Terrence judged everything she did. It's uncalled for."

"You don't know her ..."

"Please, child, I used to be her."

"No," Kenya shook her head emphatically, "you could never be her."

"Honey, please. I am from the streets of Philly. Met your father and thought I saw the sun and moon. I had to adapt to this lifestyle and all the hypocrisy it brings."

"Ma, you don't—"

"No, listen. You know why you never realized that your father and I are from two different realities? 'Cause your father treated me like a princess and cut off anyone who didn't accept it. And I did the same. We formed a bond and we respected it. But Terrence, he never stands up for his wife."

Kenya couldn't deny the truth. "No, he doesn't."

"And you think he is considerate and inclusive? You think he is someone who will put your needs first and treat you like a rare gem? Judge a man by the way he treats his family. Sweetie, I trained you better."

Kenya nodded.

Connie lowered her voice in a conspiratorial whisper. "If you need to creep around, then I have nothing to say, but running out in the middle of the night is not the smartest way to accomplish that goal."

Kenya gaped at her mother. Had she cheated on her father?

"Don't look at me that way. It's none of your damn business if I did or didn't. What is your business is effectively managing your marriage. Which means being smart enough to keep your extracurricular activities confidential and staying the hell away from the Terrences of this world."

"Stop." Kenya raised her hands, smiling. "Really— I can't take anymore." She plugged her ears and Connie laughed, pulling down her hands.

"Alright, little girl. I'll stop, for now. So where is your husband?"

Kenya shrugged.

"Then locate him. You should always know where he is—haven't I taught you anything?" Connie stood and adjusted the belt of her robe. "I will do you a onetime favor and fix this disaster, but you better watch and learn, 'because I am not in the business of regularly patching up foolishness."

Chapter Eighteen

Christopher banged on the large lion knocker to the front door of the mammoth house. He had kicked the bulbs of the stupid sensor lights as he walked up the long brick path. He contemplated kicking their front door, but chose to slam the door knocker instead. No need in harming his foot or his ankle, he would need them at full strength for when he rammed his foot up Terrence's ass.

Son of a bitch is in here. I know it. He had spoken to Lani, she called to tell him she was leaving town. She said he had come home alone, they had argued and she was leaving. Christopher hadn't directly asked about Kenya, he was too embarrassed, but he had listened to the spaces between words, the pauses between sentences. Kenya had to know her car was missing. She had to know that Christopher knew she had been with Terrence. And she hadn't come home.

Lani's phone call triggered something deep in Christopher; it focused the random anger and confusion that had been bouncing around in his mind. Enough waiting around, enough of being reactive—it was time to get proactive. This mess was getting settled tonight, on his terms. If Lani had left and Terrence hadn't followed, then Kenya might be hiding

135

out at Terrence's. Wherever they were, together or separate, Christopher would find them both tonight, and he would end this his way, tonight.

The only serene moment he had had this night came when he dropped off little Christopher over his sister Jackie's house. He hadn't called first; there was no need. Christopher knew that Darryl had kept Jackie fully informed; Darryl and Jackie were fraternal twins, there was nothing that they didn't share. When he pulled into her yard, his lights piercing the dark around her small home, the door had opened. Jackie stood waiting for him, his older sister—the only mother he had ever known.

Christopher's hands were shaking when he handed his baby to Jackie. He hadn't noticed the small tremor; Jackie held his hands for a long time, as little Christopher rested in her arms. They stood in silence. There weren't many words to be said, and Jackie wasn't much of a talker. Plus, Christopher hadn't wanted Jackie to talk him down, he needed his anger to propel him forward, his fury to allow him to stretch past reason and properly raise hell. Being around Jackie would only calm him; he needed to get away from her.

Christopher had pulled his hand back. Jackie had attempted to calm him down with soothing words. "Everything ain't what it seems Christopher."

Little Christopher's soft cocoa skin shined against hers. Sometimes, during tender moments like this, when worry surged from her wide eyes and her gentle face seemed sad, he would get a small remembrance of his mother. Just a floating nostalgia, like the gentle whiff of bread baking, that pulled up a deep sadness.

For an instant, emptiness struck at his heart. No. He could not afford to be sad, not right now. It would consume him, cause him to lose heart when he confronted Terrence and dismissed Kenya. He had left; handed Jackie the baby bag and walked out into the night, without a word.

Now he stood with his eyes pressed against the glass plates on the side of the double wooden doors. Kenya was to be dismissed. He would raise his son alone and they would be alright. *Where are they?* Christopher walked the length of the house, kicking over a few more lights. He peered through the garage window. *Shit, empty.* He kicked the garage door, leaving a large black scuff mark on the crisp white door.

Where in the hell were they?

He stood still, calculating his options in his mind. He didn't want to leave a note or any kind of warning for either of them. Right now, neither Terrence nor Kenya knew what he knew or where he stood. He had the advantage. That's how it needed to stay. There was only one person who might have more information, someone who no one would suspect he was still communicating with.

Lani. He would call Lani and find out whether she had heard from Terrence. It was obvious that Kenya had made a choice, a choice that shouldn't have been made available to her. For that option, Terrence was going to pay. As far as Christopher was concerned, Kenya would spend a life time paying.

He tapped this Bluetooth as he headed to his car. Instead of getting in, he leaned against the car and listened as the phone rang. *Pick up. Please. Pick up.*

"'Lo." Lani's voice was light and airy.

"It's me." It struck Christopher as odd that he and Lani were at a different level already, that saying "it's me" wasn't inappropriate or odd. Like two individual pieces of metal that had suddenly been twisted together and melded into a unit.

"Hey me," she giggled.

He had never heard Lani giggle before, it wasn't her style. *Is she high?* "It's Christopher."

"I know." She seemed suddenly somber, then giddy in the next moment. "Of course I know."

"Heard from Terrence?"

"Nope." Lani belched and then laughed.

"Uh, what are you doing?"

"Nothing."

Christopher waited.

Lani sighed, admission oozing out of her like gel. "Keepin' them off my mind, that's what."

He could hear it now, the slur, and the slight hiccups. She was completely drunk.

"Where are you?"

"Harione Hotel. Wilmington. Kinda." There was a long pause, as if she were trying to measure each word before it exited her lips. "Terrence was supposed to meet me, if I wanted. I think the answer is no, though."

"What?" Christopher climbed in his car.

"Huh?"

"Lani, he's coming to meet you?"

She didn't answer. Christopher didn't press; he already had the key in the ignition to his Altima and was rolling out of the driveway.

She finally continued. "He suggested."

"So he's not with Kenya?"

"Hope not. He wasn't then. I don't think. Where are you?"

"On my way to Delaware."

"Chris, Chris baby, listen."

The familiarity with which she called him 'baby' and confidently referred to him by the nickname only she had claim to caused a chill to go through him. Christopher dismissed it. "Lani, you can't hold alcohol, that's for sure. I'm listening…"

"Think about your baby, Chris. Remember him when you see her." She belched again, but no laugh this time. "You can't ruin his life, can't overreact. Please, promise me."

"Can't promise that."

"Chris, Chris please, please promise. Please." Her shrieks were loud; he pulled the Bluetooth from his ear for a second. She was still talking when he put it on again. "Think about your baby," she cried, her voice getting softer, quieter. "Poor poor baby."

Something was wrong. It was more than him, Kenya and Terrence. This event had apparently sparked some memory of another painful event. Christopher recognized the pain and the panic, like he had felt earlier when he thought about Alayna. Tonight, all the ghosts were jumping out of closets.

The phone went dead.

"Hello?"

Nothing. She was gone. Christopher tried to call back, but the call went straight to voicemail. Terrence and Kenya disappeared in the sea of worry that surged forward. Lani was alone at a hotel, drunk and hurting. Christopher wanted nothing more than to get to her, to help her. Lani's layers were peeling away and her core was exposed. She didn't deserve to be alone. He was going to Wilmington. He had to. What if Lani tried to drive, tried to seek out Terrence or Kenya. Worse yet, what if she drowned in her memories and did something permanent in response? He had to get to her. He couldn't survive another Alayna incident, couldn't stomach another loss of that magnitude, even if Lani didn't have his heart. Yet.

Chapter Nineteen

"It ain't like that, Tommy!" Sophie's shout filled the hallway outside of their apartment.

Dee and Lani glanced at each other; they hadn't expected Sophie back so soon. She had left with her best friend Rhonda, and they both had on club dresses. Lani and Dee knew the drill; they hunkered down around the television with popcorn and soda. Dee would clean it all up before they went to bed and their mother returned, like she always did.

"I know what I saw!" The deep rumbling voice echoed in Lani's mind. She stood up. She sat back down. Dee motioned her to the bedroom; Dee stood up slowly and crept down the hallway, her fingertips tracing path along the wall.

Lani didn't move.

"Get in your room, Lani."

Lani shook her head no.

"You make me so sick sometimes," Dee said, rolling her eyes. Lani paid her no attention. She was stuck to her seat, listening to the sound of Sophie beg and plead. She had never heard that sound before. Sophie was always laughing, always having fun. Sometimes cursing and wilding out. Never begging and scared. She had too much family for that, too many men in her family who would take a charge for defending Sophie without blinking. The new sound of her mother's weakness made Lani feel sick.

"I'm calling Auntie." Lani made the announcement as she headed to the small kitchenette for the phone.

"No, don't." Dee held her hand up. "You just gonna get in trouble once Auntie come all the way over here for nothing. Mommy gonna know you called then it's gone be an ass whipping for nothing."

Lani ignored her, heading for the phone anyway.

"Don't!" Dee's shout stopped Lani. "You ain't the one she gonna beat, Lani. Don't."

Lani stood still. It was true; Sophie didn't lay hands on her. She thought it was because she was the baby. Dee always said it was because she was the lighter of the two. Sophie would look at Dee in disgust, her lips curled when she observed her, and spit out, "you look just like your damn daddy." Lani suspected that was probably the real reason Dee got the spankings. Whoever Dee's father was, Sophie didn't even like the thought of him.

"I swear, I didn't do nothing. I swear it." The sound of Sophie's voice was terrifying.

Dee stepped on the small stool she kept by the door and peered into the peephole. Lani stepped into the kitchen.

"I'ma kill you, bitch." His voice held those words like they were a promise.

"Tommy, no. You gotta listen to me. It wasn't like that."

Sophie's heels clicked rapidly on the floor, she was running to the door. Dee jumped off the stool and began removing the security bar that was bolted to the floor.

"No, don't move the bar!" Lani said.

"She got to get in, Lani." Using her entire 70 pounds, Dee managed to unlatch the bar with a grunt. They could hear Sophie's key scratching the lock. Dee always removed the bar before they went to sleep, so her mother could get in later on in the night; but Lani's gut told her that this was a night to keep her mother and the man she was with locked out.

"Lani, go to the room." Dee picked up the stool as Lani tried to cut across the narrow living room to their bedroom. Neither was fast enough. The door flew open as if a powerful gust of wind had blasted through. Their mother's frail body flew in motion with the door until she slammed against the opposite wall. Tommy stepped into the apartment, filling the small hallway space as he picked Sophie up by the neck. "So what you thought, that you was going to play me?"

"No, Daddy, it wasn't like that." Sophie's face was the perfect picture of terror. Both Lani and Dee stood in one place.

"Ya'll get your asses to your room," Tommy said, without looking at them.

Neither of them moved.

Sophie turned her head to the side—despite his painful grip—and looked at them. She had blood on

143

her lips, a cut under her blackened eye. "Dee, get your asses in the room. Now." Sophie always gave the command to both of them by addressing Dee.

"Mommy," Lani stepped forward.

"Now damnit!" Sophie's shout made Lani flinch.

Dee grabbed Lani by the hand and jerked her into the bedroom. She yanked Lani from the door and slammed it. Dee stepped onto the bed, balanced on the footboard, jumped onto the dresser and leaned on the door frame. She was just tall enough to slide on the chain that their Uncle Lonzo had put in for them a couple of months ago.

"No, Dee, don't lock it. We gotta call Auntie Marie."

Dee ignored her, knowing that Lani couldn't reach the chain, even if she stood on the dresser.

"Dee … we gotta—"

"Get under the bed, Lani." Dee wasn't listening; she was already assuming her hiding position in the toy chest.

Lani could hear her mother's screams getting louder, could hear the saliva gurgling in her throat as Tommy continued to press against her esophagus.

She opened the door as hard as she could, hoping to break the chain.

"Lani, stop it!"

"He's hurting her." Lani slammed the door and pulled it open again with all her strength. The chain didn't budge. Sophie's screams got softer; Tommy's words were harsher, louder.

"Say that lie again." Tommy taunted Sophie. "It's going to be the last lie formed on your lips."

Lani yanked the door open again. The wood frame underneath it wasn't steady, she remembered Uncle Lonzo warning them not to pull on it too much. She had asked him what was the point of a chain couldn't no one pull on and he had laughed at her for being a smart ass, as usual. Tonight, thankfully, she remembered—probably because she had been so mad at him for laughing at her. Lani yanked again. The screws budged a little bit. But it was enough for her to squeeze her tiny frame through the door.

"No!" Dee's cry faded into oblivion as Lani sped out of the bedroom toward her mother. She was running blind, anger removing all sight and eliminating all fear. She had to stop Tommy from hurting Sophie.

Sophie was clawing at him; he was slapping her hands away and laughing, taunting her. Lani's hand scraped the screw driver that always sat by the television—without thinking she held it like a knife, like she had seen Dee do a million times before, and tried to plunge it into his thigh.

It didn't work. It fell to the ground.

"What the hell?" Tommy glanced down at her as the screw driver banged to the floor. He released his grip for a second. Sophie got free, gasping deeply for air, bent over at the waist, her hands bracing against her knees. Lani punched Tommy's thigh. He smiled at her, pushed her gently back. "Go on, little girl, get the fuck back…"

Lani felt nails scratch her back just before she was rocketed through the air. She screamed, stunned that

Sophie had gathered strength from an unknown source and thrown her away from Tommy. She landed on the floor by the sofa, her tooth digging into her lip. Lani screamed out in pain.

"Mommy!"

"Stay, Lani, don't move," Dee whispered.

Lani turned to look at her mother, to find out why her mother would turn on her and throw her like that.

The picture was one she would never forget. Sophie and Tommy were fighting, scrambling on the floor, knocking into furniture. It was survival now. There were no words. Both had the clear intention to kill the other one. Sophie had grown up fighting boys, she wasn't as strong, but she was holding her own. For the moment.

Dee pulled on Lani, trying to lead her into the kitchen. Lani didn't move; although she wanted to, instinct told her not to go back to her mother. The taste of blood on Lani's tongue from her lip made her nauseas. As she bent over to still her spinning head she saw Sophie's arm raised in the air. Lani saw the glint of metal against the reflection from the television screen. Sophie's arm plunged down into Tommy's flesh over and over again, blood squirting onto both of them.

Lani screamed and curled her body into the fetal position. "Stop stop stop ..." She covered her eyes with her fists as the wet stickiness of blood splashed on her.

"Help!" Dee's shrieks into the phone could barely be heard between Lani's screams and Sophie's grunts. "Please come help. He's hurting my mommy..."

Lani crawled behind the couch. "Mommy, please stop. Please, please, please stop it!" She couldn't shout anymore. Her voice was gone.

The sickeningly soft sound of metal plunging into flesh faded away; Lani heard her mother sobbing. It felt like hours passed while she sat listening to Sophie, knowing that everything had just changed irreparably.

Lani finally peeked from behind the couch. Careful not to look at the huge bloodied mass at her mother's feet, she tried to see where Dee was. Lani edged her small body to the other end of the couch and looked over at Dee, who held onto the telephone receiver.

"Dee, come here." Sophie's voice sounded resigned.

Dee shook her head 'no,' the phone receiver stuck to her ear.

"Dee, get your ass over here. You have to help me."

Dee didn't move. Lani didn't move.

"Dee, call Marie." Sophie's voice was a whisper. "Tell her I need help. Tell her to bring Lonzo."

Dee jumped, as if snapping out of a deep sleep. "Mommy—"

The knock at the door startled all three of them. Dee dropped the receiver. Lani crawled toward her bedroom, finally craving the sanctuary under the bed.

"Shit!" Sophie looked at Dee. "Who did you call?"

"911. Mommy ... I didn't know—" Lani could hear the terror in Dee's voice.

"Why—?"

147

"I didn't know what to do…" Dee sobbed. She sounded so tiny and scared that Lani wanted to help her, wished that she could comfort her. But she wasn't coming out from under that bed for anybody.

"Dee, you called the cops—?"

The rest of her words were drowned out by the sound of heavy footsteps in the hallway. Lani held her breath and prayed that this would all go away, that the night could reset itself. She held her breath until everything faded to black.

***

A ringing sound broke through Lani's darkened haze. Memories lingered around the edges of her essence; she wanted to erase them or, better yet, believe that they hadn't really happened, that it had been some other little girl who suffered so much. Normally, she kept the memories under control—busied herself to keep her mind preoccupied.

For some reason, Lani couldn't move. The ringing sounded again. She thought of Dee, of that phone call that changed everything so many years ago, of so much responsibility being placed on a baby. Lani groaned. It wasn't worth thinking about; the past couldn't be changed.

It was more ringing that pushed Lani's mind to the present, to identify the foreign sound that was scratching her eardrums. The telephone. She didn't want to answer it. *Who could be calling anyway?* She reached for her cell phone, using her toes to push forward against the edge of the bed. In that instant, the entire room flipped upside down. Nausea stirred in the pit of her belly, the back of her throat tingled. Her head hurt. *Hangover. Shit.* Lani swallowed and took a deep breath. She fought through the feeling to reach for her cell phone, but couldn't even open her eyes to look at the screen.

"Yeah."

No one answered. The ringing continued.

"Shh." Lani tucked her head against her pillow. Maybe the ringing was just in her head? She rolled over, slowly, very slowly, and peeked through squinted eyes. It rang again. *The hotel phone.* In order to answer it, she would have to turn her entire body around, so that her head was closer to the pillows. She slowly began the semicircle turn, feeling like a seal pushing around on its belly. The bed was wet. Had she vomited during the night? *Damn, that's gross.* The smell wafted past her face, causing her to lurch and vomit again.

The phone rang. It stopped for a second after every fifth ring and then started again. There was no way Lani could make it to the phone. The Ciroc she had poured and mixed with Nuvo came to mind. Dread filled her; there was no need to even think about it, it would just make things worse. She had bought huge bottles of both when she left Virginia, intent on drowning out the pain with something once she got to New York. Stopping in Delaware was just as good. She had rented a suite, with its own kitchen, living room and master bedroom. Fuck Terrence, she didn't want to see him. She just wanted to rest here, get a chance to clear her mind and think about her life and her next moves. That was her intent. That's what she was thinking with the first serving of the sweet mixed drink. But by the third serving, her goal was to clear and mind. And she had accomplished it.

149

Temporarily. Until the dreaded reliving of the past had happened and she couldn't wake herself up to make it stop.

The phone rang. Lani couldn't make it. Covered in vomit, she had to focus on getting to the bathroom, not on hearing whatever the desk clerk wanted to tell her. They had her credit card, why couldn't they just leave her alone?

A few minutes later, Lani had managed to throw one leg over the side of the bed. She wanted to snatch the damn phone out of the wall, but the thought of the physical exertion and its undoubted side effects quieted the urge. Her other leg had finally followed suit. Lani slid off the bed, only to find herself in a heap on the floor. *This is going to be bad.* Laughter spilled over, transforming into tears. Had she not been in so much pain, it would have been funny. Instead, it was just pathetic.

The ringing stopped. *Finally.* Lani took small baby crawls, but even that motion proved to be too much. Dizziness took over. She lay on the rug, disgusted that her face was against the nappy carpet. At least she didn't have to smell her waste.

"Mrs. Powell? Hello, Mrs. Powell?" The clerk's voice. *What does he want? How long does he work anyway?*

"Mrs. Powell, I'm entering the suite. Can you hear me?"

"Move out of my way." The deep voice behind the clerk echoed in Lani's mind. She knew the voice, but couldn't place it.

"No, sir, you cannot enter the suite .... you have to wait in the hall." The clerk sounded irritated.

Lani sighed. The last thing she wanted was for Terrence to find her like this. It would be just one more thing he would use to throw up in her face. There was no telling how Terrence had found her. Disappointment settled in like a heavy sponge in her stomach. He had found her; she might as well release the idea of a peaceful weekend. This was going to turn into either the Terrence pity party or a weekend defending against blame. Lani was tired, too tired to fight him anymore tonight.

The deep voice kept talking to the clerk. "Listen, don't touch me. Call security if you have to, but I am entering the suite. You've wasted enough time."

It wasn't Terrence. The cool deep voice soothed Lani and momentarily allowed her to think about something other than her splitting head. She knew it wasn't Terrence because he didn't have it in him to talk like that, to buck the status quo. The deep voice also couldn't have been any of the men in her family, because the clerk wasn't getting his ass beat, nor was he calling the police.

The deep voice came closer. "Lani are you in here? Are you alright?"

She wanted to say she was fine, but lifting her head required her neck to move and she couldn't recall how to connect with that particular muscle. A brown leather shoe turned the corner, rushed forward, lifted her. Questions filled the air, words circled her. She was oblivious, wishing this person would stop moving her, so she could open her eyes without vomiting again.

"No, no, sir, I think I found the culprit." The clerk's voice broke through, sounding politely sarcastic.

"Definitely no need for an ambulance, not just yet." The bottle of alcohol swished and the sound seemed louder than an ocean in Lani's head.

"Thank God," the deep voice had become hoarse. *Who cared this much?* She cracked her eyes, just a little, hoping it wasn't Terrence's father. The man cradling her filthy body against his clean shirt, pushing the hair back from her forehead, and rocking her ever so gently and kindly, ignoring the awful pungent smell of orange juice vomit, was Chris. Chris. Chris had come to her, despite his own needs and worries tonight.

A current of energy swept through her, like warm sunshine. She had not felt this in a long time, possible for many years. She didn't know what to call the feeling, but her mind and body went limp, and a deep sigh escaped her. At least for a little while, she would be able to rely on someone else for the first time in years.

Chapter Twenty

Terrence slammed his hand against the steering wheel. He had been driving around this Wilmington suburb for the last forty minutes, looking for Lani's car at every hotel. *Why won't she answer the damn phone? Ain't this some shit, got me all the way in Delaware and want to play games. Typical.*

Terrence pulled into the parking lot of another major chain. *Nothing.* The muscles in his neck and back ached. His eyes drooped. He needed sleep. He refused to keep driving around without direction. Terrence climbed out of the car and strolled into the lobby of the hotel. While registering, he took stock of his situation. He had started a bunch of craziness, which was for sure. He understood that much, although he didn't believe he was completely to blame. *Some night, huh?* Lani shouldn't have set him off by acting a complete fool early. When was she going to apologize for that? Here he was, pointing out all her debt, and she starts raging. *The usual temper tantrums.* Some counseling, that's what she needed. Some professional help.

He entered the wide room. Barely glancing around, he stripped down to his boxers and climbed in the bed. *Why did Lani always have to overreact? Always causing some drama.* Here he was, in this strange bed in a distant state because she had to flee to New York in true drama queen fashion. *Hell, why did she even run out of the house like that? Wanting some drama. Wanting me to chase her. That's why she ain't answering that phone.*

A part of him was pissed off. In the end, everything turned out to be about her, didn't it? In the end, his loneliness, the confusion he suffered, would be ignored. It would be all about the hurt he caused Lani. He didn't really feel like apologizing, playing the begging role tonight. Truth be told, she owed him some apologies, too. There was no telling what she and Christopher had done, not really. *She shouldn't have compromised herself like that; hell she's a married woman.*

No. I am not going to do this. When it was all said and done, no matter how he tried to rationalize it, he missed his wife. And Lani had a right to be upset, even if it was over a misunderstanding. He missed her, and it hurt deep down. He only had a right to fuss if he knew that she still belonged to him. Right now, he didn't know anything. Fading off to sleep, he grasped the pillow next time him and bunched it next to his arm, wishing it were the soft full body of his wife.

Undergrad images floated through Terrence's mind. Lani lay on the bed in the dinky hotel room on the beach. They rented those cheap $19.00 rooms regularly, the only time they could get privacy. She stared at him as he danced on the bed, naked, for this girl that had stolen his heart. She giggled and laughed, head thrown back, mouth wide open.

Then he saw her, on top of him, while he lay flat on his back, watching her in amazement. She looked like an angel and he knew he was a lucky man. While

154

she looked into his eyes, her face glowed in pleasure; he watched her eyes bright and sparkling. But she began to fade. He reached up to place his hands around her waist, but grasped at thin air. Her face transformed as it faded, years adding on, tears tumbling down her face, landing on his chest. Turmoil twisted the passionate expression into unspeakable confusion. Then she smiled, a sad smile, and whispered.

"What?" Terrence was afraid to move, afraid to lose the image. "I can't hear you, baby. Say again?"

"Goodbye," the image whispered, slightly louder.

"No!" Terrence screamed, trying to hold the face in his hands, but once again grasped air as the image, the vision of Lani, disappeared.

Terrence woke up and sat up straight. Sweat poured down his back, goose bumps all over his body. Enough. He had to find his wife. Grabbing the cell phone, he knew immediately that she had not called. Where had she gone? New York?

He repeatedly called her cell phone. If she had made her way to New York, their marriage was over.

Nausea rolled through his stomach, his damp skin felt cold. Clutching his stomach, he ran to the commode, dry heaving over the stool. The thought of having lost her weakened him and he sat on the bathroom floor, cell phone in hand.

He had to do it. There was no other choice. With a deep sigh, Terrence dialed the dreaded ten digits. True to form, she answered on the first ring, her loud voice echoing in his head.

"It's about damn time your punk ass called. I can't find my sister, she ain't answering her phone. You got some damn explaining to do!"

Chapter Twenty One

Relief washed over Christopher as her stroked Lani's cheek. He still wanted to send her to hospital and make sure the alcohol hadn't poisoned her blood. Who the hell mixes Nuvo and Ciroc and downs it all? That was some gully shit for a female. After a few minutes of staring at her, though, he was sure it was just a severe hangover.

"Uh, sir?"

The clerk waited patiently, curiosity plain on his face. He hadn't seemed so amused when Christopher came barging into the lobby, demanding he call Lani's room. Christopher had luckily spotted Lani's car, just as an RV pulled out, which had been blocking it from view. He had pleaded with the clerk, but when she didn't answer the phone, he put up such a fuss that the clerk agreed to check her room, with security. Now, with security gone, the clerk held a half empty bottle of Ciroc, eyeing Lani's ring finger and then Christopher's. But Christopher didn't give a damn what conclusion the clerk was probably coming to.

"Sir, I can have room service come and, uh, help you out."

Christopher surveyed the room and nodded. New bedding was a must; the putrid smell flooded his

157

nostrils. She had vomited a few times. In fact, she needed a bath. It was odd that he hadn't noticed that before, he normally had a sensitive sense of smell. His worry had dulled him for a moment, now awareness was flooding in like light in the middle of the night. Lani had to get in the tub.

Christopher lifted her, aware that some vomit might get on him and also aware that he didn't give a damn about that either, and moved toward the bathroom. The clerk rushed to open the bathroom door and his face held an odd expression, something kind of like admiration. Christopher nodded at the clerk. The clerk nodded back and gave him a thin, understanding smile. The clerk left the room while ordering housekeeping on the walkie talkie.

Christopher leaned Lani against his body while he folded a towel for her head and placed it at the rear of the tub. He turned the dial, momentarily frustrated by the weird handle that indicated red to blue, but ran cold to hot. Of course. The entire time she leaned against him, her body propped up by his left arm tightly around her back, her face buried in his chest. When the temperature was right, and the water filled the bottom of the tub, Christopher slowly lowered Lani into the bathtub. The cold ceramic against her back caused her eyes to fly open, panic glowing from them like beams.

Damn. Christopher sat back on the toilet seat to catch his breath. *Beautiful, no matter what.*

Lani's eyes scanned the small space. She sighed when she laid eyes on him. "Chris, you're still here." It wasn't a question, but a statement of relief. "Good." She closed her eyes again. It had only been a few minutes, but her sense of time was obviously unreliable. Christopher sat back on the commode, stretched out his legs, and watched her as the water filled the tub around her. What had she been thinking about, that made her get this trashed. What ghosts had slid out of her spiritual closet that made her try to cast out the demons by drinking away consciousness.

What was the point of all this pain? What was the point of all the saving and sacrificing and life building—working hard to provide for a future that wasn't even promised? All women claim they want a stable man who would take care of the bills and build a solid foundation. That's what Christopher had been doing for Kenya, trying to be that Black man who was handling his family and his responsibility. Wasn't that the only real way to show love? Not the flowers and candy bullshit, but by providing a secure life—wasn't that the symbol that she was his Queen? And, in the end, Kenya still ran out of the house for a chance to sniff up under Terrence, a man who couldn't even take care of his damn self. And here Lani laid, spiritually wiped out and devastated, after giving Terrence anything his heart desired. Her payment for years of tolerating him and his bullshit was to end up smashed in a hotel room all alone.

They both had it wrong, him and Lani. They both were the fools. In the end, they both had sacrificed too much to be in a world that didn't really include any of them. Terrence and Kenya had created this spiral of pain, dancing with each other in this fake friendship thing, fronting like they weren't really lovers underneath it all. And he and Lani were idiots for trying to be proper and polite and not calling the shit out for what it was years ago.

Christopher hurriedly wiped at his eyes, trying to ignore the sting that sets in just before the water might fall. It temporarily blinded him. Here he sat, in the stench of vomit, observing an emotionally spent woman, while the two real perpetrators were unharmed. There was just no logic in it, no fairness in this life. No reason to keep denying himself for the idea of doing right, when others gave over to their desires and wants and suffered no ramification.

Christopher rolled another towel and placed it under Lani's head, removing the one that was now soaked with water. Her eyes parted into a narrow slit. Their eyes locked on one another.

"Hey," he whispered.

"Hey, back," she answered, traces of a smile lingered around her full lips.

"How ya doing?"

She turned her head a little bit. "Better, now."

"Yeah," Christopher paused and then nodded his head. "Me too."

He moved to the edge of the huge tub and sat facing her, as he leaned his body against the ceramic tiles next to the nozzles. They stared at each other, hours of understanding passing between them in minutes. He had come here to be with her. It seemed so simple and so right.

A light tap at the door broke their telepathy.

"Sir? Hello?" The thick accent of a female housekeeper floated across the air. "Mr. Milton say you need some help?

Christopher stood and gave Lani a slow smile. He turned and walked out of the bathroom, closing the door behind him.

"Oh, sir," the housekeeper took a few steps back as he almost knocked into her. "I'm sorry. No meant to disturb."

"No. You didn't disturb me at all." Christopher motioned for her to calm down with his hands as she reared back from him. "Please, it's no problem."

"I no meant to be in the way."

Christopher realized that she thought she had interrupted something intimate. "No, please, don't feel like that. I'm grateful you're here."

Maybe it was the sincerity in his voice, or hearing a customer actually show humility and look her in the face, either way she stopped shifting around and actually looked at him with appreciation on her face. "What is it I can do for you, sir?"

"It's a mess in here, ma'am." Christopher pointed to the bed and carpet. "If you could change all the bedding, vacuum and remove the trash, we should be all set."

"Yep, I can see that," she added with a smile. "Rough night already, eh?"

Christopher chuckled and shook his head. "If you only knew."

He placed two one hundred dollar bills in her hand.

"No sir, I can't take this. I get in trouble if they know."

Christopher shook his head and met her eye. "Know what?"

They both smiled. She tucked the bills into her bra and headed to the bed while Christopher poked his head back into the bathroom. Lani was alright. She was still in the tub in her underwear, with her eyes closed. Christopher tried hard not to take in her curves, struggled to ignore the fullness of her body and desperately avoided tracing the lines of her hips with his eyes.

He forced a fake cough. "You need help," he asked.

She wasn't asleep. She smiled, keeping her eyes closed, obviously aware that he had been standing there. "Nope, the water feels good."

"Coffee?"

Her nose crinkled at the thought drinking anything. "Just water. Please."

Christopher closed the door and headed back to the kitchenette. It took a few minutes of fumbling around with the coffee pot and the packets before he got it right, but he finally made coffee for himself, grabbed a bottle of water off the counter for her. He went back to the bathroom and sat the water on the tub. Then Christopher sat on the couch.

As she passed him dragging a huge plastic bag that contained all the bedding, the housekeeper pointed at his shoes. Christopher glanced down. Vomit. He kicked them off and rinsed them at the kitchenette sink. Which reminded him that he had been holding Lani. Without bothering to look at himself, he stripped of the cashmere autumn orange zip up sweater he had been sporting and balled it into the trash. He would buy another one.

Christopher took a sip of his coffee. Enough thoughts about Kenya and Terrence. He was done with it, done with them. His son was safe. Lani was safe. Now he needed to get his own room, relax and try to get some sleep. Christopher whipped out his cell phone and dialed his sister Jackie. She answered on the second ring.

"Little Christopher, alright?"

"Of course," she purred in a sleepy voice. "He went to sleep right after you left."

Christopher paused. "I'm going to catch some rest, too. I'm in Delaware."

"Alright." Jackie would never ask what he was doing there and he knew it. That was why they told her everything, because she didn't cast judgment and she didn't pry. "FYI, Kenya called here about five times."

There was silence while Christopher digested that information. He wished he didn't care, that Kenya was completely irrelevant to him. But it did matter that she had tried to call. He did care. A little bit. A lot. "What she say?"

"She's worried because you aren't answering your phone. Said that she had fallen asleep at her parent's house and realized you didn't know where she was. Said she's worried because she can't find you."

"At her parent's house, huh?"

Jackie remained quiet for a second. "Yep."

Christopher was lost in thought. *How did she get to her parent's?* His mind played through the explanations, the lies wrapped within a truthful story. *There is no way she went to her parents—unless she had Terrence take her there, after I took my gotdamn car back. That's her cover.*

"Little Christopher is to stay with you until I get back. Do not give him to her."

"Christopher, you know better than that." Jackie's calm voice always soothed him. "She wouldn't even try anything like that. She just sounded relieved that I had him. I told her you needed a break."

They sat in silence while he digested that. Jackie would never ask for details, she could put what she needed to know together on her own. But she was smart and could help him avoid a mishap.

Christopher let out a heavy sigh. "Alright, sis, give it to me straight. What do you think?"

"Nothing."

"Come on, Jackie, tell me. Really."

"Really? Well, really, you and Kenya have a good thing going. We don't all get lucky enough to have love, but a decent partner is just as good, if not better."

"I don't know."

"Baby boy, sometimes the decision ain't about stay or go. Staying is the framework. The inner workings are more like 'can I move on and keep my house together' type of thinking."

"Well, then she wins, if I do that."

"It ain't about you or her winning. Either way, the only one who really wins or loses in this mess is little Christopher."

Christopher hadn't thought of that.

"Just be still for a moment, alright? Don't make any moves right now."

Christopher nodded. "I can definitely do that."

"Alright. When you're ready, she'll come back with her excuses. She's at her momma's house, so she's getting coached as we speak. You'll decide what you want to believe, toss out the rest and then make a decision based on you and little Christopher."

He nodded. He could live with that. "I can do that."

Chapter Twenty Two

Christopher tapped lightly on the bathroom door before opening it. No answer. He knocked again. *This woman is going to give me a damn heart attack.* He cracked the door and poked his head in. Lani snored lightly as she lay in the dry tub. She must have kicked the plug. All the water had drained out. He sighed. The suite had been cleaned, but the bathroom reeked. They both needed a bath to finally be done with the residue of Lani's drunken stupor.

Christopher made a quick plan of action. He would get Lani to take a bath and then call up the clerk to get a separate room. Even if he couldn't sleep, at least he could lie down and ease his body. Without having to worry about his son, he was able to ease the stress and anger from his mind. He wanted to run his own bath and let the warm water massage the tension from his back.

Christopher's phone rang softly. *Kenya.* He moved quickly to turn the ringer off, but accidentally dropped the phone on the tile floor. The loud sound woke Lani.

She glanced down at the floor and spotted the phone. "Kenya, huh?" Lani gave a small smile; her voice thin and tired.

He nodded and returned to his seat on the tub.

"Only a matter of time," Lani whispered.

"What?"

"That she would come to her senses." Lani opened her eyes fully and gazed at him.

Christopher shrugged. "I guess."

Despite himself, he wondered why Lani didn't seem bashful, lying here in a dry tub in her underwear, in front of him. Maybe the alcohol had removed any inhibitions she should have had, because she didn't appear to give a shit.

"I can't believe you drove here."

Christopher laughed a little. "Why not? I had to look out for you. Plus, I owe you an apology for earlier. I hope you didn't misunderstand … why I told you to go home. I wasn't trying to hurt you; I just didn't want … more confusion. You sounded terrible on the phone, though, so I had to check on you."

"How did you find me?"

"Luck."

They sat in silence for a few moments. "Some childhood memories came back on me. It is so sweet that you came here, Chris. That you cared at all."

"Whatever, Lani. How could I not care?"

They met eyes and smiled. Silence again.

Lani breathed. "You could..."

"Huh?"

"Not care, I mean. So please, let me thank you."

"In that case, I accept your thanks." Christopher smiled and stood up. "Well, I'm going to check into a room, because I need a bath, too. I'll call and give you the room number."

"Oh." Disappointment danced across her face.

Christopher hesitated. "Well, I need to get washed up."

Lani's eyebrows shifted, almost imperceptibly. "Do you mind staying here?" She pushed the words out fast, as if scared of his answer. "The couch is a fold out. I promise—I'll stay out of your way."

Christopher looked at her with a blank expression while he thought about it. He wanted the company, but he didn't want her to think that she had to do anything to thank him.

"Yeah. That's cool."

Lani seemed relieved. "Good," she purred and stretched her body out. "I'm glad. I don't want to be alone, not right now."

"Tell me about it." He looked around, shifting his weight. He was trying not to look at her body and the urge was pulling at him. "Alright, well, I'll go out here, call me when you're finished."

As he turned his back, he heard Lani groan. "Chris, I am stuck. My body is numb on one side." She sighed. "I'm sorry to seem so needy; I'm going to need more help."

"Needy? You? Never that."

She held out one hand and Christopher pulled her into a sitting position. She gave a low moan from moving so quickly. He smiled, and slowly helped her stand. Christopher held her up for a moment and then she raised both arms above her head.

Christopher bit his lip. *Huh? Don't play with me up in here.* Christopher gazed into Lani's eyes. Did she really want him to take her bra off? She returned the look with a steady determination.

She was challenging him, in a sexy way. And he was accepting the challenge. Slowly, gingerly, he removed her bra. Despite himself, his heart began pounding in his chest. He hesitated, only for a moment, and observed the fullness of her breasts, desiring to get lost in their promise. Under his soft glare, her nipples contracted slowly, rising toward him. Inches from his hand he looked at her, surprised at the obvious desire pouring from her eyes. Christopher held her gaze for as long as he could stand it, realizing that he had not been wanted in this way in years.

Christopher let his eyes linger on her graceful neck, defined shoulders, and the hollow between her breasts. Then his gaze returned to the breasts, which had retracted and hardened under his glare. Kenya never physically responded to him. He had to work hard to get her to this point.

He placed his hands on her waist, a thumb on each side of her panties. Slowly, he lowered them, bending his knees and slowing descending the length of her body. She placed her hands on his shoulder as he passed her hips, waist, upper thighs, legs then ankles. She stepped lightly from the panties, and the movement released a different scent, one of desire and lust. His senses blocked out all other smells, her scent pleased him.

This time there was no outrage, no righteous indignation. This time it was just her and him. He wanted to experience her softness and beauty. Find out her taste and scent, feel the touch of a woman who actually had a physical response to his presence. He wanted her, but not like before, not when the motive was revenge, so the cost would have been hard and explosive.

No! Morals slapped him across the face like a cruel Chicago wind. She was married and spoken for. He would not violate another's man wife, no matter what. He stepped back, closed his eyes and looked at the floor. He would not do this.

Lani turned her back to him as she turned on the water and tested the temperature. She seemed completely unfazed that a six foot three inch tall man stood in her bathroom, apparently suffering a moral dilemma, gaping and confused by emotional indecision.

But he couldn't take his eyes from her as she settled on a temperature and turned on the shower. With the curtain wide open, she slowly unwrapped a bar of soap and, using only her hand, rubbed it in circular motions across her body. She never looked at him.

He watched her hand and the white soap, foaming against her brown skin, covering every inch of her body, until she stood covered with white suds. She stepped further into the water, splashing it everywhere, letting it run in and out of her mouth, as she rinsed the thick lather from her skin.

Wiping her face with her hands, she started the process again. His eyes once again followed the hand and soap, as it darted in between her thighs. His mouth was slightly open and he leaned back to the far wall, the towel rack digging into his shoulder. He didn't notice it. Again, completely covered in suds, she rinsed off, spraying water on him, the floor, and everywhere else. The water splashing on his face did not cause him to blink.

This time, when she opened her eyes, and wiped her face with her hands, she looked fully into his eyes. He closed his mouth, feeling as though he had been caught, like a peeping tom. *Maybe she forgot I was here.* She looked at him for a second and then stepped out of the tub. Walking forward, she pressed her body into his, and stood there for what seemed an eternity.

Her fresh clean scent filled his nostrils; the thick steamy air released his tension. She stood on her toes and kissed him lightly on the lips. Then, taking a step back, she confidently raised his t-shirt over his head. He ripped it off without hesitation and she rested her hands on his chest and leaned into him.

Pulling apart, she kissed him again, her hands feeling up and down the length of his torso. Resting on the waistband of his sweats, she lowered his sweatpants, slowly, observing every inch of him. He stepped out of the pants and she raised her body again and gave him a full hug. Then she returned to the shower. Smiling, she reached out a hand to Christopher. It was a request, a blatant invitation, a very real offer.

Chapter Twenty Three

Terrence's head ached and his ear throbbed, yet, Dee continued talking. Actually she yelled, screamed, hissed and issued threat after threat. No one in his life had ever called him so many "motherfuckers" at one time. He had stopped replying ten minutes ago, giving up and resigning himself to listen to the never ending rant. She sounded just like Lani—she would wear herself out eventually. And if she didn't, he would finally just hang up.

Silence finally filled the line. Terrence breathed and unclenched his fist.

"Are you still there?"

His heart dropped. He almost didn't answer. "Yeah, I'm here."

"Don't you have anything to say? Anything at all?"

Hell yeah. Stop talking shit and help me find my damn wife. And I am not scared by your ghetto threats. By the way, I am not going to be too many more assholes, you hear me you nagging, rude, narcissistic bitch. Terrence swallowed. He wouldn't say that. It wasn't out of fear, but out of basic respect for women. No matter how good or poorly trained they were. Dee was still a woman, still a mother, still his sister-in-law. What good would

172

disrespecting her in the same manner that she had just disrespected him in do? If anything, she would just go back and repeat that he had called her out of her name, conveniently ignoring how her tongue had started the battle of words, and he would have to fight her family and Lani. It was a losing proposition and things were already bad enough. "What do you want me to say?"

"What do I want you to say?" Dee shrieked so loud into the headset that Terrence snatched it from his ear. "No wonder my sister is losing her mind! Is this what you do, tune her out, ignore her ass to death, and now you wondering why you can't find her?"

That was enough. Enough. Terrence wanted to strangle both Lani and her inconsiderate, ill mannered big sister. "Listen. I am a damn good husband. I am faithful, do you understand, I have never cheated on my wife!"

"And you don't damnit listen, either. I didn't even say cheat, I said *you neglect her.* That means Terrence," she spoke slowly, as if Terrence were mentally disabled, "you don't listen to her. Then you answered to something I didn't even say. You know what; she needs to leave your ass."

"Yeah, that's what you been telling her for years. That's one of the reasons we're in this situation."

"Boy please, ain't no one told her to leave your bourgie ass. But be real with yourself, pretty boy, you are the reason you are in this situation."

"Enough of your bullshit, Dee. I'm out."

"Yeah, you always are." Dee slammed down the phone.

Terrence shook his head. Calling Dee had been completely unproductive. He was no closer to finding Lani, and he had listened to an earful of nonsense for nothing. The entire situation caused him aggravation. He had enough of Lani's shit. Why would Lani tell him she would wait, and then not answer her phone? What had he missed? This seemed too juvenile; even Lani wouldn't go this far.

He had to find Lani and get some damn answers. If this is where they ended, then so be it; it was time to draw the line in the gotdamn sand. Lani would find out how good she had it, how lucky she had been, once he decided to leave her. Once she had to get back out there in the world and deal with the assholes that played the dating game like chess. Then she would realize. But what he wasn't going to do is allow her to keep the power in her court, having him run around in circles; searching for her while she sat back and enjoyed the chaos.

While he dressed the cell phone rang. Terrence glanced at the caller ID. *Kenya.* What did she want? Hadn't she done enough? He didn't feel like dealing with another woman's drama right now, at least she and her husband were in the comfort of their own home. He couldn't even find his wife, thanks to Kenya's scheming ways. He pressed End, sending her straight to voicemail.

He tucked the phone in his jacket pocket, gathered his things, and left the hotel. Terrence patted his pockets as he waited for the elevator. The electronic checkout spared him from having to go to the main lobby. Hunger pounded at his gut. It had been a long night. He needed to grab a bite in the lounge area before driving around parking lots, locating Lani. And he wasn't going to do that much longer either.

His hip felt lighter than usual. Something was missing. Standing still, Terrence patted all of his pockets. His wallet. *Damnit.* He turned back down the hall to his room. The card key still worked—he entered and searched for the wallet. *Where in the hell is it?* Terrence eyed the dresser and the bathroom countertop. He felt around the floor, on the bed, under the crumpled sheets and the blanket. Nothing. Sitting down on his bed, Terrence tried to calm himself. His heart began racing and his hands were shaking.

What the hell? Where is my wallet! Where is my damn wife! What is happening to my life? "Aww!!" The scream of frustration that escaped his emotional wound was a guttural sound, and it pushed from his mouth before he could stop it. Tears filled his eyes, but he brushed them away quickly. He refused to break down so easily, he couldn't do it. He had to make this right. He would find a way to make it right.

Terrence placed his head in his hands in an attempt to regulate his breathing. The cell phone in his pocket vibrated. It had to be Lani. Finally. He checked the caller ID again. *Kenya's parents.* Terrence fought the temptation to pick up the phone and yell at her to leave him alone, for a second at least. What the hell was wrong with her that she kept calling back to back when she was obviously being sent to voicemail? What the hell did she want anyway?

Fear gripped his gut, something must be dreadfully wrong.

He pressed Talk and waited while the phone dialed back Kenya's mother's house.

"Hello?" Kenya sounded breathless.

"Yeah, what's up?"

"I don't know. I, I can't find Christopher."

Terrence wanted to shake her. "Kenya, I can't worry about him right now. I'm looking for my damn wife."

It took a second, just a second, before the fear rumbling in his stomach silenced and the dull aching in his head stopped. The sudden realization stilled everything in him, turned his blood into ice.

"Oh. Oh no," whispered Kenya.

The cold intensified, until he felt pain searing throughout his entire body. The cold somehow burned him and his mind became a blank slate.

Kenya said what Terrence would have never been able to say. "Oh no, Terrence. Their together, aren't they?"

He dropped the phone. Nothing mattered, but the burning pain. He sat down on the bed and stared directly into the mirror in front of him.

Chapter Twenty Four

"You alright?" Christopher whispered with his eyes closed, afraid to breathe until he heard the answer.

"Wonderful," Lani inadvertently tightened her legs around his waist. "You?"

She hoped that the question sounded light, but the tension and worry were evident. She deeply hoped he wouldn't regret what they had just done, what she had led him to do.

She knew he heard her worry, because he opened his eyes and looked fully into hers. Lani fought the urge to blink and look away. Christopher smoothed down her hair, still wet and frizzy from their long shower. He smiled. Then, before she could catch her breath, he lifted her in one scoop and placed her directly on top of him, so that her torso laid the length of his. Placing his hands on her hips, he slowly moved her hips down, until she could feel his length, pulsing and throbbing against her inner lips as it rose in the air.

"That's how I'm doing." A small smile played around his lips.

Lani smiled back, her legs straddling his, her lips resting against his. He wrapped his arms around her. "I'm glad to be here with you. No worries, okay?"

She nodded, biting her lip to quiet her emotion. She didn't want to fall in love with this man. That would be impossible, wouldn't it? But he made her feel so wanted.

Christopher kept talking. "We can do whatever you want, even if that's nothing at all. I feel good just like this."

Lani slowly raised her torso, coming nose to nose with him. A tear escaped her eye as she sat up, her hips spread against his pelvis, his thick mass bouncing against her behind. Christopher didn't flinch.

"No thoughts about him or her, for the rest of today, okay?" Lani's voice was quiet and sensual. She just wanted to get lost in the erotic space that the two of them had created, where their bodies unique rhythm felt so perfect. Who knew that Christopher was more sexually compatible with her than any other man she had ever felt? It was amazing, and something she wanted to cherish for now and, if she had to feel guilty about, then feel guilty later.

"Okay. I promise. I was just about to say the same thing." He reached for the small pillow behind his head and readjusted it, as if preparing to continue snuggling.

He pulled at Lani, to bring her back down to lie on his chest, but she shook her head no and remained sitting upright, looking down at him. Lani kissed him lightly, at first, then deeply. His hands gripped her hips firmly, while she continued kissing him. He groaned deeply, one hand rubbed her back and the other lightly pressed against her stomach.

His touch felt so light and new to Lani that her desire mounted instantly. Her mind went blank and her body yielded to the sensations as he cupped her breasts and caused a slight implosion. She couldn't take anymore. She lifted her hips and slid back slowly, letting the tip of his length tickle her moistness.

"Are you sure—" he never finished the question as Lani submerged the full length of him into her depths.

Yeah, I'm sure.

Christopher's eyes were wide for a second. Using her inner muscles, she gripped his wide mass. He smiled broadly and closed his eyes as she slowly rolled her hips, enjoying every inch of him. Holding hands, they both held on tightly and succumbed to the current and vibration carrying them forward.

***

Lani lay very still; her head flush against Christopher's bare chest, listening to his light snore. She couldn't believe he would willingly lie on his side on this narrow couch, at such an awkward angle, just to keep his arms around her. They hadn't bothered to pull the couch bed out to lie freely on it. Instead she felt protected, tucked between his wide body and the back of the couch. Her legs were still open, wrapped loose around his and her arms clung to his torso. She felt exhausted, but refused to sleep. She had to remember this feeling of comfort, of security, of being wanted. Hopefully, she would be able to recall every second of the tender moments they had shared from the tub to the bedroom, to the narrow kitchen and then here, in the living room. Experience taught her that moments of security were always fleeting, so she remained determined to absorb every bit of this while she could.

Christopher's heavy breathing subsided. She knew that he lay there awake, with his eyes closed. *Please don't look at me with disgust, or blame. If I see any regret, I'm leaving.* No more rejection. She simply couldn't handle it. Especially not from him, the one person who had treated her like a woman all these years. Lani had no more fight left in her, no more resistance to the snubs and backbiting, the whispers and blatant cruelty. Her confidence was splintered.

Truth be told, Terrence had left her long ago. She hadn't noticed when it happened, just found herself alone at his parties and family functions, floating on an empty boat with no paddle. No life line. No husband support. When he earned six figures, they were all good. But when he walked away for a chance to develop his career with an upstart, things began to change. Yeah, it had been somewhere around then. To minimize the sudden loss in income, she took her chances, taking loans and maxing credit cards, to maintain the illusion. Her credit extended, Terrence even blamed her for their debt, pointed the finger as if he had no involvement.

Resentment built slowly but surely. Lani hadn't known what to do, how to respond, so she began shouting, hitting, throwing things. Anything to break through his wall of silence; his apathetic treatment. How could everything always be her fault? Did he really believe that? And why didn't her pain affect him, hurt him? Shouldn't he want his wife to be happy? Instead, she had been acting a damn fool. She realized that now.

No. I will not think about Terrence at this moment. I will not ruin this. I will enjoy Christopher and what we shared. It is mine, something special for me, and has nothing to do with Terrence.

Lani had a lifetime to think about Terrence. A lifetime to swallow regrets. She wouldn't do it now.

Lani wondered if the normal Christopher would return; the one who seemed to have life down perfect and had the answers to everything. She wondered if the relaxed one who lay here now, who had taken her to orgasm beyond orgasm, would disappear and the judgmental one would return. She waited for him to utter one word, make one face, attempt to hide one look and shatter the small peace she clung to.

She had needed this. Needed someone to take the time to kiss her, rub her, watch her reactions and study her every move. Pay attention to her. It had been months since she and Terrence had made love. Lately, he crawled in the bed, after whispered conversations with Kenya, flipped her over and handled his business. No foreplay, no words of love, no touch of affection. A dry kiss, a few humps, him snoring. Her left holding a bag of emptiness. That's why she put him out. Hoped that in his own room he would miss the intimacy, would re-evaluate his approach and carelessness and would come back to her with hunger or fire. But, as usual, he blamed her and, as usual, her "punishment" hadn't worked. Maybe it was time for her to understand that a man can't be punished, just like he can't be changed. All a woman can do is decide what she will and won't accept and let the chips fall where they may. Had she had that approach she would have done what she had to do when Terrence started ignoring her, instead of acting like a fool to try to make him change his ways. The fault was her own.

She sighed and buried her head into Christopher's chest. Finally, Christopher cracked his eyelids. He looked at her slowly, like taking a deep sip of wine, and smiled gently. He leaned forward and kissed her forehead. Instantly, she felt like a woman. The strong urge to flirt, smile, bat her eyes and bite her lip flooded her at once. He had always had that affect on her, but she avoided it while their spouses played friends.

Today. Today had not been about Terrence. Not about Kenya. No, this had been a gift to her, a restoral. A reminder of love and tenderness. The intimate pull and pressure of a man yearning for her. Christopher's intensity had filled Lani's void.

Chapter Twenty Five

Kenya dropped the phone. She didn't hear it land against the wooden surface, didn't notice Connie padding lightly into the spacious kitchen behind her. All she could hear was Terrence's deep breath before his phone disconnected.

"What? What happened?" Connie's worry made Kenya panic.

Kenya lowered her head, ignoring her mother. *That bitch is with my husband. That tacky tramp has snatched another man from me.*

"Kenya! What is going on," her mother shrieked. "Is he alright, did you find him?"

"He's with her!" Kenya shouted at the top of her lungs, throwing her head.

"Damn." Connie took a seat at the round table next to her daughter. Kenya looked at her mother in pain. Connie shook her head, not trying to sugar coat her distress. "How do you know?"

"I just know, Mom, alright. I can feel it." The tears ran down Kenya's face. "I've lost him."

"No. He might be screwing, but that does not mean you lost him."

Kenya just stared at her mother. "I don't know what you mean and I am too tired for this."

"Neither one of you know shit. That's the real problem here. Fools playing grown up games. He thinks you slept with Terrence, you think he slept with Lani. No one knows anything." Connie stood suddenly, her face drawn in a tight knot. "Get your stuff together, you're going home."

"Oh, now you're putting me out."

Connie observed her daughter quietly. Kenya thought, for half a second, that Connie was going to slap her. Instead Connie spoke slowly, her voice cold and thin.

"You better pull yourself together. Stop calling the world looking for him. Piece together some suggestion of dignity, damnit." Connie walked quickly to the counter and reached for her purse. "I will take you home. You will remember that he is your husband; he cannot be taken, only given up. And you, little girl, better not give him up."

Connie pulled Kenya from the seat. Kenya had forgotten how much taller than her mother she stood, because Connie had such a strong personality.

Connie looked up at her daughter with her finger pointed. "When he returns, you will not question him about what he has done. Don't give up information about yourself that he doesn't request. Life goes on."

"No, I didn't sleep with another man. I need to know if he slept with her."

"Why? *You* opened this door and allowed in this situation. You better dig in your heels and repair this thing, even if you gotta use scotch tape and a staple gun, cause my grandbaby ain't living in no torn home because of you wanting Terrence's flaky ass." Connie marched out of the kitchen. "You got ten minutes, meet me in the car." Her voice carried into the kitchen.

Kenya felt ridiculous. Of course her mother wouldn't understand her position. But she had to admit that her mother made a good point. She knew no more than Christopher. Except that Terrence's head had returned to Lani, and her husband might be with Lani, leaving her alone in this. Her only trump card was the marriage and her home. She would have to return home and set up her counterattack from there.

Chapter Twenty Six

Terrence had lost track of time. His mind pictured his wife on top of Christopher, beneath Christopher; in every position he had every experienced with her, he now saw Christopher. He wanted to vomit while he imagined all the ways that man would probably take his wife. Terrence seethed with anger.

He could've taken Christopher's wife, had he wanted. Could have flipped her upside down or bent over backward in the damn parking lot, if he wanted. *This is the* disrespect *I get, after not taking his wife?* All he could envision was pummeling Christopher's face in.

And Lani. He had been faithful, if nothing else. How easily she took everything that defined him and laid it at another brother's feet. The dark, twisting anger that swirled though his mind scared him. The bile in the back of his throat made his head hurt. He hated Lani.

In the next second, Terrence fought to get a grip. Lani wouldn't do this to him. Not his Lani. He had her completely and totally. She wouldn't be this bold; the most she would do is disappear, just to make him go crazy with worry. He sat up. *That's what this is, just another game. Another temper tantrum. They probably planned their retaliation together.*

But Christopher had gone hard core, had really believed Kenya had left. Hell, he had actually taken her car. No doubt, he would try sexing Lani, taking out his anger on Terrence's sexy wife. And if so, was Lani capable of sleeping around like that? He shook his head. Lani would be easily fooled; the truth was she was a hood rat. What did she know?

Terrence couldn't figure out what to do. Go after Christopher? Go after Lani? Say fuck them both and go home?

Hell, he could have any woman he wanted. To hell with Lani and this situation. If she wanted to play it like this, then fine. He damn sure didn't plan on sitting around crying about it. He would go home, put her shit on the curb and start over. Simple. Whether she screwed Christopher or not seemed irrelevant, now he had become fed up with the hassle. Bending over, he picked up the cell phone and noticed his wallet under a pillow on the floor.

How did I miss it before, I swear I looked under that pillow. He scooped it up and headed to the counter to checkout, since he had missed the morning deadline. Terrence paid the clerk the extra fee and stepped out into the evening sun. A brilliant sunset splattered the sky. Lani would have insisted on watching it. He stared at the orange ribbons, remembering how Lani always observed skylines, trees, clouds and all type of irrelevant shit. But lately, she had stopped sharing her observations with him.

The baby. The last baby changed everything. After he screamed, cursed and cried, she stood there, frozen and in shock. When he finished screaming, she tried to explain but he didn't want to listen to a word. Why did she keep doing this? Getting pregnant, slipping up, and, with each abortion, he felt like he lost something. It angered him, that she repeatedly put him in this situation. When he had finally been ready to begin a family and financially able to support one, she had aborted it without his permission.

Yeah, there had been no more shared sunsets after that. And all the warring between them had started then, too. Terrence walked across the parking lot. For the life of him, he could not remember where he'd parked. The lot had been full before, so he had parked on the side of the building.

He spotted his car when he turned the corner of the building. He jumped in and gunned the engine. Tonight, he would sleep in his master suite, not in a guest room. Tonight, Lani could pick *her* shit up off the floor and find somewhere else to go.

Almost out of the parking lot, he noticed a car parked haphazardly against the iron gate. He instantly knew the car. *Christopher.* Slamming on his brakes, Terrence stared at the car. Then he hopped out of the car and slowly scanned the lot. Just behind Christopher's car, tucked to the back, sat Lani's BMW.

"Son of a bitch!" Terrence's mind went blank. What were his options? There weren't too many that didn't land him in jail. He chuckled at the irony of the situation. He could wait in the parking lot and run them both over. He could knife their tires. He could straight out ask the clerk for her room key and surprise them. He parked next to Christopher.

Terrence walked to Lani's car and used her spare key that he kept to disable the alarm. Maybe he should take *her* car, let them see how that shit feels. He opened the car and sat very still. Her smell filled his nostrils. A box of tissue rested in the passenger seat and loose tissue were scattered everywhere. He sat there for hours, inhaling her scent, occupying her space. Finally, near tears, he opened her compartment and removed the pen and small pad she always kept there.

"Lani please come home. I am sorry. Let me make this right."

He left the note on her seat, replaced the pad and pen in the glove compartment, and slowly shut the door and locked it. Terrence kicked Christopher's car as he passed; the small dent in the door caused him some satisfaction. He climbed back into his car, started the ignition, buckled his seatbelt. Then he cried the silent tears of a man defeated.

Terrence pulled himself together and left the lot. Back on I95 he pulled out his cell phone. There was no answer at Kenya's mother's house, so he called Kenya's house. She answered on the first ring.

"It's me," Terrence couldn't hide the pain in his voice. "I found them."

Chapter Twenty-Seven

"There is a difference, you know." Lani lay against Christopher's shoulder, the warm blue blanket wrapped around her body as they sat on the floor at the end of the bed.

"What's that?" The question was unnecessary; he knew what she was going to say. There were so many differences, too many to name. But one that made their circumstance altogether different. One that required he return home, while her future lay up in the air.

She hesitated. "You have a beautiful son."

He didn't respond. She looked up at him, waiting. He could feel her body become tense, saw the worry in her eyes. He didn't mind her mentioning his baby boy. He just wondered if it pained her, to have lost her baby. Of course Terrence had given both he and Kenya an earful about her decision to abort without him. How selfish and inconsiderate her decision had been, how she seemed intent on ruining his life. Christopher remembered that at the time that he had wanted to punch Terrence in the gut and throw him out of his house. He had lost respect for him that day, for making his wife out to take all the blame and not forgiving her and her mistake, the way that a husband should. If anything, he and Kenya had later agreed that Lani had her hands full trying to take care of Terrence's spoiled ass, although neither of them believed in abortion.

"Yep, my baby boy." *He changes everything.* Christopher knew that he could get lost in Lani; make her his and never look back. A part of him felt in tune with the younger him that had lost Alayna so many years ago. Some small part of him felt awakened from a deep hibernation, thawing out the deep infatuated love that had been buried within him. If he were childless, he would take whatever time he had left and splurge, overindulge, allow himself to get lost in Lani. Kenya and Terrence, with their selfish friendship and their hidden agenda, would be easy to walk away from.

But little Christopher existed and he mattered more than Christopher's own life. Raising him would not allow Christopher the luxury of being lost in love's daze. "Changes things." Christopher repeated.

Lani pressed. "Like..."

"Like me wanting to keep you for myself. Wrap you into my life. I can't. Not right now."

She nodded. "Not right now," she repeated softly.

Christopher's phone buzzed angrily on the dresser in front of them. Lani reached over and grabbed it. He didn't seem to care whether she looked at it or not. He just looked at her. She smiled and handed it to him, without looking at the screen. There was no doubt who it was, anyway. Lani kissed him on his cheek and moved slowly toward the bathroom with the blanket wrapped around her.

This is the real difference between me and you. I still gotta have access to the world and leave my phone on. Christopher thought.

Lani had turned her phone completely off, denying any and every one entry into their comfort zone. But his phone had to remain on, just in case Jackie called, in case little Christopher needed him.

For his son, he would deal with Kenya and work it out. Weekend visitations and every other holidays were not an option. Since she had been calling around looking for him, Christopher figured she wanted to return and had a good lie in place to minimize the damage. Having spent time with her family, she would be armed and ready, just like Jackie said. Maybe he couldn't totally dismiss her, but she would have to work her way back into his home. And his heart felt forever sealed from her.

He flipped the phone open. "Yeah."

"Are you with her?" Kenya's voice trembled.

"What?" Christopher felt a deep rage swirling within him. He took a deep breath.

"I said, are you with her?"

Christopher couldn't believe that Kenya had the nerve to repeat the question. "Wait a minute. You ran out of my house in the middle of the night to be up under your boyfriend. Didn't call me or answer any of my calls to you. And the first thing you think is appropriate to say to me is whether I am with someone?"

He had never spoken to her so aggressively before, never exposed the angry side of himself. But he had lost respect for his wife, and their dry relationship seemed more boring, more plastic and brittle than ever now that he had experienced Lani. Things had changed and it was best that she realize it.

Kenya sighed. "Come home, Christopher. This is all just a big misunderstanding. We just need to talk."

"No, Kenya, you have me severely twisted, thinking I am the same fool as your new boyfriend. Let me be very clear: I am coming home. Damn straight. To my house. My son's home. You, on the other hand, need to be gone when I get there."

"What, you can't..."

"Go to your folks, since that's where you probably are claiming you were last night, right? Go over there and get your lies straight."

"Christopher, this is my home too." Her voice sounded shrill, as if she were going to start screaming.

"Kenya, you left. The grass apparently is not green enough on my side of the world. You didn't come back, didn't call. You made a choice."

"No, it wasn't like that. Listen, where are you? I'll come to you so we can talk."

"Let me be very clear before I hang up this phone. Little Christopher with stay with Jackie until I go pick him up—"

"He is ... I left him—"

"—and," Christopher continued, interrupting her, "you need to be gone when I get there."

"Christopher, why are you—"

"Goodbye, Kenya."

"You're hanging up on me? I am your wife!"

"I am not hanging up on you. I am ending the conversation and I am telling you goodbye." Christopher paused. "Goodbye."

He snapped the phone shut and exhaled deeply. Jackie had taught him well. He could tell Kenya had her story already rehearsed. He didn't want to hear it and didn't want to think about it. He just wanted to enjoy the small peace he had found. Besides, he needed to throw Kenya for a loop until he returned home. She could never put him through this again. If anything, she should know that there would be repercussion for her decision to turn her back on them for Terrence.

Christopher stood up and looked in the bathroom, but it was empty. He backtracked and walked into the living room. Lani sat wrapped in the blanket in a corner of the couch.

Lani spoke as he walked toward her. "So, you got to go, huh?"

"Nope." He collapsed on the couch and laid his head in her lap. "Not unless you're putting me out."

"I could hear you, you know..."

Christopher shrugged and remained quiet.

"...I don't want to deal with either of them," Lani continued.

"Then don't." Christopher squeezed her thigh. "This space right here is ours and we won't give it to them. Don't answer questions about it. Don't speak on it. Keep it here." He tapped her chest lightly, indicating her heart.

"You mean here?" she giggled and playfully thumped his chest back.

"No, I mean here." Christopher leaned forward, lowered the blanket and scooped her breast into his mouth.

"Ah, I get it now." Lani laughed and then grasped his head between both hands. "Seriously, how much longer, before you have to go?" She suddenly looked sad, as if she thought he was leaving in the next few minutes.

"We have the rest of tonight."

Lani nodded, the sadness in her eyes lightened. "Then give me all of you tonight."

Chapter Twenty Eight

Terrence sat quietly behind the wheel of his parked car and listened to the whirring of the closing garage door. He longed to get out of the seat, go in the house and rest his head. His body wouldn't move. For the past three hours he had driven on mental autopilot, unthinkingly going through the motions.

Lani is with Christopher. Just like that. *Just that simple.* How easily she had found the poisonous dagger and sliced it through his heart. *This is what she does? I leave for a few hours and she shares a hotel room with my best friend's husband?*

He opened the car door and leaned his legs into the garage, stepping on bird seed that was scattered on the floor.

Gotta clean that up.

Lani always stored bird feed sloppily on the shelf, where it inevitably spilled over onto the cement floor. She had asked him to clean the garage, but he hadn't had time. There was no reason she couldn't do it herself, which was the real reason he hadn't bothered.

Terrence stood up and stretched out his arms. This day, this entire weekend, felt surreal. Like he was simply a character in a bad play. So much had

196

happened in the last two days that he really couldn't think about it; couldn't put it all together. How had he wound up here and what in the world had he done to deserve a cheating tramp for a wife?

Fury pushed in his chest and threatened to erupt. He didn't want to give in to it because he knew that if he lost himself to the frenzy, he might not recover. Terrence took slow steps around the bird seed and accidentally bumped into the boxes against the back wall. He passed the empty space in the garage that was usually filled by Lani's car. Terrence kept his eyes on the door in front of him. He entered the house, barely noticing his surroundings.

Sunlight poured into the large picture window in the family room. Terrence sank into his soft leather couch and spread his legs out in front of him. He didn't really know where to begin or what to do. Should he put her stuff out? Should he go back to Delaware and beat Christopher's ass? Should he let her know that he knew where she was? Maybe he should just pretend he didn't know anything and ruin her stupid little game.

He had left a note, though, so it was too late to play it cool now. At least she would panic when she saw it.

In the back of his mind, Terrence felt amazed that he hadn't flipped out and hadn't done anything stupid. He didn't really believe Lani would sleep with Christopher. How could she? What would that say about her? About him? But he couldn't stop himself from trying to remember the last time he had made love to his wife. It had been months ago, before she started rejecting him, stiffening in his arms. The slow manic panic began to crowd his mind. Maybe Christopher was the real reason she had been pushing him away. It was possible that they had been creeping together all this time and the truth was just now coming to light. It wasn't impossible to think that Lani had a double life going on. It would explain all her drama and temper tantrums; simple diversions to cover her real deceit.

The truth was so simple. That was it: Lani and Christopher had been cheating all along! Terrence pounded his fist into the couch, the jumped up and ran down the narrow hallway into Lani's personal office. Lani had dubbed it her "femme fatale space" swearing that she needed some area in the house to herself. He remembered the raised eyebrow and look of disdain that crossed Kenya's face when he told her that Lani had turned the room into her "private space." Obviously, Kenya had thought that was too much, maybe even suspicious. He should have paid more attention to Kenya's insinuations and told Lani "no." Realistically, since when did a woman need their own space in a house, the entire house belonged to them anyway?

If Lani was doing dirt, the proof would be in her office. He snorted as he pushed open the office door, stepping into Lani's "girly" world. The walls were a deep shade of gold. He bumped past the fluffy tan love seat and knocked his knee into the large crimson ottoman. Cussing as he tripped over the tweed braided rug, he stepped onto satin covered pillows with a mixture of autumn colors and slipped, knocking his hip into the oak desk.

"Shit!" Terrence roared as he rubbed his palm on his bruised hip. The damn room was booby trapped with frilly nonsense. Terrence leaned against the desk and pulled each drawer out, throwing the contents all around. He had no idea what he was searching for, but there had to be something, anything that would explain this predicament.

I have been a good husband; I take care of her ass. I'm faithful. I buy her whatever she wants. What the hell else does she think she can get? Does she think she can find better than me? That another man is going to tolerate her moody spoiled ass?

In frustration, he dumped the drawers on the floor. He tapped power button on her computer while he thumbed through her rolodex. After a few minutes, his surge of energy fueled by anger faded. Terrence plopped into the rolling leather chair, hitting his knee on the desk.

"Damnit!" he shouted and lowered the seat. The screen saver popped up and momentarily stunning Terrence. A picture of him, immediately after college graduation, covered the entire screen. His robe rested wide open; the flat hat and diploma were in one hand, reaching toward the camera. His free hand rested lightly against his heart, while his mouth shaped in the form of the words he had muttered just as she snapped the picture, "Forever you."

Forever her. Forever Lani. He had loved her so much, then; the sight of her had made his body tense and his breath short. That day came back to him with sudden force. He and Kenya were mobbed by their families, merged into a familiar unit. They had been taken pictures, together and apart, and with their family members. Lani stood off to the side with Dee and one of Dee's daughters. It was the only family that Lani had invited to the graduation.

Lani had glanced at Terrence several times and although he saw her, he felt helpless. He had stood surrounded by so many people, so many obligations. He had decided that she would just have to wait. But ten minutes later, he couldn't find her. In the middle of another round of pictures with Kenya, he looked over to get a glimpse of her and realized that she and Dee had disappeared.

Terrence remembered walking away, in the middle of posing with Kenya for the picture. He smiled, despite himself, remembering how furious his mother had been later. She had shouted that he'd embarrassed Kenya by walking away like that. He hadn't cared. His heart had begun hurting, because he knew that he had hurt Lani, even thought he wasn't quite sure how.

Then he had spotted Dee's daughter, bobbing in and out of the crowd. Following, he quickly realized she was lost, although she hadn't started crying and didn't really seem worried. She was just as cool in confusion and chaos as her mean ass momma.

"Are you okay?" Terrence touched her arm, but immediately removed his hand when the little girl looked like she was going to punch him. Terrence had to fight back his smile. She looked like a miniature Lani.

"I'm good, my mother will find me," she had said with a little eye roll that made him smile.

They walked together, although she refused to take his hand, until they found Dee searching wildly for her.

"Lani, Lani, I see her!" Dee had screamed across the crowded lobby. He turned, following the direction of her voice, spotting his beautiful girlfriend. He opened his arms wide for a hug.

"Congratulations," he said softly, "we made it."

She entered his arms, as she always used to do, even when she felt upset. "Yep, we did."

Terrence caressed her cheek. "What's wrong?"

"Nothing." Lani lied, her pain evident on her face.

Terrence needed to know. "What?"

"You just now telling her congratulations, trying to finally acknowledge her?" Dee's voice grated against his nerves and scraped them raw. "After all this time. While you were with your family and your little girlfriend, I guess Lani wasn't that important, huh?"

"Huh?" He stared at Lani. He hadn't even thought about it that way. Family pictures and "immediately after" stuff was an obligation. It wasn't his fault that she didn't have any family.

Lani shrugged her shoulders and looked just past him. "It would have been nice to have met your family, that's all," she mumbled.

Then he understood. He remembered his heart had stopped as he realized Lani had never met his mother. He had never formally introduced her as his girlfriend to any of his people. He had actually felt guilty, because he would never treated a girlfriend from his social circle like that. It wouldn't have been an option; their families would have made contact way before graduation. He didn't want to be real with himself about why he hadn't introduced Lani, about how he was afraid that his family wouldn't approve of her.

Terrence pulled her over, broke through the family crowd, and introduced her proudly. His mother had been kind, but obviously surprised. But his father had grinned, the devilish grin that let him know exactly what his father had in mind. Even now, Terrence laughed, thinking about his father's bright eyes as he took in Lani. Even Kenya's mother had been gracious, had hugged Lani, kissed her on the cheek, commented on her beauty and expressed sincere congratulations. Only Kenya hadn't responded at all, the cool aloof gloss returning while she stared down her nose at Lani.

Interesting, I never thought about it that way before. She always has that look when Lani comes around, a detached cold thing. Not really mean, not really obviously rude, but something...

Leaning back in the seat, Terrence couldn't believe Lani still had this picture. After the introductions, Lani made small talk for a few minutes with the family, while his father winked at him and his mother elbowed his father in the ribs. He hadn't rushed her, and when Lani felt ready, he had walked her to Dee's car, kissed her and made arrangements to meet later. Terrence remembered Lani's scent as he whispered in her ear that he was proud of her, proud to introduce her to his parents. Then he had told her how beautiful he found her every time he looked at her. He remembered how Lani blushed, leaned into him, grinned adoringly at him. Then Lani snatched Dee's camera and told him to pose. His heart skipped as he recalled extending his degree to her, putting his hand on his heart, whispering "forever you." He had meant it and he never thought she had any clue how deep that moment felt to him. He had never seen the picture, yet, here it sat, on Lani's computer. And the picture had captured the moment, his intensity, and his love.

Lani looks at this every day?

Terrence leaned back into the large leather chair. He and Lani were so similar now to that day. Every major function still played the same, Terrence surrounded by family and friends and Lani off to the side, waiting to be acknowledged. Even Kenya's reaction to Lani hadn't changed over the years. Still the cold, cool gloss. But he had blamed Lani, thought it was her fault for sitting there quietly. Figured she was moping because she selfishly wanted all the attention. Or he assumed that people stayed away from Lani because of her moodiness.

The truth is, I have never bothered to bring Lani into the fold. I never let anyone but Lani know how much she means to me. No wonder Kenya could be all up on me like that. It's my fault.

Terrence leaned forward, his head in his hands, his elbows rested on the desk. Tears rolled down his face and landed on the keyboard in front of him. *What have I done?*

Chapter Twenty Nine

Christopher had left a few hours earlier. Lani insisted that he leave first, so that she could have some time alone to process everything that had happened. She had thought Christopher would leave first thing in the morning, but he hadn't. After touching base with Jackie, he insisted on feeding her breakfast and giving her a massage.

It was cute to Lani that Christopher kept trying to find reasons to stay. It felt good to have a man want to be in her presence and want to spend his energy making her feel special. They had hugged and kissed and Christopher had cradled her in his lap and whispered his intimate thoughts to her. She found out about Alayna; the first time he had ever discussed it. Lani told Christopher about her mother and her life with Dee. She explained for the first time how Dee had sacrificed her childhood to raise Lani. Lani admitted how guilty she felt that she had settled for a man who didn't make her sister feel welcome, who never took the time to really understand how much Dee meant to her.

The more they talked, the closer they felt. It no longer seemed like a dismissible affair, once history had been shared and skeletons revealed. They talked about the danger of what they had created and how it might haunt them one day. But Christopher adamantly refused to feel guilty or bad about it.

"This is love and I will enjoy it while I can. Most people don't get this in a lifetime," he had mumbled as he kissed her on the cheek.

Even now, in the room by herself, she didn't feel guilt. They had discussed hiding their romance, but then Christopher said that the hiding would make it seem dark and stained; something it wasn't. Rather than hide it, he had said he wanted to keep it sacred and safe. To himself. Lani liked the way he put that, although she found herself amazed how easily men compartmentalized emotion. But, in this case, his method felt easier to swallow, and she agreed to it.

Around noon, Kenya had begun calling every ten minutes. To his credit, Christopher never yelled at her, or disrespected her in front of Lani. Even when he didn't answer the phone, he didn't discuss Kenya at all. Lani had watched him and prepared her heart for the probable disappointment of him gossiping about his wife, but he never did. It made Lani love Christopher more. Despite everything, he manned up and kept his wife's flaws to himself. Unlike Terrence, who would have told every detail of every discussion and interaction, and would have called her out of her name a million times by now.

The few times Christopher answered Kenya, he took the small cellular phone off the wall charger and marched into the bathroom, shut the door, ran the water. Even then she could hear the anger in his low voice, the direct commands and his limited patience. She could only imagine how Kenya, Mrs. Princess, was responding to this new side of her husband that now recognized her without the rose colored lenses. Oddly enough, Lani didn't feel satisfied or vindicated. If anything, the thought of Kenya just made her sad. Because, in the end, it was Christopher who was really hurt. Just like her. Despite all the antics Terrence was going through, she was the one who was hurt.

But Lani knew herself well. She might feel sad thinking about Kenya, but in person she would undoubtedly want to attack her. She still thought Kenya was fool to run out in the middle of the night after a married man, leaving a baby and her own husband at home. In Lani's way of thinking, Kenya needed her ass whipped.

Eventually, Kenya wouldn't stop calling and obviously refused to give her husband up to whatever situation he was in. Lani admired her fight. She figured Kenya's mother must have talked some sense into her. Eventually, Christopher gave in and prepared to leave so that Kenya would stop interrupting their time together. Neither wanted their memory of this weekend to end with nonstop calls from Kenya.

Sighing, Lani lifted her travel bag, laying it across her chest, and grabbed her small hand bag. She had stayed past that day's check in and would still be billed for the night, but it was time to go. Christopher had renewed her and she felt prepared face whatever awaited her. If she stayed another night in this hotel, she might never go home at all.

She hadn't decided whether she would put Terrence out, or just leave. She needed to talk to one of her girlfriends for some legal advice and find out how best to play it. Marriage to Terrence had depleted her finances; if she didn't extricate herself carefully she would be bankrupt. Lani stopped walking.

Is that what I've decided? Am I leaving him?

One part of her yelled, "*of course*," the other remained silent. *Do I still love him?* Love was really irrelevant at this point; love had kept her on this painful path for far too long. *Does he love me? No. Does he respect me? Hell no. Does he feel lucky to have me?* She snorted at the thought of Terrence feeling lucky to have anything, or believing anything was not his inherent right to enjoy.

At the lobby checkout, Lani turned in the plastic key.

"Ma'am you can keep those as a souvenir. Your bill has been covered, already paid for. Looks like your all set." The clerk smiled amicably at her. She felt thankful that the young man who had worked the night Christopher came was not there.

My bill paid, huh? Only Christopher.

She headed to her car, slowly stepping into the parking lot. Lani didn't look forward to the drive home; she didn't want to think about her life.

If I could just think about the last 24 hours, about Christopher. You know what, I am not even going to talk to Terrence when I get home. Nothing to say tonight. I am just going to try to rest, think out a strategy in the morning.

Lani's stomach dropped at the idea. She would be a fool if she believed Terrence would give her any rest tonight. Clenching her jaw, she made it to her car and threw the bags in the backseat. She climbed in the car she started the engine and began driving forward before she noticed it.

She hit the brakes. A small business card sat tucked under the left windshield. She plucked it gingerly, thinking it was some unwanted advertisement.

Lani, I don't want us to end. Not yet. Stay in my world, when and how you can... Luv Chris

The tiny sentence was scribbled on the back of the card; the front had his office numbers, all his professional contact information.

So this is how it will play, huh? We will stay secret lovers? She smiled.

Christopher could do it without any problems, she knew that. Kenya had never really had all of him, anyway. But could she? She loved so completely, could she have a fake life with Terrence and maintain love with Christopher. *Well, I can damn sure try!*

Lani tucked the tiny card into her wallet, just behind her license, under the flap. Smiling, she patted the wallet and slid back into the seat. She never noticed the light flap of paper that had been waiting for her on the seat that slid out of the open door when she reached for Christopher's card, which now rested lightly on the pavement. Shutting the door, Lani pulled off into the night, heading for what remained of her life.

Chapter Thirty

"Nothing is the same. I just don't feel the same, you know?" Christopher inhaled, enjoying the smell of bread cooking in Jackie's house.

Jackie didn't respond as she tucked little Christopher's blankets into the tiny bag.

"So, what, I am just supposed to go back now, like nothing is wrong?" Christopher pounded the soft baby pillow that he was attempting to ram into the front of the diaper bag.

Jackie softly took it from him and placed a gentle hand on his arm and slowly removed the bag from his grasp.

"Jackie, say something. Please."

"I don't know what to say," Jackie paused and looked at him, then shifted her eyes to the sleeping baby. "I mean, why has everything changed?"

"I don't know." Christopher looked away.

"Who were you with, Christopher?" Jackie pushed her little brother. "It's all over you."

His head snapped up sharply. It was rare to hear judgment from Jackie—she normally didn't go there.

He glanced at her questioningly, but her gaze remained even and undisturbed.

"You went to her, didn't you?" It wasn't a question.

Christopher wouldn't deny it and she knew it.

"So now what?" she asked softly.

"I don't know. That's what I'm asking you."

"What about Kenya, your home, your life?"

"Doesn't matter anymore. Not worth it. Feels like a job, something I got to do. Just turn off my mind and do it. Don't expect nothing in return, no benefit other than a pat on the head."

Jackie asked very slowly, "Do you love Kenya?"

Christopher sat still and eyeing his baby. "Of course, I love my wife. But, I am not feeling that "in love" thing, anymore."

"Nobody does, after a while Christopher."

"I know. But, I mean, I just realized that we never really had that, that thing..."

Jackie started grinning as she shook her head. "That sister must've worked it on you."

Embarrassment flooded his mind. He kept his head down. "It's not about her."

"I know. I know it's not. I'm sorry for teasing."

They sat in silence while Jackie bundled baby Christopher into the warm cover.

Christopher pressed the words out of his chest that had been playing in his mind all this time. "I'm leaving Kenya."

Jackie shook her head. "Christopher, give it some time. Wait a second."

"No need. I finally remembered what I was missing. I remember this feeling. I want this feeling. I have never had it with Kenya. I, I am not going to lose any more time, just doing what's right. Missing out on life."

Jackie nodded. She knew that feeling; she remembered when the sight of her husband, Miles, made the pit of her stomach drop. It was a long time ago. What could she say?

"So, I'm like Daddy, huh? All this education and opportunity, and I am still searching for the next thrill."

"Never, baby boy. Never look at it like that. You are too young to give up on what life has to offer. Maybe you and Kenya will find something and stay together. Maybe not. Either way, I got you."

He smiled and kissed his older sister on the cheek. "I know."

Chapter Thirty One

Miles sighed deeply as he turned off the engine and leaned back in the seat. Christopher's car was in the yard, which could only mean one thing—he was picking up the baby. The baby. Life, joy, a bundle that he had never had the chance to call his own, had resided in his house over the weekend. And he had done alright. Miles had found out that he could pick him up without breaking him, could feed him without choking him. It had felt good to have a baby in the house.

Jackie was going to be upset. Miles knew his wife would play it cool; she would seem simple and unfazed. That was the persona Jackie projected to everyone. Never judgmental, never shaken. Not in public. Not even to her little brothers. Jackie had raised them after all, and still thought she had to be strong for them. Only with Miles did she unravel, just a bit. He always knew he was still only getting surface stuff, though. Jackie was deep. Too deep. Rivers of pain flowed through his wife that he didn't even want to know about.

The only time Miles had seen Jackie break down and cry was after the fertility shots didn't work. All that money and time wasted. Taking her temperature three times a day; demanding sex on a certain date at a certain time by a certain angle; bending over and handing him the needle to have it stuck in her hip. It crushed Miles that she would do so much; go so far, just to have a baby. Shots? It seemed unreal to him. Black folks didn't have to work this hard to get pregnant. It just happened.

Truth was, pregnancy hadn't happened for years. And he had agreed to meet with the fertility doctors, to take the tests, make those humiliating deposits. Still nothing. It wasn't him. That was one thing they both knew. So she bent over while he jabbed her with the needle, a part of him crying while he watched his wife sit on a sore behind. The cold sex, without meaning. He couldn't do it. He had stopped, demanded she stop. They would have to accept it, they would never have children.

It worked out pretty well. They lived a comfortable simple life. A clean life. Not too many complications. Never any drama, until Kenya became pregnant. Jackie hadn't said anything, smiled politely, kissed her baby brother and continued sipping her drink. But Miles could feel her heart sinking, the hurt burning like and uncontrollable flame. When they got home she had refused to comment, wouldn't even talk about it. But that night, she ground her teeth so hard that he woke in the middle of the night. It sounded like metal scraping against pavement. Miles had folded her in his arms, waking her, massaging her jaw line. In the dead of the night, in absolute silence, Jackie had finally cried. Finally, released years of frustration and disappointment. Finally, conceded that this was her fate.

I guess I got to go in here. He didn't want to see them pack up little Christopher and walk him out of the house. It would tear Jackie apart. Later. But what choice did they have. Sighing again, he climbed slowly from the truck just as the front door opened.

"What's up, Miles?"

"Nothing man. You back?"

"Yeah man." Christopher averted his eyes.

What's that all about? One thing he appreciated about his wife's family, they were honest folks. The truth sat right on them; they couldn't hide it if they wanted to.

"What's up?" Miles asked, leaning over the car seat and adjusting little Christopher's blanket.

"Man, I don't know. Things have changed."

Miles nodded. "We'll talk."

Christopher met his eyes, "Yeah, I'll call."

Oh shit! Miles didn't have to ask, the simple defeat on Christopher's face gave it away. It had to have been another woman.

"Keep my baby safe," Jackie called from the front door.

Christopher grinned sadly and waved at her. "I will, I will..." Carefully carrying the baby he nodded at Miles before moving slowly down the driveway.

Miles watched him load the car seat into its cradle, jump into the driver seat and slowly pull away. Only then did he have the courage to look at his wife. He glanced slowly toward the door, just in time to see

Jackie's shoulder's slump, her brave attempt at nonchalance passing away in the breeze.

Chapter Thirty Two

Lani rode slowly down the street. She couldn't figure out where else to go, although she definitely didn't want to go home.

Maybe Terrence won't be there. Probably with his Kenya anyway. She kept up the stream of "what if's" and "probably's" building her nerve. The weekend with Christopher had fortified her, made her feel able to conquer the world. But much of that had faded over the past few hours.

The truth was Christopher wouldn't be with her when she faced Terrence, wouldn't have her back. No telling how things would change once he went back to his wife, anyway.

Terrence's car sat in the driveway. The lights were on. He was there.

Damn! Lani pulled slowly into the yard. *How do I do this? The truth is that he is the one in the wrong. Hell, he is the one that walked out, left me. Went to another man's wife for comfort.*

But in that same instant, a glimpse of Christopher's naked frame filled her mind, her hand filled with all of his manness and her tongue exploring the gentle curve of his ear.

216

Stop it! She cracked the window to let the evening coolness clear her mind. Maybe she should just leave. Stay at a hotel. Live at the hotel. Go to work like everything was normal until she found another living arrangement. That would be the easiest thing. Then she could work past what she had done, how much she had enjoyed it, how much she had believed she deserved it. It had all made sense, just a few hours ago. Now right and wrong were not so clearly defined.

Even if Terrence had done something, it definitely wasn't what she and Christopher had enjoyed. She knew that. It seemed almost funny; in cheating she actually got a better deal. Kenya's frigid self could never compare to the experience of her and Christopher. She could tell that by how Christopher responded to the very simple things she did, the basic loving, and the standard stuff.

Tilting her head, she imagined when she sat on Christopher's lap, her legs open, wrapped around each one of his, while he kissed the back of her neck, reached around her torso and gently caressed her blossom...

Stop it!

Lani shook her head. She could still feel Christopher, smell him and taste him. She wasn't prepared for Terrence. Not yet anyway. She would just leave.

"How long you gonna sit in the car?"

Lani froze in terror. Terrence's voice sounded thin and tired.

Where is he? She turned her head quickly, scanning behind the car, expecting him to jump out the bushes or something equally terrifying.

Terrence responded to the unspoken question. "I'm right here."

"Where?" Lani hadn't meant to ask the question out loud, but fear allowed the word to slip past.

He didn't answer. In the early evening light she finally spotted him, sitting in plain sight on the stoop in front of the front door.

What the hell, why didn't I see him? Because he never, ever sits outside.

Terrence's voice sounded like water hitting hot oil. "Are you getting out of the car?"

His face held no expression, gave her no indication of his thoughts. Something deep down in Lani felt frozen and she could hear her heart beating.

Lani shivered.

They sat in silence for several minutes. She heard a bird chirping somewhere.

Terrence tapped a twig against the brick steps. "Where have you been?"

"Delaware."

"Yeah, I know."

Something in his voice made her look up, lock eyes and try to read him. *Of course he knew I was in Delaware. Get a grip; he was supposed to meet me.*

But some other part of her warned her not to say anything, not to do anything. Wait him out. She ignored the mental warning. "You know? You never showed up."

"Yeah," the twig snapped. "I did."

Impossible. He couldn't know. If he did, why didn't he do anything in Delaware? Lani shrugged again. "How long you been sitting out here?"

"Long enough."

"Long enough for what?"

"Long enough to get all the information I needed to know..." he paused, squinting at her. "So you did it."

Lani gasped. "Did what?" Playing stupid was her safest bet.

Terrence stood suddenly, stepping off the stoop into the grass. "Lani, what did you do?"

"Terrence, you're confusing me. I don't know..."

"WHAT DID YOU DO!" he screamed like a maniac with one hand in the air, point at her. "SAY IT. TELL ME. WHAT DID YOU DO?"

Lani sat very still. Her eyes watered as she watched Terrence scream at the top of his lungs, waving his fists in the air, losing all control in the middle of their front lawn.

Chapter Thirty Three

Kenya sat at the kitchen table, gripping the mug of cold coffee. She released her grip and placed her hands flat on the table. It didn't matter how long it took, she was going to sit there and wait for Christopher. She couldn't believe Christopher would do this, would go to Lani—a classless bitch.

Before, it felt unfair that Lani had Terrence, unfair that someone so undeserving had such a great catch. But Christopher was different. He belonged to her. They had a life, a commitment, a belief in family.

And just like that, the tacky wench wrecked it. Somehow, Lani had lured her Christopher into the worst mistake of his life. Earlier, Kenya had panicked. Her own lust and guilt had overwhelmed her senses. *What was I thinking?* The past 36 hours had been complete hell, her waiting by the telephone trying to catch up with Terrence and figure out what to do, while he chased his own wife. But then she turned to her own man and tried to reach out to him, and he too had gone to Lani's aid. At least, that's where she suspected he was. His sister wouldn't tell. And she hadn't wanted to cause more fuss by snatching little Christopher from Jackie.

Truth be told, she needed a break and knew her baby boy was in good hands. So, she sat at the kitchen table and thought about her life. About the sacrifices Christopher made for her. How good a man and father he was. She wouldn't give him up without a fight. She certainly wouldn't let Lani infiltrate her home.

A misunderstanding. That's it, it is all a misunderstanding. I should have told Christopher I was going to meet Terrence. He overreacted. I can explain that, get him to understand. Then he better make it very clear what he did with Lani and how far he let it go. I bet they didn't do anything; he just went up there to make me worry, to scare me.

She turned the cup slowly, blocking out all thoughts of her interaction with Terrence, her temporary weakness, her own indiscretions. They no longer existed and were not relevant. She hadn't crossed the line of no return and she felt confident that Christopher hadn't either. But Lani was the problem. Her moral values were nonexistent, allowing Christopher to scare Kenya by staying with her.

Didn't she care about her own reputation? Didn't she know how trifling that was, to even allow Christopher to stay there, to give out that image?

The garage door opened. Kenya took a deep breath as she listened to Christopher's heavy footsteps cross the garage platform. He opened the side door and looked at her without smiling. He carried the baby carrier to the far side of the kitchen and began to unbuckle their baby boy. To Kenya, the silence felt deafening. Little Christopher whimpered and tried to suck on his fist. Despite expressing milk and wasting and discarding most of it through the weekend, her breasts remained painfully full. She stood up, determined to feed her son.

"I told you not to be here." Christopher placed his body between her and her baby.

"This is my home, Christopher."

"Really?"

Kenya stared at him. *What does that mean?* She grasped her son, kissed and hugged him, then cradled him in her arms while she fed him, pulling a small nursing towel over him.

"Kenya, I don't want you here. "

"Christopher, that's crazy. I don't understand where this is coming from."

"Crazy? Crazy is leaving your son to be with Terrence," he said loudly. "Crazy is walking out on a husband to be with a fool!"

She wouldn't argue while nursing. The tension could poison her milk and make it unhealthy.

She started calmly, in a low voice, "You misunderstood. I didn't rush to be with him. I never left—"

"Kenya," Christopher interrupted, "It doesn't matter, now. Not anymore. Actually, I don't care enough to hear about it."

He turned on his heel and walked out of the house.

Chapter Thirty Four

Kenya should have stayed at her parents, like he told her to. He knew it sounded illogical, but at least that way he would feel different now. The sight of her enraged him; he hadn't expected it. He had thought he would be able to cope with her, would possibly feel anger. Instead, the sight of her at the kitchen table with her back straight and face devoid of expression, made him want to throw something. She seemed to think Christopher owed her an explanation.

He needed some time away from her. That much was clear. And he wasn't leaving his home. He hadn't expected her to make a stand. If it weren't for his baby boy, he would have carried her out of there.

My baby boy. Damn. That changed everything. His son. He couldn't risk his son suffering from any rip that he caused. The boy needed his mother, how could he deny that?

Christopher ran his hand over his head and leaned back in the car seat. Here he was, driving around in circles for no apparent reason. His mind felt like one continuous loop, replaying his anger at Kenya, his weekend with Lani.

Lani. He could still taste her, smell her. He wanted to hear her voice, just one more time. But no, he didn't want to press up. This weekend had been a one-time thing. It was late Sunday evening, what would he say. They didn't have anything in common, except they had both married self absorbed people.

He sighed deeply. He was a man, after all, and he wasn't playing games. If she didn't want to talk to him she could just not answer the phone. But he would take the chance and make the call. He dialed her number by memory. He hadn't saved it in the phone. Not yet. He still had to be discreet. The phone rang twice. On the third ring, he heard a click then noise.

"Hello?"

No one answered, but the noise was loud. *Maybe I dialed the wrong number.* Then he heard screaming, definitely Lani.

"Lani, Lani?" Christopher yelled into the phone.

"Stop it, Terrence. Stop it!" she shrieked. He could hear Terrence's voice in the background, although he couldn't make out the words.

"I'll call the police. I swear..."

That was all Christopher needed to hear. He signaled right and headed for Lani's house. Keeping the connection open, he could hear Lani screaming and shouting and Terrence answering.

It sounded ugly. Christopher's head burned. Terrence had no right. None. He had left Lani, walked out and broken her heart. He had called Christopher's wife out of the house in the middle of the night to meet his own selfish need. Now he was ranting and raving and raising hell. Terrence was nothing but a punk. He certainly could put his wife through hell, but would he be bold enough to face Christopher? Christopher didn't think so, but he was certainly going to find out.

***

"Get out of the car, Lani." Terrence smiled at Lani as if he were completely calm and negotiating a new advertising deal.

"Hell no, Terrence." Lani slammed her hand against the window.

His fake smile disappeared.

"Damn you. Do you hear me? Damn you, Terrence." Her hand slapped repeatedly against the window.

"Damn me?" He couldn't believe his ears. "You fucking tramp! Get the hell out of my car!"

Lani sat up straight, her finger pointing in the air, spite glowing from her eyes. "Yeah, I'll be a tramp Terrence. That's what you want to hear. I'm a tramp now, alright? After you went running out of this house in the middle of the night. After you went to her. You're calling me a tramp?"

"HOW MANY TIMES DO I HAVE TO SAY IT?" Terrence jumped up and down as if a sea of rats nipped at his ankles. "I DIDNT GO TO HER."

"And you're a liar. Take your lying ass in the house."

"No." Terrence folded his arms. "You get out of the car."

She pressed her lips together and crossed her arms.

225

Terrence lifted his eyebrows; noting she was calling his bluff. He shrugged and pulled a long screw driver out of his back pocket.

"What do you think you're going to do with that, Terrence?"

He didn't answer as he walked to the front driver side tire and stabbed it. He hummed Method Man and Mary J. Blige's anthem, "You're All I Need," as he slammed the screw driver in the front passenger tire.

"Terrence, have you lost your mind?"

Lani pressed both of her hands against her window and stared at him with her mouth open as he plunged the screw driver in the rear tires as well.

She was trapped.

Terrence wanted to laugh at the surprised expression on his wife's face. She and Dee thought he was such a punk, just because he wasn't as hood rat as the men they seemed to like. Well, how did she like her suburban punk now?

"Isn't this what you want, Lani? To be disrespected; yelled at and fighting in the streets. Yeah, this is what you always wanted. Them ghetto ways of yours. Always throwing my shit around, tearing up my home and ruining my clothes … this is what you want."

"No it's not, Terrence!"

"Sure it is." The front tire was deflating quickly enough, but Terrence stuck it again, for good measure. "I try not to argue with you. I try to keep the peace. But nooo…" Terrence put his arms in the air and waved them like a clown, "…you got to keep pressing the punk, keep disrespecting the punk in his own home, and keep treating him like the punk you think he is. Is that it?"

"I never said I thought you were a punk."

"You disrespect me!" Terrence pointed the screwdriver at her. "Over and over again, I swallow your bullshit. No, say little slick shit out your mouth with me sitting right there. Mumble all loud about how much you hate me and our life while you stomp your selfish ass around the house."

Lani was stupefied. His words were true and wrong at the same time. She did act like that, but only in response to him being selfish and cold. He had caused it, not her!

"Keep treating me like shit to my face and then get mad because I *want* to be around my family and friends. Because I loved *you* and I married *you* but I got to escape your depressed ass to keep some sanity."

Silence.

"Ah, you don't want to discuss that, do you?" Terrence stabbed the passenger tire again. "No, you got to be the victim—'ah my husband doesn't love me, he doesn't pay me enough attention, he won't talk to me'—what about all those days you get lost in that head of yours, huh, Lani? What happens to me and us on those days? How many times have I had to drag you out of the bed and wash you from head to toe, after you shut down for days at a time? How many weeks did I go to work, unsure if I was going to come home to you with slit wrists or hanging somewhere because your depressed ass won't go see a psychiatrist? Shit, you ain't even take me to meet your mother!

After all these years! What the fuck does that mean? What does that say about me and how little respect you have for me?"

"Terrence..."

He couldn't stop it, couldn't stop himself. He felt a black gaping hole in his chest, it hurt to breathe. The hole stretched throughout his body, a huge tear in his soul.

Lani had done it. She had slept with another man. His godson's father at that. Someone he was forever tied to. It was the biggest insult. He knew it now, although he had tried to convince himself otherwise. He had waited for her, thought of how he would apologize, how he would work to make everything alright. He had left that hotel when he should have caught them both. He should have raised hell then. But he had believed in her—he had still trusted her.

Then Lani sat in the car, closed her eyes, and Terrence could see visions of lovemaking playing out across her face by her sensuous expressions. She had actually pulled into their yard and reminisced on her sexual tryst. And Terrence had watched her. Quietly watched. And every calm logical thought, every gesture of love, every guilty feeling about his own wrongs, his own neglect, his own faults, evaporated at the realization that Lani had no respect for him at all.

Terrence wanted her out the car. He wanted her to engage him, so he could unleash his fury. He had never hit a woman before; but he certainly wanted to strangle her ass.

He had seen her fumbling with the phone. He didn't care. In a second he was going to break the windshield and pull her ass out.

Lani sobbed. "Go back in the house, Terrence, or I swear I will call the police."

He felt his eyes widen like saucers. Is that what she had just said? Just when he had thought she couldn't stoop any lower, now she was turning into that type of black woman who would actually call the police on a decent, hard working brother? The type who would create legal complications for him after he had achieved a lifetime of remaining under the cop's radar?

"That's what I get for dealing with a roller. The police? You're going to call the police?" Terrence studied Lani for a minute as he paced back and forth in front of the car. "You know what, call them. Shit, adultery may be illegal in Virginia any damn way. Call them and tell them to help you pack your shit."

He couldn't believe Lani had undermined his life like this. Threatening to call Virginia police on a black man was tantamount to requesting he get lynched. After she already disrespected him in every way possible. An irrational burning began to explode in his chest. Hate. *I actually hate her.*

Terrence began walking backward into the garage. "How long were you with Christopher, huh? How long?" He turned his back on her, looking for the stones that were in the back somewhere. Terrence had bought them to line the garden; he could slam them through her windshield. "You were with him for days..." he whispered. "For days."

He spotted them, right next to the old golf clubs. *Damn the stones, the clubs will be better.* The golf club pleased him, it was a better option. He swung it in the air like a baton as he marched back to her car.

"You were with that son of a bitch for days. You don't have any respect for me. I mean none. Bet you'll respect my ass now." He pulled club above his hand and began beating the hood of the car and the windshield. "GET THE FUCK OUT OF MY CAR!"

"STOP TERRENCE, STOP. I SWEAR I'LL CALL THE POLICE!" That infuriated him more. He pointed at her. "I want you out of my car and off my property. Now. Leave now."

"This is my car. My property. You leave now; I am dialing 911."

Why couldn't she ever give in? Even just once. Why could she never let him win one battle or one argument? Why wouldn't she just do as she was told and get out of the car? Terrence continued to smash the windshield while Lani screamed at the top of her lungs. He had forgotten about neighbors and random passersby, nothing could penetrate his shell.

He climbed on the hood of the car. "Last warning." Terrence twirled the golf club.

"Damn you, Terrence!" she shrieked, as he slammed the club against the windshield with all his might, splintering it.

He heard the door open, despite her screams. Finally. She finally had to give in. The small victory felt so sweet that Terrence raised the club over his head for one final blow, a broad smile across his deranged face.

A massive figure dove across the hood of the car, tackling Terrence. They both rolled off the other side of the car and the club fell from his hand as his head slammed against the pavement.

Terrence lay breathless for a second. Lani couldn't have tackled him like that. He looked up into the eyes of his attacker just as Christopher landed a punch across his cheek. Terrence pushed himself back, stumbled a bit as he got his footing.

"Are you serious?" The question flew out of Terrence's mouth. "You of all people want some of this ..." Bending low, he tackled Christopher, knocking him off balance. Terrence pummeled Christopher's chest and rib cage. But Christopher was too big for him. He picked Terrence up and slammed his body against the pavement again. Holding his arm behind his back, Christopher leaned into Terrence.

"You defile my wife and then attack your own. You're less of a man than I thought."

With everything he had, Terrence reared back and head butted Christopher, who released his grip as his nose stung and eyes watered. Terrence took a few steps back, preparing to attack again. His eyes searched the yard. Lani had disappeared. He was still furious, still wanted to kill Christopher, but he had to make one thing clear and set the record straight.

"You motherfucker. I did not sleep with your wife. Not now, not ever. Never tried. Never thought about it. I respected you. I called Kenya to talk. Called my best friend to talk about my wife. And this, this is what you do? This is how you do me? You've taken everything from me..."

Something inside of Terrence cracked. It was an admission and a realization. He had lost everything. Terrence pulled at his shirt and then his hair. Tears ran from his eyes and sweat poured from his brow. Terrence was out of his mind. He stared at Christopher in agony. "You've taken everything from me..."

Chapter Thirty Five

Terrence stared at Christopher. The stupid look on his face outraged Terrence. *Where is my golf club?* Terrence swung wildly around, his eyes scanning the ground.

"Do you hear yourself?" Christopher shook his head, a look of utter disbelief shattering his normal calm exterior. "Seriously, man. Do you hear yourself?"

Terrence swung back around. "Get off my property."

"No, you're going to listen to me."

"Get off my property." Terrence spotted the covered handle protruding from the hedge separating his yard from the neighbors. "Now."

"No. You are lying to yourself. You called my wife. My *wife*. In the middle of the night. You were with her and you think I don't know." Christopher's index finger violently jabbed the air with each word, and he spat the words out as if he were gagging on them. "I trusted you. And you were with my wife."

"I WASN'T WITH HER." Terrence paced in a small circle, hands on his head. "IT WASN'T LIKE THAT."

"It was like that." Christopher took a step closer. "You took my wife out of my house? What, to hit her off in the parking lot?"

Terrence's lips spread into a slow smile, but his eyes remained frantic, cold and distant. "Did she tell you? Did she say how it went down?"

Christopher stared at him. Terrence knew he wouldn't ask; that he didn't really want to know. What man did? But this was his chance to tell it, to make Christopher felt as low as he did.

"She wanted it, man. Tried to grab for my piece and everything." Terrence smiled fully, shrugged his shoulders and whispered, "I had to snatch her hands out of my pants."

Terrence watched Christopher's face with satisfaction, watched him flinch at the mere mention of what had happened. *Yeah, you ain't so high and mighty now.*

Terrence turned his back to Christopher and headed to his garage. Terrence intended to close the garage door, shutting him in the house with Lani, if that's where she was. He had a mission now. They were both going to feel what he felt.

"I don't believe you." Christopher called to his back.

"Believe it." Terrence turned back around and watched the huge man standing there, covered in defeat. There was something about Christopher in that moment that reminded Terrence of himself. *Lani really wasn't that much different than Kenya after. They did this. They both had ulterior motives and both went for self and disregarded marriage for their own desire.* Terrence knew that

Christopher could never have fought off Lani if she decided to go after him. On some level, it probably wasn't even his fault.

"Get off my property."

"Did you do it? Did you...?" Christopher pushed forward, "Did you...?"

Terrence wanted to bury the dagger in Christopher's heart and twist it. But he couldn't. Christopher had been the only brother he'd known.

"No, I didn't do your wife. I went the hell off on her. On my so called best friend. I took her hands out of my pants and told her to get it together." Terrence took a few steps closer to Christopher. "Since we're being so honest, what happened between you and Lani?"

Christopher didn't answer, his eyes focused on the pavement.

"Answer me. I want to hear it."

Christopher raised his head and leveled his eyes with Terrence. His face shifted slightly as he glanced at the house. Terrence followed his eyes to see Lani watching out of the front window. The sight of her must have given Christopher strength, because when his eyes met Terrence's again they were defiant, his jaw set and his neck straight.

"Say it," Terrence whispered through clenched teeth. "I dare you to say it."

"Lani and I..."

Before Christopher could finish, Terrence punched him on the chin, right in the spot that his father taught him would take down any man.

Christopher stumbled, took two steps, and then collapsed on the pavement.

"Big ass man with a glass chin. Ha!" Terrence chuckled, and turned to face the house. Lani had left the window.

He grabbed the bent golf club from the hedge and walked to the front door. As he reached it, he could hear the massive lock turn and click into place.

"Lani. Open the door." Terrence took three breaths and wrapping his hand firmly around the club. It was all good. She would probably lock all the doors. He strolled calmly to the picture window and hit it methodically with the club. He was getting in his house. And he would put her out, even if he had to drag her by her hair.

Lost within the deep echoes of his own mind, and focused on entering the house, Terrence didn't hear the sirens until it was too late.

"Drop the club. Hands on your head." It took Terrence a moment to realize there was a patrol car in his yard and two officers were standing behind him, shouting at him with their guns drawn. He glanced in the window again. Lani met his eyes, her face frozen with panic.

"This is how low I have sunk." Terrence shouted. "This is what I get for ever having loved you."

Chapter Thirty Six

Miles stood next to the water cooler while he observed his wife. *What do I say?* He wasn't a man of many words. The house felt empty to him and the baby's scent still clung to the air. Jackie moved around the house quietly, cleaning their already sterile living space. Miles sighed and turned his head to survey the kitchen. It was small, but cozy.

Time for a new paint job. "Any dinner?" *No need to ask, really.*

She had returned to her zombie state; cleaning in silence. "No."

Miles kept questioning. "Did you eat anything?"

She deeply exhaled, as if his questions were annoying her. "No."

"Jackie, you should have told me you weren't going to cook." He moved to the refrigerator.

For the first time she looked up and glared at him. "You are a grown man, Miles. You can figure out how to feed yourself for one night."

Miles opened the refrigerator so that Jackie wouldn't see his face. *Damnit. This is what I get every time a child stays over here. This silent blame bullshit.*

237

Miles stood still, trying to decide what to eat. If he was going to have to cook, he might as well go all out. *Maybe I'll fry up that whiting Tim brought over. No, I don't feel like cleaning fish.* He removed the collard greens that were in a Ziploc bag in the freezer. *I think I might have me some greens with rice, fry up some fish after all. Yeah, that'll work.*

Miles washed his hands. Going back to the freezer, he pulled out the whiting. Then he scanned the cabinets for corn meal. Miles placed the cornmeal, pepper and seasonings on the counter. *Hot sauce. I need some hot sauce for this whiting.*

Jackie's voice broke into his thoughts. "What are you doing?"

Huh? "I'm cooking, woman! Didn't you just tell me to feed myself?"

"No, Miles, I just cleaned in here."

"Jackie, I got to eat. Now listen, you didn't cook and I'm hungry."

"Then you better get yourself some carry out. I do not want the house smelling like fish."

Jackie walked past him into the living room.

Miles followed. "Listen. I ain't going through this every time one of your nephews comes over. I mean, I understand how you feel. But you ain't got to torture me."

Her expression was unreadable. "So now I am torturing you? Because I asked you not to fry fish in a kitchen I just scrubbed."

"Jackie, what the hell does it matter if you cleaned it or not. Ain't it a kitchen? Don't we eat in here? I'll clean up after myself."

"Why are you always ruining what I try to do? Why would you try to dirty up what I just cleaned? It's just like you to come in here and do this..."

Miles crossed his arms and leaned against the table. "What are you talking about?"

"What do you mean, what am I talking about? You never listen to me."

"Baby, listen." Miles lowered his voice. *I am not going to argue.* "I know you are upset. I know it. There is nothing I can do about it.

"Maybe that's just the problem." She walked out of the kitchen.

Miles felt his stomach ball into knots. He wasn't used to this. It wasn't how he grew up. The women in his family did everything, took care of everything. They didn't go through depression, as far as he knew. They couldn't afford to. But Jackie would disappear into pockets of quietness, as if she were possessed. One minute Jackie seemed fine, the next she was argumentative. Miles knew Jackie seemed mad, but was really sad. Probably devastated. And he would pay the price for the next few days; the price for a debt that wasn't his. For whatever had happened that had caused her to be unable to carry children.

Miles slowly placed the collards and the fish back in the freezer. He sat at the kitchen table for a moment and his head leaned back on the chair. He didn't know how much of this he could take. He wanted a child, too. But his emotions were never discussed; his disappointment was a non-issue to his wife.

Truth be told, I can have kids. I am sacrificing that to be with her. Doesn't that count for anything? He stood up and headed for the back door. He would get something to eat somewhere else after all. Where someone didn't mind listening to him for a change.

Chapter Thirty Seven

Lani sat in the car seat and stared straight ahead. This night had played out like a terrible movie scene, similar to the night she was separated from her mother. Her life had come back full circle and she was right back to where she had started. Police and their weighted questions, neighbors, siren lights and the inner feeling of panic had all returned. The commotion was too much to bear.

Terrence sat in the patrol car, his eyes fixed on her like a wounded animal. She wished he would look away, or at least blink. He simply stared at her like a child transfixed on a television screen. But Lani knew better than to try to reach out to him, to try to console him or to try to explain that she hadn't called the police.

Lani had never seen Terrence like this before. After all these years, she didn't even recognize him.

What would he have done had he broken through that window? What was he going to do if he had gotten into the house? She didn't want to think about it. It made her sad, actually. Maybe she should have felt fear, but she didn't. She wasn't going to die at the hands of Terrence. If she knew nothing else, life had taught her that. Had Terrence gotten into that house, Lani might

241

have been forced to kill him. And that reality saddened her. Her husband had become her most dangerous enemy. The one person she had given her heart to, and would have handed over her soul for just some attention and reinforced love. Now she had to treat him like every other man in her life. She had to be wary, watch his every move and plan for the worse.

He has no idea how to do this. But I have been here before. I don't want to hurt him. But I will, if I have to...

"Are you alright?"

Christopher stood at the window of her car, watching the patrol cars pull off. Both she and Christopher had refused to press charges and refused medical care. The police took Terrence anyway, stating that in cases of domestic violence someone had to leave.

Christopher had the good sense to stay away from her until the patrol car was out of sight. Lani's fingertips fluttered to her chest. "Have you ever actually felt your heart ache?" she asked softly, her hand resting lightly over her heart. "My heart actually hurts. It feels like my chest is cracking."

Christopher remained silent. After a few minutes he faced her again, his face still but his voice wavering.

"It will be alright. He will be alright."

"I know." She knew better than even Christopher.

Christopher coughed and then looked up into the dark sky. He coughed again. "Uh, Lani. I need to know. What did you tell him?"

For the first time, Lani locked her full gaze on Christopher. *Why?* Was he afraid of Terrence? She gazed at the knot near his chin, the speed bump over his eye. *How in the world did you let Terrence beat your big ass?* Shaking her head, Lani looked at the ground. In the end, everyone was for themselves.

Christopher stood next to her, but he was worried about his own marriage, his own reputation. Why else would he ask that now?

"Lani, I need to know. I need to prepare."

"I didn't tell him anything, Christopher." She couldn't hide the cynicism she felt. "He just knew."

Christopher lowered his head. "What are you going to do?"

Lani had no answers right now. "I don't know."

"Where are you going to stay?"

"I don't know. I guess I could stay here."

"No." Christopher seemed worried. "They will release him and he won't call, so you won't know when. You won't have time to leave..."

Lani glanced at Christopher again. *He seems more shook up than me. I guess that's what a shot to a glass jaw will do.* Lani immediately felt bad for thinking less of Christopher. This wasn't his fault and she would have been angry at him had he hurt Terrence. *What could he have done, really?* But some part of her felt annoyed at him, although she didn't know why.

"Can I stay with you and Kenya?" she asked dryly. He faced her again, his face pained.

"Lani, why are you attacking me? We are all in this. This whole thing is..." he exhaled, leaned back on the car again and faced her mammoth house. "If you want to come home with me, you can."

"How would that work?"

"Lani, I don't give a damn. I need to know you are safe." They remained silent for a few minutes. "For all I know, Kenya has left me anyway."

"Don't count on it. She won't give up that easy." Lani chuckled a little, but Christopher didn't respond.

"I am going to have to call into work," Lani sighed, determined to be civil. When it was all said and done, Christopher had tried to come to her rescue. A second time. "I can't go like this. And I don't know if I will have to bail Terrence out tomorrow or what. I am just going to stay at a hotel again."

"Let me drive you."

Lani nodded. "I just need to get some things from the house."

They walked into the house together. Lani stepped into the large foyer and turned on the lights. She ran lightly upstairs to their bedroom to collect her things, while Christopher stood uneasily at the base of the steps.

As she entered her master bedroom, her senses were overtaken by a sweet smell. Glancing around her room for the first time, Lani's mouth fell open. The bed was covered in pink rose petals and Godiva chocolates. Candles, waiting to be lit, sat in the candle holders on the night stands. A picture of Lani in college, one she had never seen before, sat framed on the nightstand next to the leather trimmed ice bucket, now filled with cool water. A new pink negligee was draped across the chair, waiting for her.

Terrence had done something for her that he had never done before; he had created the romantic atmosphere with the intent to seduce her.

Lani stumbled backward and leaned on the doorframe. Terrence never did this. He always relied on Lani's love of him and addiction to their lovemaking. He never pulled out the romantic stuff unless he felt ready to beg. Had he been ready to apologize, to makeup, to start again?

No wonder he was so hurt. No wonder he seemed so betrayed. He had laid all this out for her, only to have her indiscretion tossed in his face. Had she just waited, just held on, he had been home waiting for her; preparing to love her again.

The weight of the truth crashed in on her. *I am the cheater. I crossed the line. What if he really didn't do anything with Kenya? Maybe Christopher and I were the only ones who really violated. How could that be?*

Lani walked to the large bed and sat on the edge. Running her hand across the plush pink rose petals, she began to cry.

Chapter Thirty Eight

Christopher stood in the huge foyer of the empty house. It didn't feel like a home, although he couldn't put his finger on what was missing. It was too new, too shiny and too perfect. Too empty. Christopher though that his home had a cozy vibe; it was a space where he could be comfortable. He didn't feel comfortable here.

What am I thinking? Of course, he didn't feel comfortable here. He had just witnessed Terrence's total meltdown after having spent the weekend with the man's wife. *I need to have my head examined. Things are so ... complicated.* The entire thing felt too twisted and confused. He'd had enough. A sudden unexpected longing for his simple life invaded him. The focus on his family: enjoying his career, wife and baby boy, had sustained him for so long. It had been enough.

Then Terrence crossed the line and called on his wife. Kenya responded. Christopher retaliated. Leaving them here, touching down in the midst of an emotional hurricane.

Christopher leaned against the banister of the impressive curved staircase. The house echoed and he could here Lani whimpering. She had a reason to cry. This whole thing had turned into a nightmare. *What had she told Terrence for him to lose it like that? How had he figured it out?*

Terrence had been mortally wounded, that much he felt sure of. Even he hadn't realized that Terrence loved Lani so deeply. Terrence always seemed detached from her, socializing and partying while she sat in isolation. For the first time, Christopher realized how deeply connected to Lani Terrence was. Terrence hadn't just flipped out because his ego was bruised or because another man had laid claim to his wife. Terrence's torment derived from a rip in his very spirit, which held a deep raw soul reliance on Lani. While Christopher stood in front of Terrence, he could see Terrence's eyes shifting, searching for Lani, and wondering about Lani and the betrayal. In the end, even Christopher hadn't mattered that much to Terrence. His mind had only been aware of Lani.

Have I ever felt that way about Kenya. They had a very convenient thing. But would he lose his mind if she cheated? Probably. *What if she just walked away?* His heart did not skip a beat. He felt nothing. Maybe he could do it. Maybe he could walk away. *No, not now, not with a baby.* The thought of her cheating infuriated him, but what Terrence had said made him feel nauseous.

"She wanted it." The words and Terrence's stunning clarity at that moment had frightened him. He hadn't been delirious or just taunting Christopher. It was one thing to believe that she left to console her friend and made a crucial mistake. It was another to find that she had pursued something that wasn't available to her, had risked everything they had for the one chance to get near Lani's husband.

What do we have? Really. Besides the image, the house and the child. What do we have?

Lani's whimpering quieted, snapping him out of his thoughts. *What was she up there doing?* "Lani?"

He didn't hear anything for a moment. "Lani?"

"Yeah?"

"Do you need me ... to come up?"

Christopher stood at the base of the stairs, waiting for her answer. He heard her sniff again. He didn't know how deep her pain would take her. He didn't want her to sink back into the despair he had found her in the hotel room.

"I'm okay," Lani answered softly.

Sighing, he walked back to the middle of the foyer and stared straight ahead into the two story family room. Taking a few steps forward, he was still amazed at this house. *They don't deny themselves much that is for sure.* He felt his shoes sink deep into the plush carpet as he walked gingerly to the mantelpiece. Christopher felt like he was invading; staring into Terrence's private layers with a microscope. The mantle contained a few pictures, some of Lani's plaques. Two heavy candle stick holders. And he was here. In a framed picture in this mammoth house, sitting next to Kenya.

Picking up the picture frame, he felt his head hurt at the sight of Kenya. There she sat, chin in the air, eyes focused on Terrence. Smile pasted across her face. He sat next to her, laughing and holding his beer. Terrence was leaning forward, sharing the laughter with Kenya. Lani sat next to him, a plastic smile plastered across her face. But her eyes were cold.

248

Had Lani known then? Women know women. She must've suspected Kenya of wanting Terrence then. Either way, why was Kenya's face always held in that uptight way? She seemed so ... mean.

"That picture was two years ago. One of your mother-in-laws infamous gatherings." Lani's voice floated down. Her voice sounded so soft that Christopher didn't jump. Gently returning the frame, he turned to find Lani standing on the high bridge of the second level, overlooking the family room.

"I remember," he said softly.

"I'm not leaving," she shook her head.

"Why?"

Lani smiled. "I don't know. I just am not going to run from my home."

"He will be back, Lani."

"I can handle him."

Christopher felt riveted to the spot. *What should I say or do?* He didn't want to speak about Terrence in a negative way. *But, the boy is clearly out of his mind.* "He will hurt you, if he can."

"He can't do any more to me than he already has."

"Well..." He hadn't thought about where he was going or what he should do. While he tried to play hero here, the truth was that he and Kenya were on the outs. He didn't want to go home either.

"Come here," She blinked as she spoke. She always seemed so sincere when she spoke to him. "I have something to show you."

Chapter Thirty Nine

It was her clear skin. That's what Terrence remembered. Even now, even while he wanted to strangle her, he thought about her clear skin. It made him think of honey. Terrence had wanted to taste her as soon as he laid eyes on it. Inside the cafeteria on a warm Sunday morning, he and his frat brothers were still funky from the party the night before. It didn't matter, no one bothered to wash before coming to breakfast. The goal was to get there and claim one of the four waffle irons before the line became unbearable.

He had a hangover. That much he remembered clearly as well. But that didn't stop him from wanting one of those waffles. The cafeteria would sit out yellow batter in buckets. Students would line up, pour them in the griddle, cook them and walk right out.

Terrence stood behind Lani in line. He had waited and waited, baseball cap pulled low, eyes on the floor. His headache began to throb and two of his homeboys already had their waffles and were heading out the door.

He remembered turning and looking over her shoulder, wondering what was causing the delay. His line had been shorter than his friends, and he was next, once the honey colored female in front of him moved. That's when Terrence realized that she had cooked a stack of waffles and was using the machine over and over again.

"Hey!" his friend Robert yelled from behind him. "Tell that chick she can't hog the iron like that man."

Terrence had glanced up, intent on telling this wavy haired girl to get out of the way. But she turned around with her eyes flashing like diamonds.

"Excuse me?" Her neck moved with the two words, and her wavy hair bounced. The expression on her face looked like she dared anyone to say anything to her.

It was a statement, not a question. Terrence laid eyes on her cheeks and on her forehead. He grinned. He wanted to kiss her, wanted to find out if she tasted like she looked. Robert kept talking because his manhood was on the line in front of the brothers. He wasn't going to drop it.

"You heard me. You need to move."

"Yo, you don't know me, so you need to watch who you talking to." Her New York accent sounded so sharp against the sleepy Virginia morning.

Terrence had laughed at the honey girl, who knew she was dead wrong for taking over the waffle machine like that, but still rolled her eyes and eyeballed the six foot four inch tall frat brother in front of everyone.

"Alright, Honey, with all the b-girl attitude. You need to hurry up," Robert had laughed. He obviously wanted her, too. Robert normally never backed down when someone got between him and his food.

"I'm finished anyway," she stated, with a final head roll, grabbing the stack of waffles, and deliberately strolling past Robert with the plate held high. For dreadful moment, Terrence thought Robert might knock the plate out of her hand, but she kept her eyes on him as if she were daring him to do just that. Robert just smiled.

"I see you," Robert had said, his eyes fixed on her behind as she walked past. They both watched her stroll to the table and hand the waffles out to her friends.

"Damn," Robert had said. Terrence remembered thinking the same thing.

Lani had so much spunk then. She was loud with weird rules of loyalty and friendship. He tried to talk to her, but she didn't pay him any attention at first. He asked her name the next day as she walked past him on campus.

She had stopped, looked him up and down, and replied, "Who wants to know?"

"You know me. Don't front."

She smirked and walked off. For a second, he felt surprised. He had never had a girl walk away from him before. He watched her heading to the dorms off campus; she was a Queen Street girl. As she rounded the corner, she looked back. Their eyes met. It was what he needed to know. She had looked back, she was definitely interested.

Two days later, he asked again what her name was, although he had already found out through other sources. How she had escaped his radar before he didn't know, but now he was determined to have her.

"So, are you going to tell me your name," he approached her as she sat outside the math building, looking over Calculus 3 class notes.

"No." She hadn't even bothered to look up at him.

Terrence had smiled. "Why not?"

He wanted to laugh now, remembering how she had gazed at him then, smiled and said in her sweetest voice, "'Cuz, you are a little too pretty for me."

Terrence couldn't believe it. He laughed outright and walked away but, looked back at her. He wanted her even more. Then she happened to be at a frat party. He spotted her and wondered whether she was a frat groupie. Disappointment lingered on the edges of his mind, and he almost wrote her off. But then Atomic Dog came on and the frat men in the party went crazy. Going straight doggie style, Lani had gotten licked by someone. Her loud voice, cussing out all of them because she couldn't identify who had actually licked her, had been hilarious. He had approached her then, and pulled her out of the thick den of the dance floor. She looked him up and down, her eyebrows questioning him, but this time she didn't get smart. In fact she hadn't had much to say as he walked her to the bathroom so she could wash herself off. He remembered how odd it seemed that she was so offended, when most of the party groupies seemed thrilled by being the center of attention like that. When she came out of the bathroom, with her pride bruised, Terrence had danced with her and she let him touch her skin, her cheek, during that dance. He was consumed by her. He could watch her talk, dance and laugh. He found himself always observing her. He had never seen anybody live life like Lani, so unconcerned with others. In the beginning. But she changed. She lost her edge and became more demure, quiet like all the other women he knew. The only time he saw her colors, felt her fire, was during lovemaking or the ridiculous arguments. And he didn't argue.

Now, he was just sick of it. Either she was raising hell or moping. Loud or withdrawn. And what about tonight? She actually came home, sat in their yard, and thought of Christopher. She had been with Christopher. If she would sleep with him, what else would she do? Didn't she stand for anything? He had thought having a different background would keep them alive, but, in the end, he was wrong. They were too different and she had no respect for him. She had no respect for herself. No matter how hard he tried, he couldn't force culture into her. And now he knew, she really was beneath him after all.

He heard his name called. Looking up, Terrence walked slowly to the cell doors and stood back as they rolled open.

His heart fell when he looked into the eyes of Darryl Simmons, a deacon at his parent's church and a police officer. He dropped his eyes.

"Terrence? I thought that was you…"

Terrence bit his lip and felt his eyes burn. This was the type of humiliation that he wanted to avoid. "Deacon Simmons."

"What are you doing in here, son?" The deacon led him out of the holding area and down a tiny hall to his small office, which he shared with three other officers. None of them paid him any attention.

Terrence shook his head. There was no explanation he could offer that wouldn't make things worse. He shrugged.

"Have a seat." Deacon Simmons pointed to the small chair that was squeezed between his desk and the wall.

Terrence shrugged himself into the seat.

"Does your family know you're alright?"

"They don't know I'm in here." There was a long pause. "I don't want them to know I am here."

Deacon Simmons leaned back in his chair and watched Terrence. Terrence glanced at him and then through the window into the dark night.

"I can respect your privacy, Terrence. But you need to make it right—I read the report; were you attacking your wife?"

"No." Terrence rubbed his arm. "Yes—to tell you the truth, I don't know. We're just going through a lot."

"Be careful, Terrence. You hear me son. Don't do anything that's going to jeopardize your freedom or your ability to take care of yourself in the future."

"I hear you, Deacon."

"Listen, call your family and have someone come to get you. I hate to see you in here, Terrence."

"Thank you, Deacon. I appreciate it."

"I expect you to give me a call this week, to let me know if things are working out."

"I definitely will, Deacon Simmons."

Turning the phone so that it faced Terrence, he motioned again with his hand. "Go ahead. I want to get you out of here before my shift ends."

Chapter Forty

Kenya didn't talk with her father much. Not that she didn't love him. Her mother was always around, and he just spoke through Connie. Connie was the center of all communication in the household. She had become so used to the arrangement that the sight of him at her front door, alone nearly made her jump out of her skin.

"Daddy?"

"Don't Daddy me, like I never come by." He smiled lightly, sarcasm in his voice. "May I come in, or are you going to stand there with your mouth open?"

"Where is Mom, parking the car?"

"No. I am not an invalid, you know. Not yet, anyway. Your mother hasn't figured out how to make me totally dependent on her just yet." He stepped into the house, brushing past Kenya. "I came alone."

"Oh." Kenya closed the door quietly behind her. "Uhm. Have a seat, Daddy, Okay?"

She was going to call Connie and find out exactly what was happening here. Her father did not just show up at her front door. Maybe Connie had put him out.

"Listen, I came to see you. So don't run in there to call your mother." He sat down on the couch and observing the painting above the fireplace. "I can visit my baby girl, can't I?"

"Of course." Kenya laughed.

He knew her well, although he never had much to say.

"You've changed things since I was last here."

"Daddy, you never come over here. I always come to you. It's been like this for almost a year."

"Well, as long as I see you, make sure you're alright, I don't need to see the house. Right?" He removed his cap and sat it next to him on the couch.

"You thirsty?"

"I could drink something."

Kenya moved into the kitchen and grabbed him a beer and a glass. When she returned, he was standing at the mantel.

"Beautiful family you got here."

"Thanks, Daddy." Kenya sat the beer and glass on two coasters on the end table. Then she planted herself into the chair.

"Beautiful family," he muttered again, more to himself, as he returned to the couch. "Where is my grandbaby?"

"Upstairs. Napping. He should be up soon."

"Sleeping through the night, yet?"

"Kinda sorta."

"In other words, 'no.' And I bet you don't have him on any type of schedule." James clucked his tongue.

"Well, he had a long weekend, so..." The room fell silent. *A long weekend, what am I talking about. A hellified weekend. The worst weekend of my life.*

"Yeah, I heard."

Kenya looked at her father sharply. *What does he know?*

"Oh, you assumed that I don't know what it means when a married woman with a new baby shows up at her parent's house in the middle of the night. And she climbs out of her best friend's car. In the middle of the night. The best friend she has had a crush on for years."

"Daddy, I don't like Terrence like that. We are just friends."

James took a slow long drink of his beer and then sat the bottle down on the end table. "Bullshit."

Kenya gasped. Her father never talked like that to her.

"Excuse me?"

"You heard me. I said bullshit."

"Daddy it's not like that."

"Then what is it?"

"I don't know, actually. I just got confused."

"Well, let me unconfuse you. Christopher is a good man. You have a good life. My grandbaby will be well taken care of. You will be well taken care of. With

Christopher. Not Terrence. I love him, but not as a son-in-law."

"I know, Daddy."

"You can't put your life at risk."

"Daddy, it's not me. I think Christopher may have ... you know."

"You think so, huh?"

Kenya nodded and kept her eyes on the rug. This was so embarrassing; but he was easier to talk to than she remembered.

"Before or after your midnight drop off?"

"After."

That sat in silence while James finished his beer. Kenya hugged the pillow and tucked her legs under her body. She felt like a little girl again, knowing her Daddy would protect her from everything.

When he finally finished, James looked his only daughter in the eye. "Kenya, I don't have the answers for life. I don't know a lot. But I do know that you don't throw out the baby with the bath water."

"Yuck, I hate that expression." Kenya wrinkled her nose.

He laughed. Then he stared at her. "Do you hear me baby girl?"

She nodded. "I hear you, Daddy."

"I am always here for you. You know that?"

"Yeah, I know it."

"Good. Now turn on the television. I am going to watch my game over here, so I don't miss any of the first half."

Kenya laughed and stood to get the remote. As she handed it to him, he grabbed her hand and patted it. "We are always here for you."

"I know, Daddy. I know." The telephone rang and Kenya jumped. *Please be Christopher.* "Hello?"

"Kenya. It's me, I need your help."

***

"Why are you calling me?" Kenya whispered into the phone, hoping her father couldn't hear her.

"What, I can't call you now?" Terrence's irritation was evident.

"No, you can't. I can't do this with you anymore. I…" her voice faltered. "I have to look out for my family."

"Kenya, listen I can't even go there with you. I didn't do anything to hurt your family."

"My family is in shambles."

"Listen, Kenya, I need your help."

"No." Kenya placed the phone back on the base. Her parents were right. Terrence couldn't call and disrupt her life anymore. That wasn't friendship, it was selfishness. She was no different than the typical 'other woman,' except she got none of the benefits. He didn't want her sexually, but he sure didn't mind using her emotionally and mentally. She had to end it.

The phone rang again and she stood looking at it. The caller ID screen wasn't working, for some reason it was cracked.

"Hello." *Please be Christopher.*

Terrence spoke in a rush. "Kenya, please don't hang up, I'm in jail."

"What?"

"I'm in jail. That's why I am calling."

"Where is—" Kenya formed her mouth to say Lani, and then realized how foreign the name sounded on her tongue. She hadn't called her by name in years. "Where is your wife?" she pushed out.

"Not relevant. I need you to come get me."

"No. Why are you in jail?"

"Fight."

"You and Lani got into a fight that bad, Terrence that you had to go to jail?"

"Yeah."

Kenya put the receiver close to her mouth. "Figures."

"What figures?"

"That this is where you would wind up. That she would lead to jail."

The line was silent. Kenya felt a small panic stirring in her stomach, maybe she had said too much. Even now, she didn't really want Terrence upset with her; she didn't want him to cut her off.

"Kenya, I ... I am not even going to respond to that."

"Listen, Terrence, I can't do anything. I have to be here when Christopher gets back, so we can talk things out. He misunderstands. I can't leave."

"He isn't back, yet?"

"Back from what? From where? What are you talking about?"

Terrence chuckled. "Come get me and I'll tell you."

"No. Tell me now."

"Nothing to tell, really."

Kenya felt stupid. "Then why did you say it?"

"Say what?"

Kenya shouted into the phone. "Say that Christopher hadn't gotten back." There was another pause. "Terrence, why did you say it?"

"He was at my house."

"Christopher came over there?" Kenya's hand flew to her mouth. She couldn't believe that Christopher had gone after Terrence in an effort to fight for her, to defend her honor. She knew he still cared about her. *He probably threatened Terrence, demanded he stay away from me. That's what Terrence deserves.*

Warmth spread through her. "Well, that's more reason why I can't come get you. I definitely need to wait, to let him know it's alright. That I am okay."

"Huh? Kenya, what are you talking about?"

"I can't come get you after he confronted you about the other night and had you put in jail. I want to be here when he gets back."

Terrence growled into the phone. "Kenya, you have got to grow up, baby sis. You've got it confused. He just showed up, jumped into an argument between Lani and me. A marital argument and he jumped in to protect Lani, I guess. It got ugly and someone called the police. I am in jail. He hasn't come home, yet. Do the math..."

Her brain wouldn't accept that explanation. She had to see for herself. "What precinct are you at," she asked quietly.

Chapter Forty One

Miles took another sip of beer. It was late. But Jackie wouldn't say anything when he finally stumbled into the house. He wanted her to. He wanted her to open her mouth and ask, just once. He wanted her to be concerned, just once. He needed some emotion from her, something other than unquestioning faith and belief. It almost felt like she didn't ask because she really didn't care. Or she thought he was incapable of having other options.

"I have other options, damnit!" Miles slammed the beer onto the counter.

"Well, I am sure you do." The young lady looked at him and winked. He had forgotten she was standing there. *Were we talking?* He took another sip from the beer and kept his eyes on her.

She chitchatted with a friend standing next to her and then she glanced at Miles again, smiling.

Miles shook his head. It amazed him how young women threw themselves at him. All the rules had changed. He didn't have to pursue them. They found him confident; they sought comfort in his age. Miles was old enough to be steady, but not to be considered an old man.

"So, what options do you have?" she asked, leaning forward.

"Just thinking out loud." Miles waved his hand in the air and looking around for his cousin Butch.

She wouldn't let it go. "I don't have so many options. Not tonight, anyway."

He didn't answer, just looked at her and shrugged a little bit. He wanted her to leave him alone, to stop tempting him. He glanced at the strapless dress she wore, her breast protruding from the square cut of the dress. Miles wondered what her breasts felt like, if they were heavy like Jackie's' or light and perky. He knew the answer to that, actually, without having to see.

"My name is Alma. What's yours?"

"Miles."

"Nice to meet you, Miles."

"Yeah, you too."

He wanted to be rescued from Alma, with the blossoming breasts. He normally wouldn't even consider it, but he was tired of being sad, tired of entering a miserable home. The depression would take months to get her through, and when she was better, did she thank him? Did she every once consider his feelings.

"So, what are your plans tonight?"

Miles looked into her face. "Nothing. I had a hard day."

"Really?" She adjusted slightly, turning fully toward him, the plump rise of her breasts bubbling in his face.

"Really." He tapped his heart. "Hurts, here."

266

"Yeah, I know that feeling." She sighed and glanced around the room. She was browner than Jackie and long braids cascaded down her shoulders. He didn't like braids. He didn't like any type of fake hair. But something about Alma seemed genuine.

"I hurt right here, often." She tapped her left breast.

Miles shook his head. He assumed she meant to tap her heart, but the last thing he wanted to see was the cleavage jiggling softly. He smiled.

She glanced down at her chest and smile at him.

They sat there for a minute. "Miles, right?"

"Yep."

"Maybe, we can make each other feel better." He stared at her, watched her lips on the rim of the glass as she took a sip. She leaned close to him. "You know?"

He didn't want to do this. He hadn't messed around in years. Before they were grown and he appreciated his wife. Before he took the time to learn her. But this might be what he needed. Just to taste something new, something young and lively.

"Whoa partner, what's up?" Butch stepped up next to him and eyeing the young woman.

Miles didn't respond.

She smiled.

"Who is your friend?" Butch looked her up and down.

Miles didn't answer. He couldn't remember her name. He took another sip of beer and kept his eyes on the mound of cleavage in front of him. She took the hint, slid Miles a scrap of paper and turned back toward her friends.

"Damn man. I leave for a few minutes and you about to get laid." Butch tapped him on the arm.

"I wasn't going to do nothing." Miles felt relief that Butch had made it back. "Shit, I'm glad you got back when you did."

"Yeah, I bet you are. Let me get you home, alright." Miles glanced at Butch appreciatively. They had known each other for a life time and Butch always helped him, always supported him and kept him out of trouble. "I'm going to have Malinda follow us in my car. Come on, let's go."

Miles sighed, stood up and headed for the door. He needed to be with his wife. He needed to be there for his wife. *Who am I to judge her?*

Chapter Forty Two

Kenya's face did not give Terrence the relief he expected. With her eyes wide open, her nose pointed high, she approached him as if her were the scum of the earth or her latest social project. The officer handed him some forms which he signed and he met her in the waiting area. She didn't speak, just watched him walk towards her as if he was a criminal and she was his only salvation.

"Thanks for coming." He wished he hadn't called her.

"Whatever," Kenya snapped. "I had to leave my baby with my father."

"Your pops, huh? Did you tell him where you were going?"

"Yes and no. I said you needed something."

Terrence sighed. The last thing he wanted his parents to know was that he had spent even a few hours in jail.

"This is the second time I am running around in the middle of the night for you," Kenya continued softly. "And I don't appreciate it."

Terrence remained silent. *She's not worth arguing with. She has returned to never never land, painting the world her own unique shade of confusion.* Terrence bit his lip as they walked toward the car in silence.

They both climbed into the car, Kenya started the engine and pulled forward in one smooth motion. Terrence stared out of the window, listening to Kenya' quiet sniffs. He needed quiet right now, an opportunity to think and sort things through. He didn't have a plan of action and couldn't figure out how to deal with Lani. His eyes stung every time he thought about her.

"What if you and your wife had gotten my husband mixed up in this mess, huh? I am sure she is used to dealing with police, but..." Kenya hesitated, sniffing again.

"Listen, Christopher came to my house and played hero. We didn't ask him to come over there; I damn sure didn't, anyway."

"No. She had to have called him. She had to have lured him over there."

Terrence squinted, his eyes and stared at Kenya. Was she serious? Does she really play the victim in every circumstance?

"Listen, he is a grown ass man. Trust me; I was looking at her the entire time. She didn't call him."

Kenya remained silent, but laid her foot heavy on the gas. Her mere presence annoyed Terrence. It was the first time in his life that he absolutely didn't want to be near her.

"That bitch did something to him..." As infuriated as he was at his wife, he felt a deep contempt for Kenya at that moment. She had some nerve to sit there and talk as if her own shit didn't stink.

"She is still my wife," he said softly.

"Yeah, your wife is a trashy, stank little street gutter tramp who has ruined her own marriage and is trying to ruin mine."

"Kenya, what the fuck are you talking about? Like you had good intentions. Or don't you remember? Shit, she didn't do anymore than you, had I let you, that's for damn sure."

They sat in awkward silence for a moment, Kenya's jaw clamped shut, her eyes focused forward. She gripped the steering as if she were getting ready to throttle it.

"I am doing you a favor and that's how you talk to me? In my car. Like she is..."

"Her name is Lani. Lani. Not 'she,' not 'your wife,' not 'her,' Lani."

"I know her name," Kenya muttered.

"You know what," Terrence leaned back in his sit and closed his eyes, "just keep any mention of her out of your mouth,"

"Or what?" shrieked Kenya. "Or what?

"I'm telling you Kenya, I don't give a damn if you came to pick me up or not, don't speak on my wife again."

Kenya slammed on the brakes. "Or what, Terrence? What you going to do? You can call me whenever you need to talk. Well, I got something to say now and you won't listen."

"Kenya..."

"No, I am going to tell you. Your wife is a no good ho that never deserved to be with you in the first place. You can't open your eyes and see all the devastation she has caused, all the problems? You were sitting in jail like a thug, my husband is nowhere to be found, and now you are making threats against our lifelong friendship. So what, after a lifetime, we aren't friends anymore? You're choosing her over me?" Kenya's eyes bulged while her finger jabbed at the air. "Me!" she shrieked. "You are choosing her over me?"

Terrence stared at her as if it was the first time really seeing her. She had never spoken like this and, although he knew Kenya could be rude, he never understood until this exact moment how she really felt about Lani. *All this time this woman held my wife in contempt. It is one thing to not be a fan of Lani's, another to utterly despise her. And it's clear that Kenya hates her.*

Terrence closed his eyes and blocked Kenya out. *Why didn't I see this before?* Terrence felt the energy sinking from him. It was all too much. He had learned too much about himself, about his wife and about Kenya in the past 72 hours. He couldn't take anymore. He opened the car door and slid out of the seat. Shutting it gently behind him, he began walking home.

"Get in the car." Kenya rode along side Terrence as he walked down along the shoulder. "The last thing I want you to do is get killed walking along the damn shoulder at night."

"Thanks for your concern." Terrence didn't look at Kenya. "But I'm alright. My house is another ten minutes anyway."

"Ten minute drive, 45 minute walk. At a minimum."

Kenya had a point. He hadn't thought about it. The long never ending roads were quickly navigated in a car, but the distance was insurmountable by foot. Either way, he didn't want to deal with Kenya. He would rather hitchhike.

Kenya breathed hard. "I am going to your house anyway."

"What?" Terrence stopped walking and looked into the car. "For what?"

"Looking for Christopher. I am going to put an end to this game he and Lani are playing, trying to get a reaction out of us."

Terrence shook his head. "Just leave it alone."

"No."

He stood there in silence for a few minutes. Then he opened the door and slid back into the seat.

They drove in silence until Kenya turned on the radio. Neither noticed the music.

Chapter Forty Three

"You rescued me. Again."

"No." Christopher shook his head, staring up at Lani. She had washed her face and pulled her hair back into a ponytail. Her clothes were different, too. She had changed into a coffee brown tank top and crème drawstring cotton pants. The clothes hugged her body like she was going to work out, and his eyes rested on her hips. Lani looked fresh, although her eyes were still pink.

Christopher smiled. "You don't need rescuing."

"I did today. I felt trapped in that car."

Christopher nodded. He had forgotten that part—the car, the tires and the golf club.

Lani disappeared for a second and he realized that she was coming down the huge staircase. Her voice drafted lightly through the house while she continued to talk.

"I've never seen him like that." Lani's reference to Terrence was met with silence.

Christopher remained planted in the family room and watched Lani walk toward him, under the high bridge.

274

"I bet." Christopher didn't want to ask again, but he had to know. "How did he find out?"

Lani shrugged. "Kenya, maybe. I don't know. He was watching me while I sat in the car. I thought about you. He might have seen my face..."

Ouch. No wonder Terrence had acted out. Christopher couldn't imagine watching his wife as she glowed in the aftermath of another man's love, unaware that he was there. That had to feel horrible.

Lani stood in front of Christopher and grasped both his hands in hers. "So, you did rescue me."

"I guess," Christopher said with a smile, feeling foolish for allowing her to actual make him feel like a hero. Lani ran her hand along the smooth ridge of his jaw.

"You need some ice."

"Yes, I do." The side of Christopher's face felt tender to the touch, and Lani's touch came with its own special fire. He gritted his teeth to keep from jumping in pain.

"Let's get some ice."

Christopher followed her into the wide kitchen and noticed that the black appliances and cherry wood cabinets gleamed. She opened the freezer, reached in and emerged with a handful of ice cubes while Christopher leaned against the marble island, watching her. *I could watch her forever.* She stopped while wrapping the ice in a towel and eyed him.

"Whatchu thinkin'?"

"Nothing."

Lani grinned again, and then focused on finding a Ziploc bag to fold the toweled ice in. She approached him, holding the bag up. He didn't want her to press it to his face because he didn't want to flinch in front of her, so he blocked her with his hand.

"Stop being a baby." Lani laughed and pushed his hand out of the way.

"Aww." The cold hurt, and he couldn't contain it.

Lani laughed.

Christopher took the bag from her and placed it against his face again, but Lani didn't move.

"Chris. You are the first person to be there for me like this. Well, other than my sister, Dee."

He shook his head.

Lani leaned her head to the side. "I am sorry I was rude earlier. I am so stressed out."

"Rude? Who, you? I didn't even notice."

She laughed again and stood on her tip toes. They stared at each other for a second, tension building in her pause, and then Lani placed a light kiss on his lips.

The kiss shocked him. *She still wants to kiss me, with everything that has happened. With Terrence's melt down.* He stared at her for a moment.

Lani wrapped her arms around his large frame and leaned into him. His body relaxed, although his mind still felt on alert. He wrapped his free arm around her curvaceous frame.

"We end up together, alone, again."

"Again." He repeated his voice barely above a whisper.

Lani continued to rest against him, kissing him every now and then. He desperately held on to the bag of ice, using it as a distraction to prevent getting lost in the warmth of her body.

"Come on." Lani departed suddenly, pulling him by the hand.

He didn't ask where. He didn't care. She led him up a back staircase that he didn't even know existed and down the hall to the master suite.

"I want to show you what Terrence did."

Christopher glanced around the room. *The man was preparing a serious rendezvous.* He had to give it to him. Terrence had laid out a nice atmosphere.

"This is why I was crying earlier."

"You regret, now, what we did."

"Absolutely not. I regretted not waiting for him to get to this point. Then I realized how much longer I would have waited. The truth is, we had to go through all of this for him to even want to do this for me. And now, it feels like 'too little, too late'."

Christopher shifted. He didn't know what to say.

"I just wanted to show you. Wanted you to know why I was crying. Being with you made me remember, I don't have to be thankful for leftover crumbs from Terrence. For after thoughts of love."

Christopher took in the luscious suite and glanced at the arched cathedral ceiling. "So, what now?"

"I don't know."

The telephone rang and they both jumped. Lani ran to the phone near the bed while Christopher waited at the door.

"Dee! I know. I tried to call you earlier. I know, just ... hold on okay?" Lani looked at Christopher pleadingly, "I am so sorry. I got to take this."

"No problem." Christopher took a few steps down the hallway and stopped at the overlook to view the family room. *Impressive.* He went to the steps and sat on the top step, waiting for Lani.

Chapter Forty Four

"Dee, where are you?"

"No. you have been ignoring my calls. After I put my foot up Terrence's ass, I am going to put my other foot in yours."

Lani felt her heart stop. "What do you mean? Are you driving down here?"

"Damn straight." Dee popped her gum.

Lani's mind raced. "Who?"

"Who what? What are you talking about? Me!" Dee shouted at her.

"Dee, who all are you bringing?"

"Just me and Ricky. I had to have a man in case we have to put that fool husband of yours in his place."

Lani sighed. "Where are my babies?"

"Girl please, grown lady one and two are over Reedi's. You know I don't trust just anybody with my girls, but she is the most drama free person I know." Dee hesitated and then continued, her tone sounding lighter. "I spoke to Terrence. Figured I needed to come down there."

Lani stumbled into her bed. "When?"

"Night before last. When I still didn't hear from you and he wouldn't call back, well..."

Lani knew Dee had probably stayed up, worried sick about her. She hoped her nieces hadn't seen the pain she caused their mother. They didn't need the stress.

"I, I wasn't thinking. I'm sorry."

"Where's he at, now?"

"Who?"

"Lani, what the hell is wrong with you? Terrence, where is he at right now?"

"Jail."

"Jail—did he hit you?" Lani removed the phone from her ear to spare her eardrums the loud shrieks.

"No, Dee, Terrence didn't—"

"What!"

"No, he didn't hit me."

"Why'd you call the police?"

"I didn't. We got into a big fight in the yard. The neighbors must have called."

"See, I knew it." Lani realized that Dee was talking to Ricky. "I am so glad I listened to you, babe that fool is in jail."

Lani rolled her eyes. She didn't want to keep Christopher waiting if Dee was going to talk to Ricky. "Dee, are you talking to me?"

"Yeah, I'm almost there anyway. We are in Columbia. Maryland, right Ricky? I will be there in about an hour or so."

Lani sighed. She would have never asked her to come, but she felt relief. She would be able to sleep for a few days now without worrying about Terrence. Lani sniffled and a burning feeling crept into her sinuses, just before tears fell down her face.

"Lani, Lani you still there?"

"Yeah."

"What's wrong?" Dee never missed a thing.

"Nothing. I just feel ... I'm glad you came, that's all."

"Aw girl, whatever. You know I am down for you, no matter what. Of course I'm going to come check on my baby sister." Lani laughed through tears as Dee talked. "Alright, girlie, I'll call you when we get into Virginia. I got to convince Ricky that we shouldn't be going nowhere near that bridge he likes to cross."

"What ... the Woodrow Wilson?"

"Yeah, he likes to see the monuments in the distance. Almost crashes every time we cross that thing. We are going around I495 the other way. Let me go, so I can keep this man of mine in the right direction."

Lani said a silent prayer of thanks. There would be no more destruction by Terrence's hand when Dee was there, that was for certain.

Lani walked into the hallway and spotted Christopher sitting on the top stairs.

He lifted his head as she walked toward him. "That was my sister. She's coming."

"Good. That will be good." He leaned his back against the wall, his legs spread out in front of him down the stairs. "When will she be here?"

"In about an hour."

"Fine, I will wait for her. Because there is no way I am leaving you in this house alone."

Chapter Forty Five

Lani sighed again. She had two protectors tonight. It felt like a rare luxury to have two people worry over her and want to protect her. She glanced appreciatively at Christopher. *I can't believe he is still here. Despite it all. After seeing Terrence, I would have thought Christopher would have made an exit. Most men would have.*

Although she normally would never admit it, Terrence had shaken her to the core. She hadn't been scared of him, just scared about how far he would go, how far she would have to go. How far Sophie had gone; had been forced to go.

Lani was willing to go all the way there, to fight to the death. She didn't want to be the black "War of the Roses," but she might not have had a choice. When Terrence had jumped on the hood of the car, Lani realized she would have to abandon ship. The windshield was caving under every blow and the already shattered glass would crumble on her at any given moment. Frantic, she had glanced around and noticed Christopher's car pull up. Opening her door, she took a deep breath and made a dash for Christopher's car, expecting Terrence to follow her. She had hoped to jump in, lock the door, and ride away.

283

Instead, Christopher had jumped out, without turning off the ignition, ran past her and tackled Terrence. Lani stood there in shock. For a second she thought they both were dead, broken necks or severe concussions. She actually heard their heads slam against the pavement. She had felt astounded that calm, peaceful Christopher, who had been the slowest of all of them to react, to enter this painful square of deception, had become the aggressive attacker. The football player in him was a different animal, she realized that now.

While they lay on the ground, Lani had made a dash for the house, fumbling with the door that Terrence had thankfully left unlocked. She locked herself in and watched them from the window. Christopher made eye contact with her immediately, signaling for her to lay low. While he looked at her, Terrence tackled him and knocked him to the ground. She watched a little longer and heard Terrence screaming. She had run through the house then, to the master suite, past the closet to the bathroom. The commode was housed in its only tiny room, and a flat panel of the wall in front of it provided access to the plumbing for the tub. Lani threw herself on her knees, pressed the panel in, and reached her arm into the tiny area. She withdrew a small locked case.

It took her a moment to remember the combination. She hadn't thought about the case in so long. Terrence's shouts were tearing through the tense air, his voice anguished. She glanced out the window to see him walking in circles, rubbing his hands through his soft hair. Lani had a momentary desire to protect him, to hug him and comfort him. But she was the cause of his pain, and if he caught sight of her, things would only get worse.

Lani had fidgeted with the combo, finally unlocking the case and examining the tiny 22mm that Dee had given her years ago. Just in case. She and Dee had lived a lifetime the first ten years of life; they left nothing else to chance. Lani would do what she had to do to protect herself.

She loaded the small pistol, held it in her hand, and ran back downstairs and glanced out of the picture window. Christopher looked right at her, making immediate contact. He began to talk, but Terrence moved so fast, so suddenly, that Christopher caught a deadly blow to the chin, stumbled backward and fell on to the pavement.

Lani's heartbeat raced as she watched Terrence trying to enter the house, heard him singsong and call her name.

"I'm gonna have to shoot this man." The thought ricocheted through her. She couldn't find any other option, any alternative. She heard him whistling, like a madman. She wouldn't try to kill him. But she would shoot him. She heard the golf club slam against the window and she watched the pained smile on Terrence's face. Lani jumped back and positioned the gun, aiming it at the window. If he tried to enter through it she would shoot. When the glass cracked, she removed the safety and steadied her hands. Her mind went to her mother and that night. The night her mother went to jail. For years Lani had carried the shame of being an inmate's child. People didn't understand how someone's mother could go to jail. Father's, they understood, but her mother? People

treated her different, they automatically assumed she was going to be wild or didn't have a chance at being a successful person because her *mother* was incarcerated. She felt so isolated and alone, and she despised her mother for leaving her and Dee alone in the world. For choosing the path that led to her stabbing and killing a lover and destroying their lives.

Yet, here she stood, in a similar circumstance, with similar options. For the first time, she felt sorry for her mother, for having to choose her own life and their lives, over a possessed, selfish, man. Here she stood, about to shoot the love of her life, stepping into the circle of generational curses that would lead her to the same end as her mother.

A piece of the club made it through the glass. Just barely. But as Terrence yanked it back, the glass shattered. She widened her legs to brace herself for the explosion, but, in the same instant, heard sirens. Thankful, Lani had run upstairs, returned the gun to its case, locked it, and placed it back into the small space. By the time she returned, the police had Terrence under arrest.

Standing here now, watching Christopher, she smiled at how wonderful he was. How strong he had defended her. How he chose to not hurt Terrence, even thought Terrence was in full attack.

"Come here," Christopher patted the space next to him on the stair. "Sit with me for a second."

"You want to go downstairs?"

"Nope." he grinned.

Lani walked slowly to the stairs, aware that he watched her waist and her breasts with every move.

She smiled. *How can his mind even go there right now?* She sat down next to him and leaned into his large frame. He wrapped an arm around her.

"So are you going to be alright when I leave?"

Lani traced his fingers with her own. "Where are you going?"

"My sister Jackie's place. You met her before."

His fingers ran lightly up and down her neck. She moved in front of him and sat one step below him. He massaged her shoulders and his hands traced her neck bone.

"What are we going to do?" he asked softly.

"I don't know," she answered with a slight chuckle. "How are we the ones in this position?"

"Life, I guess."

"Will you stay in mine?" she asked softly.

"Do you still want me to? I mean, after tonight."

"More than ever." Lani answered without hesitation.

"Are you staying with Terrence?" It was the million dollar question.

Lani slowly shook her head "no." That was the only clear answer, the only real resolution that she had reached. Staying with him was now impossible. Too much had happened, and the positives just didn't compare to the negatives. That she had almost wound up just like her mother terrified her. It was the last sign that Terrence's presence in her life would only bring her pain and misfortune. And she had tolerated enough of that to last a lifetime.

Lani didn't ask whether he was staying with Kenya, and she didn't care. Lani didn't need another husband either. What Christopher decided to do was separate and apart from her realization and acceptance that her marriage had been over for years.

Chapter Forty Six

Christopher's hands continued to massage her neck, rub her shoulders lightly and play with her ponytail. Sighing, Lani closed her eyes and followed the trail of his hands with her mind's eye.

This man makes me feel like heaven.

"Lani?" Christopher's voice sounded thick.

"Huh?"

"Aren't you going to ask me?"

Lani was lost at tingle of his touch. Her mind was blank. "Ask you what?"

"What I have decided..."

Lani waited, hating that she had to ruin the moment by speaking and focusing on thoughts. She had wanted to release herself to his hands. They only had a little under an hour left before Dee arrived and a different kind of confusion, a welcome distraction, but confusion all the same, was going to come with her. Dee always brought welcomed chaos. Then tomorrow Lani would have to deal with Terrence: the separating, the insults, the attacks and the misplaced blame.

Certainly, in his mind, he and Kenya will not be at all to blame for this mess. So, as far as she was concerned, her

289

peace was now, at the hands of this man whom she was falling in love with. A man who was married with a newborn baby and loving him would lead to a dead end.

Lani turned slowly, her knees on the steps, and looked Christopher in his eyes.

"No, I didn't ask." She caressed his cheek with the back of her hand. "I am not going to ask."

She leaned toward him and stared into his deep brown eyes as her fingertips traced a light path around his forehead. "Remember your words, 'stay in my world when and how you can'? That's all I ask."

"You're beautiful," he whispered.

"Your wonderful," she answered.

Their noses touched, their lips met. She kissed him lightly on the lips, again and again; then turned her head slightly, opened her mouth and enjoyed the full taste of him. She felt his hands on her waist, lifting her up the one step while he moved back just a bit and leaned his back against the wall. Lani was lost in the kiss. The heat of his body against her cause soft moans to escape her, and his soft lips captivated her. Never had a kiss tasted so perfect.

Christopher broke the kiss to bury his head in her neck. She felt his tongue trace a path of fire along her throat, enjoyed his teeth gently tugging at her skin. Their mouths met again, until Lani pulled back to touch him. She stroked his face, as she licked his lips, kissed the tip of his nose, ran her fingers along the length of his neck and kissed him gently on the forehead.

Christopher smiled at her, shaking his head. "We had better stop, before we get started."

That made Lani laugh. She didn't want to stop. But she agreed—they were out of time, they needed much longer than less than an hour to fully enjoy one another. There was no need in starting something they couldn't finish.

Lani turned slowly and sat in his lap—she leaned her back into his chest, one leg leaning against his down the steps, the other leg, leaning against his on the carpeted floor. They were both facing the banister, turned sideways on the top step. She loved being tucked against his huge frame, like this. He wrapped his arms around her and rested his hands against her stomach. Christopher lifter her tank top and rubbed the soft skin around her belly button.

Lani felt so protected and safe within his arms. His strong hands stroked her stomach, while she sighed appreciatively.

"Lani," Christopher whispered. "You have my mind messed up."

She chuckled.

"Don't laugh," his voice sounded so heavy, "I am serious."

She lifted one of his hands and placed it over her breast, with her hand covering it. "I am serious, too."

She heard him sigh in resignation as he released himself to the desire that they both felt. Lani closed her eyes while he kissed her neck and rubbing her breasts with both hands. Lost in ecstasy, Lani felt his hand slip under her drawstring waist, curve over her pelvic bone and stroke between her legs. She reached back and grabbed the back of his head. She rubbed the perfect shape of his head and his square neck as she released her inhibitions and spread her legs wide open.

Christopher's thick length throbbed against the small of her back with a pounding urgency to melt inside of her, and she desperately wanted to feel him. Her mind went blank, given over to the intense passion that surged through her.

She forgot everything around her, her mind was only in tune with the intense desire to consume Christopher. Rocking to their own unique rhythm, Lani didn't recall how Christopher's pants came undone and how her pants were slid down to her knees.

She only remembered the heat surging from his hands as they delicately held her waist, lifted her on top of him and guiding him into her depths. She only remembered feeling his unique pulse, riding his rhythm until they both exploded, his hands remaining on her waist, her hands resting on his thighs. She only remembered smiling, feeling as if she were floating and hearing him pant her name continuously, his mouth pressed against her ear as he told her he loved her over and over again. She only remembered opening her eyes to respond and, while her eyes focused in the dim light, she happened to glance out the huge picture window directly in front of them. She only remembered trying to respond to Christopher words of love and realizing, a second too late, that she was staring through the window into the eyes of Terrence.

Chapter Forty Seven

Terrence rode in silence. He wondered whether Lani was still in the house. He doubted Christopher was still there, even if he hadn't gone home to Kenya. *Hell, I wouldn't have gone home to Kenya either.* The tension in the car was worse than sitting in that jail cell. Her jaw seemed locked and her eyes wide and frantic. Kenya seemed to be on the verge of a break down.

Terrence didn't want to argue with her anymore. He couldn't keep pointing fingers or passing blame. They had both messed this thing up. He realized that, sitting in the cell for the past couple of hours. He shouldn't have left Lani and he shouldn't have called Kenya. He should've have spoken with Christopher.

Or better yet, I should have just stayed my ass at home. And Kenya, she shouldn't have lied to Christopher.

Those two things had caused all this. But he knew that things would get back to normal. He just had to decide what to do with Lani, now. He always said he would never stay with a woman who cheated on him. But Lani was his wife. And she had always protected him and stood by him. Maybe he could get past it. Not tonight, but someday, if Lani worked hard enough for his forgiveness. But some things were going to have to change.

First of all, she needs to get some psychological help. That much was certain. It wasn't an option. He would demand it. He thought he might still make her move out, separate for a little while. That way he could have time to work out how he felt, whether he could forgive her or not. And then they would have to work out this situation with Kenya's husband. What would happen to their relationship with Kenya and Christopher? He never wanted Lani near Christopher again, that much was certain. And, after this weekend, he realized that he really didn't know Kenya at all.

They turned onto Terrence's street and drove slowly down the quiet neighborhood. Terrence was sure he and Lani were the talk of the street. Police never came down this quiet street. He wondered, now, who actually called the police on him. He didn't really believe it was Lani, not in hindsight. She had never called them before.

With a start, Terrence realized that Christopher's car still sat parked at an awkward angle along the curb, near Lani's car. Kenya began grinding her teeth, the loud crunching sound made Terrence wrinkle his nose in disgust.

"Why is my husband's car still here?"

Terrence didn't answer. He didn't consider it an actual question. But his heart had sunk, too. He hadn't expected to have to deal with Christopher again. And he knew that he wouldn't get in a lucky chin shot a second time.

"Kenya, thanks for coming to get me."

He pushed the door open and leaned his long frame out of the car.

"Terrence, I ... listen, just tell my husband to please come outside."

Terrence nodded and closed the door. He stood at the end of the driveway for a moment, checking out the damage he had done to Lani's car. What had he been thinking? He was going to wind up fixing the entire thing. A waste of money. His eye travelled to the picture glass in the living room window. He had acted a fool. He hadn't realized until now.

Terrence looked at his house for the first time. The mansion he and Lani built. He rarely looked at it now and took it for granted. His eyes surveyed his property, looking at the front columns and the dim landscape lighting. A warm soft glow of light sprinkled through the huge picture window in the foyers.

Lani and Christopher must be in the family room. He took a few more steps before he glanced up at the house again.

At that distance, he could see them, sitting on the floor of the stairway. Christopher's head was barely visible behind Lani's shoulder.

Terrence squinted. *Is she sitting backward in his lap?*

Lani was leaning back into Christopher's chest. He was talking, his hands wrapped around her. Lani never sat like that with him, never leaned into his chest. He stood riveted in one spot, watching them like a movie. Kenya jumped out of the car. Terrence could hear her cough and impatiently tap her nails on the car.

"Terrence, what are you waiting on?"

He didn't answer. They were only visible from this one spot, this one security breach that he had allowed so that the magnificent view of that window wouldn't be blocked and the sun wouldn't be shut out. Now he had a clear, unwanted view of his wife placing Christopher's hand on her breast and arching her back as she lay against him, the back of her shoulders pressed firmly into his chest. He stood mesmerized, as her arms reached behind her, elbows straight up, and rubbed the back of his head while he sucked on her neck.

"Terrence!"

"Kenya, get back in the car. Now."

Suddenly, Lani's torso leaned forward and she seemed to be lifted in the air.

"No," he whispered. "No, Lani. No."

"Terrence, why are you just standing there—?"

"Gotdamnit. Get in the fucking car, Kenya. Now!" Terrence roared at her, turning his head from the scene that was wrenching his insides.

He was going to be sick. He could feel the bile pressing against the pit of his stomach; burning against the back of his throat.

But Terrence had to watch. He turned back around and forced himself to watch Christopher leaning back against the wall and Lani's body rising and falling, as she leaned slightly forward, their torso's forming a 'V'. A position he had never experienced with Lani. Had never dared asked. Christopher was exploring his wife in ways he hadn't even thought of.

Terrence staggered slightly, riveted to the spot, unable to move. They stopped, eventually, Terrence's eyes absorbing every minute detail. Christopher kept kissing her.

"Terrence?" Kenya had walked up to Terrence. "What is wrong?" She sounded so small. He had scared her, by screaming. He had quieted her. At least she hadn't seen them, hadn't had to stomach the sight of that terror.

Terrence forced himself to stand still and keep his eyes on them. As they shifted and kissed and Lani once again leaned back into Christopher's chest, Kenya followed Terrence's eyes, looking up at the house.

"Oh my Lord..."

Chapter Forty Eight

Kenya took a step forward, a very small step. She actually almost lost her balance and the tiny step was to help shift her weight. Her eyes had to be deceiving her. As she stood next to Terrence she became aware of Lani, leaning back smiling, her eyes closed, and her breasts protruding over the top of a chocolate covered tank top. For an awful second, Kenya felt embarrassed for Terrence, imagining her friend's humiliation that his wife was sitting on the top step of the stair case, in full view of the huge picture window, obviously pleasing herself.

Damn, even I didn't realize how much of a trick she was. Why, with her husband in jail, would Lani be sitting on the steps thinking about sex anyway? And why hadn't she found a more private spot, in this unbelievably huge house? *A house that I deserve much more than her, that's for damn sure.*

"Kenya, go home." She could hear the pleading in Terrence's voice, the complete destruction of him. She looked into his eyes and he turned his body, attempting to shield her and obstruct her view. In that instant, she noticed a third hand, a much larger hand, covering the front of Lani's breast. The quick intake of air almost caused her to choke. She pushed Terrence away and focused more carefully. Christopher's face was barely visible over Lani's shoulder, because it was pressed into her neck. Lani's eyes were open now. She seemed to be looking right at Kenya and Terrence. Her face seemed frozen.

Only Christopher was unaware. Only Christopher continued to kiss and rub, suck and massage. For those awful few seconds, Kenya felt that the world had stopped rotating and time stood still.

***

"Chris. Chris," Lani whispered his name, but he wasn't listening. His head was buried in the side of her neck, sucking and kissing. "Christopher..."

"Yeah, babe." His warm voice tickled her ear, any other time she would have found comfort in it. But not tonight.

"Christopher, they're here." Lani hadn't meant to sound so clichéd, but it was the most she could utter.

Terrence's eyes were boring into her without blinking or flinching. Her heart dropped when she realized that he could really see her and she could feel panic beginning to stir in the pit of her stomach as she wondered how long he had stood there, at that one point in the driveway that was angled just right to see the top step.

She had forgotten all about it.

"What...?" Lani could feel Christopher jump.

"Christopher." She could feel his head adjust on the side of hers as his chin grazed her shoulder. That tenth of a second felt like a lifetime.

Terrence watched her, Kenya's eyes frantically spanned from her to Christopher; Lani's impassive eyes watched Terrence and Christopher stared into the night. It was the longest quiet moment of Lani's life.

"Shit. Oh shit." Christopher sounded oddly calm. His tone didn't match the words falling out of his mouth. "Oh shit."

Lani shifted and quickly slid out of his lap but his hands were still on her hips. Even now, he didn't push her away or knock her over trying to hide. But he felt stiff and very cold.

"Oh shit," Christopher said again and quickly jumped off of the step onto the landing. Lani caught a glimpse of him as he disappeared around the corner, but, at the same time, she realized that the front door wasn't locked.

Terrence's back was turned now; he seemed to be struggling with Kenya. Lani's hands were cold and the hairs on her arm stood on end. She raced down the stairs, across the foyer and turned the deadbolt on the front door. She had never seen Terrence like this before. His eyes appeared dead, lifeless, and expressionless. There was no telling what he would do.

Sophie flashed into her mind again. She was less than Sophie. What Sophie had done had protected two little girls, had kept herself from being killed by a murderer who she had relied on and loved, without realizing the cruelty in his soul. Lani was worse than that. She had no children to defend or protect. No man had pretended to love her just to torture and terrify her for his own gain. No, she had a husband who had loved her at some point. And she had just subjected him to watching her reenact a porn scene in his home. On top of the lavish balcony that he had demanded be built a certain way, that he had taken days to draw out with the architect—the focus of his pride.

Lani leaned against the wall next to the entrance. If Terrence tried to come this way, at least she would know. Instead of Terrence, Lani heard Kenya, screaming and crying. She listened as Kenya called her every name imaginable.

We were wrong. Even though they had initially been the victims, even though her husband had left and this scandalous, two faced, evil woman had run to his side, Lani and Christopher were still in the wrong. Now, no matter who had started it, Christopher and Lani would be blamed for the entire thing.

Sophie would be ashamed of her. Dee would be ashamed of her. Damn, she was ashamed of her damn self.

What were we thinking? Right here in the house? In front of the damn window? Lani shook her head and then looked up toward the ceiling. The empty ache that had taken up residence in her essence during the last abortion seemed to stretch. She had been trying to fill it for months now, first by ignoring it, then by willing it to go away, then by trying to make Terrence different—more attentive—to make her feel better. To make that hole that felt like it was flipping her inside out go away. It expanded. Lani couldn't breathe. She was going to drown, to pass out, and to die.

Lani hadn't prayed in months. Hadn't had time for church recently. She had felt tired of getting dressed to go listen to the same sermons, and watch the same phony people socialize, who were mostly Terrence's family and friends. But now, those all seemed to be empty reasons. Now, her life could be at risk, but certainly her life was about to change. She had done something so selfish, so completely self absorbed and greedy, that she had to question herself. Maybe she was a monster. Maybe Terrence was right—maybe the problem was her. Maybe she had pushed him to Kenya—what type of woman was she, with what she had just done?

Panic had etched its way into her heart. Lani was completely lost.

"God, please. Please, please, please … please help me." The screech came from her; she felt the words, felt the call out to the Almighty, before she heard herself.

Lani couldn't find any more words, didn't know what to say to account for all the hurt and pain over the last few years. She felt as though her chest was opening and spewing forth all of her fears. "Please, God, please … please. I am so sorry."

Christopher shouted from the foyer, "Lani, come up here."

"No. I have to face whatever it is that I deserve, Christopher. I ain't shit, and Terrence knows it, now. I deserve whatever I get."

"Lani, just come upstairs, I'll handle them both." She couldn't see him. She wondered what he was upstairs doing.

"No." Lani would wait for whatever punishment Terrence served up.

***

Kenya looked at Terrence for an explanation, something that would make sense. For a second all four seemed to be moving in slow motion and then suddenly time returned and Kenya felt her sense come alive.

You son of a bitch! She turned on her heel and stumbled back to her car, tears falling from her eyes. How could he do this? He was a bastard to cheat on her in the open, where everyone could see. And the way he held Lani. All the kissing and rubbing. *He doesn't even make love like that!*

She slammed her car door shut and revved her engine. She threw the gear into reverse and backed out of the driveway. Kenya's blood was racing and her mind was a jumble of thoughts. How could he do this to her? Why? Why would he do this? He had to have been with her the entire weekend. It was true. She had asked, had threatened, but she never really believed it. Not really. But Lani had Christopher. *Lani took another man from me!*

"THAT BITCH!" Kenya screamed as she switched gears. *I am not leaving. No. I am not running from this bitch.* She swung a U-turn and pulled back into Terrence's yard. Kenya slammed the car into park and jumped out, leaving the car running. She ran past Terrence, who was slowly walking toward the house, his eyes on Lani, as if he were in a trance.

Kenya sprinted to the front door.

"Open the door. Open the goddamn door." Kenya slammed against the door with her fists. "I saw you, Christopher, you cheating bastard. I saw you. Open this mother fucking door."

Kenya felt the sobs tear at her chest and realized that the front of her shirt was wet. She was sobbing. "Open the door! That bitch. You bitch. You hear me, Lani? I am going to kill you, bitch. Open this gotdamn door."

Kenya kicked the door over and over again. She took a step back and kicked, using her heel, her leg fully extended. The door barely shook. The more she kicked, the more she screamed and the more enraged she became.

"Open this goddamn door, you sneaking, lying asshole. For this bitch? For this low level, trashy ghetto bitch. You're going cheat on me? ON ME! For this bitch!" Kenya screamed the words in unison with each kick.

The door swung open, causing her to lose balance in mid kick. She fell into the doorway, knocking into Lani, who stepped back and stared down at her.

"I am not going to be too many more bitches. Not in my own house. Stop kicking my goddamn door."

Kenya felt her eyes widen so much that they were bulging. "How dare you talk to me like that? I saw you..." Kenya scrambled to her feet. "I saw you on my husband, you stupid tramp. Stay away from my husband."

Lani did not blink. Her cool demeanor was enraging Kenya more. Kenya glanced around the huge foyer. "Christopher! Where are you, damnit? Christopher?"

"This is the last time I tell you," Lani spoke slowly. "You are not going to call me too many more names on my property."

"Fuck you!" Kenya turned suddenly and faced Lani. "What, I am supposed to be afraid of the ghetto girl. Fuck you. You ruined your life, now you're trying to fuck with—"

Fire blazed across Kenya's cheek and a powerful blast hit her stomach before she could react. Kenya didn't even realize she had been hit, until Lani punched her a third time and then pushed her against the far wall.

"Do you know how long I have wanted to whip your ass?" Lani hissed quietly.

Kenya was struck by how controlled Lani's rage seemed, not loud illogical attacks like Terrence used to complain about.

Lani was in full control now. "You don't think I have watched you all these years, knowing you wanted Terrence. Don't you ever in your life call me out of my name where I can hear you."

Lani pressed Kenya against the wall by her throat. Kenya pushed her with all her might and Lani punched her in the chest. Kenya was swinging wildly; Lani punched strategically.

Christopher came out of nowhere.

"What the—" He grabbed Lani, held both her arms and shielded her body from Kenya, who was still wildly attacking. Lani immediately subsided and stared at Kenya with a shadow of a smirk on her face.

Christopher had gone to her first. He had run to Lani first, grabbed her arms and shielded her. And Kenya realized that Lani noticed it.

The air rushed out of Kenya. She felt defeated. Christopher turned around and faced her. "Let's go."

"Get away from me." Kenya stumbled across the large foyer.

"Kenya, let me drive you home. I'm sorry you saw that..."

"Fuck you, Christopher." She pushed him away from her. Embarrassment flooded her body and hate surged through her in spasms. "Get away from me."

Kenya ran out of the front door. For an awful moment, she didn't think Christopher was going to follow. She stepped outside into the cool night air and ran to her car with nobody following. But then she could saw Christopher's large frame running across the lawn, taking an angle to cut her off. Kenya wouldn't make it to her car.

Chapter Forty Nine

Lani had her back against the wall of the foyer and tried to focus her mind, remember something. She had lost herself in the emotion of retaliating against Kenya and had forgotten something. Some very important thing. Despite her remorse, she wasn't going to listen to Kenya continue to call her names. How much from one woman could she take? Lani might have owed Terrence an explanation but she didn't owe Kenya anything. But after Christopher had hesitated in the doorway, meeting her eyes with question, and she had signaled for him to go after his wife, Lani remained still, trying to remember the thing that had her deeply terrified.

Terrence. She whispered his name and, at the same moment, he entered the foyer through the front door, his eyes still expressionless. Lani met his eyes and wondered what she should say that would make it better, would make him understand. But there were no words.

Her lips parted, but he spoke first.

"Get out," he whispered, a dry hoarse whisper that sound like an old man. "I gave you a chance earlier, but I won't now."

Lani continued to stare at him without responding.

307

"Do you hear me, you trifling bitch." Terrence's voice became louder, a raspy soft sound. "Get the fuck out."

"No." Terrence had called her a trifling bitch. Her husband had called her a trifling bitch. Under other circumstances she would have raised hell. But she couldn't. Not tonight. Because she and Christopher were dead ass wrong.

"What?" Finally, his eyes changed. They contained an expression. Rage.

"No, I ... I—" Lani wasn't going to say sorry, that would be admitting more than she was ready to admit. She still didn't know how much he'd actually seen. Saying sorry wouldn't make a difference anyway. "—I am not leaving my home. Not after you left. Remember, you started all of this when you left."

Lani needed to leave this area, to get somewhere safer away from him. She walked up a couple of steps and her eyes locked on him. "I don't know what to say, Terrence. I don't know what you need to hear. Tonight is just one night of many miserable ones in this marriage. But you left me and went to her. What do you expect me to say?"

"I don't give a fuck about what you have to say. You thought I was in jail and you sat here and fucked another man in my house. My home."

Lani walked up two more steps.

Terrence started to follow her. "Get the fuck out now."

"No." She turned and walked faster up the stairs. He moved so quickly that it took her a second to realize he was running toward her. She jumped and sprinted up the stairs, trying to take them two at a time. Terrence reached Lani near the top, tripping over her feet. They both fell and he landed slightly on top of her, while she frantically tried to crawl up the last two steps. Terrence pressed his body weight into Lani and pinned her face down on the stairs.

"So you like fucking on my staircase, huh? You got that man's cum all in my fucking carpet?"

"Get off me," Lani struggled and desperately tried to separate from his weight crushing her into the stairs.

"No, bitch." Terrence pushed more. "Isn't this how you like it?"

"Get off me," Lani screamed as she struggled up one more stair. She felt his hand grip the back of her neck.

"Here is the spot, right here. This is where you were." Before she could stop him, he had mashed her head into the thick plush fibers of the carpet, like she was a dog he was training. "Isn't this where you were?"

"I can't breathe, Terrence."

His grip loosened, but he kept his hand on the back of her neck, kept her body pinned to the rug. She lifted her head and attempted to climb up the steps. His hand clamped onto her head again, pushing it back into the rug.

"Stop!" she screamed. "Stop it!" A claustrophobic fit over took her. She couldn't stand being pinned down in the tight space, his body leaning over half of hers, her face in the rug. Lani began to wildly push and kick, elbowing and kicking, screaming at the top of her lungs. Terrence released his grip in shock, and Lani took advantage, lunging forward and throwing her body onto the upstairs landing.

He reached for her and grabbed her ankle as she tried to stand up. Lani fell again, but scrambled back up just as he reached the spot she had been in, and ran as fast as she could to the master bathroom.

***

"Kenya, baby, I'm sorry you saw that."

"You're sorry I saw it? But you aren't sorry you did it? Oh my God." Kenya hit him in the chest, her arms pounding out a rhythm of her pain. "How could you do this? How could you..."

"You have to calm down. Please. Let me take you home."

"Calm down? Are you out of your fucking mind?"

"Kenya, we can't do this here. Not on this front lawn. Get in the car. I will drive you home."

"I HATE YOU!" she bellowed, hitting at him again. She felt Christopher's arms wrap around her and knew that it looked like he was hugging her. But the hug actually restricted her arm movement and caused her to stand still in the pit of his chest.

"Kenya, you have got to calm down."

"I can smell her on you. Don't tell me to calm down, you fucking loser."

For a second, his grip around her loosened and she struggled to separate from him.

"What can you say? Huh? I got to calm down for what? I saw you."

Christopher stood there staring at her. She took a few steps back to her car. "I am your wife. We have a son. And you are over my friend's house, fucking his whore ass wife. What can you say?"

"Kenya, that's not how this happened. You know that."

"Oh what, are you saying I didn't see you fucking her? I didn't see you sucking on her neck?"

"Kenya, what led me here? Huh? How did I get here?"

"What the hell are you talking about?"

"What got me here?" Christopher demanded. His voice was louder. Her hysterics were rubbing off on him; he was reacting and becoming angry. *Good. Now he will know how I feel.*

"You got you here, Christopher. This was your choice. I've never cheated." She turned her back and walked the final steps to her car. She stopped at the door. "I've never cheated. And this is what you do—"

"You never cheated?"

"Hell no."

"But you wanted to. Say you didn't." Christopher spoke through clenched teeth and tight lips. "I dare you to stand there and lie. Terrence told me. You wanted it. And I know it's true. So save that sanctimonious bullshit for your girlfriends. Spare me. You walked the fuck out. You begged a married man for his dick. Fuck me? No. Fuck you!"

Kenya stared at him with her mouth open. He had become someone else, someone unrecognizable. The way he spoke, the way he stood, she didn't know this man. And she felt afraid of him.

Christopher motioned to her car. "Get in the car. I will follow you home. We will talk about this later."

"Don't tell me what to do," she said, trying to sound brave, but hearing herself sound like a child. "You are in the wrong, here, not..."

"Get in the FUCKING CAR!" he screamed.

She stared at him for a second and then lowered her frame into the car, fresh tears pouring down her face. Christopher walked toward his car. For a second, Kenya imagined laying her foot on the gas and ramming him into the side of his car. But she would never do that. He must have thought about it though, because he watched her as he walked to his car. Christopher opened the door and began to climb in when an awful crack ripped through the air, slicing the quiet of the night like lightning. Kenya saw Christopher look at the house and then she realized what that sound might have been.

***

In the bathroom, she locked the door and sat on the commode and tried to catch her breath. She couldn't believe that Terrence had just treated her that way or said those things.

"Oh my God, oh my God," Lani whispered frantically as she paced back and forth in front of the large Jacuzzi. A cracking feeling tore across her chest and she couldn't fight the tremors that consumed her.

312

"I love you, you bastard." Lani threw her vanity mirror against the door as she screamed. "I love you. No matter that you fucked her. No matter that you left me. I never treated you like that."

"You don't love me." Terrence shouted through the door. "You don't love me. You don't even know what love is."

"I hate you!" Lani screamed again and the force caused her to choke. Sputtering and coughing, she threw herself against the door. "How much can you do to me? Huh? Why? Why do you treat me—?"

"No, fuck that. You love me then you hate me. That's the problem with you. You don't know what the fuck you want. But you damn sure made a choice tonight and IT WASN'T ME. Get the fuck out of my bathroom."

"You bastard. You mother fucking bastard." Lani ran over to Terrence's sink and cabinet. She threw everything she could find at the door. She couldn't control herself; she wanted to hurt him, to make him feel her pain and she couldn't.

"I'm a bastard, but you are a low life whore. I married a tramp whore!"

"Fuck you, Terrence," mumbled Lani weakly, her energy a volcanic eruption that left her dizzy. She leaned against the wall and slid to the floor, crying. "Even now, even now you don't care."

"Open the door, Lani."

Lani didn't respond. She had to get control of herself. She had trapped herself in the bathroom. *Dumb dumb dumb. Pull it together, girl.*

"Lani, open the door."

Lani sat very quiet, wondering what he would do if she committed suicide. She wouldn't, she wouldn't even consider it. But she just wondered whether he would care, or would he be happy to finally be rid of her.

"Lani, answer me."

How was she going to get out of the bathroom? This was life or death. Her heart jumped when she heard him kick the door.

"Open the fucking door. Where is your boyfriend now, huh? With his wife, that's where. I can't believe you would do this to me. I SACRIFICED EVERYTHING FOR YOU. TO PLEASE YOU!"

Lani stared at the small panel in the wall. She didn't have any other choice. She was backed into a corner, trapped like a wounded animal. The small gun was her only way out.

"Terrence." Lani kept her voice steady and controlled. "I am telling you right now, you need to leave."

"Fuck you. You're going to get the fuck out of my house. Since you're such a tramp, maybe I'll have you blow me first, before I throw your ass out. Open this goddamn door."

For Lani, that was the final insult. She crawled across the bathroom, into the little room and pushed in the panel. As she pulled out the small case her hands were shaking and the case fell onto the tile floor.

"What are you in there doing?"

This time she had no problem remembering the combination. She took out the small gun and removed the safety. "Terrence, I am asking you to leave. I do not want to have to hurt you."

Terrence laughed an insane maniacal sound. "Hurt me, bitch. You have already destroyed me."

She aimed at what she hoped was higher than his head. Bracing herself, she pointed the gun and fired.

"What the fuck?"

"Terrence, that was a warning shot—"

The door shook as Terrence tried to kick it in.

"Motherfuck. Are you shooting at me? Son of a bitch, you're shooting at me in my house?"

"Leave! Terrence, I swear I will shoot you. I am aiming lower this time." Lani took a deep breath; she had to steady her nerves. The sound of his body slamming into the wood made her jump. The door cracked; a splintering sound like ice crackling in the tray.

Lani yelled and her anguish sounded like a wolf's howl. Hearing Terrence kick the door again and watching the splintered crack spread down the center of the door petrified Lani. She aimed at where his midsection should be.

"Terrence," Lani gasped. "Please..." she whispered.

His body slammed into the door again. The wood groaned and the split widened.

She pulled the trigger.

Lani listened to Terrence's yells as they torpedoed through the house. "Terrence," Lani gasped. "Please…," she whispered.

His body slammed into the door again. The wood groaned and the split widened.

She pulled the trigger.

His yell bounced off the cathedral ceilings. Lani glanced at her reflection in the mirror. Sophie stared back at her, her grey eyes glinting. Lani staggered and leaned her frame against the door. Her heart was pounding in her chest, she couldn't catch her breath. She gulped air, trying to slow her racing heart. After all this, she was no different than Sophie—and she was about to wind up in the same place. She was cursed; there was no way to fight it.

***

"Terrence," Kenya whispered, clutching the steering wheel, as a second explosive rip crackled against the dark night.

Christopher began running toward the house.

"Christopher, no!" Kenya jumped out of the car and watched in amazement as Christopher sprinted *toward* the sound of gunshots.

A moment later, Christopher stopped running and stood in the middle of the yard as Terrence's lean figure raced out of the house, running for his life. He didn't seem to see Christopher, but ran in the opposite direction across the neighbor's yard. Kenya sat still, holding her breath. Had Terrence killed Lani? She didn't want to go into the house and she could tell

Christopher didn't either. He just stood in the yard, frozen like a statue.

Lani's thick frame appeared in the doorway, gun in her hand, looking out into the night.

Kenya watched Christopher staring at Lani. He never even looked back at her.

Fuck him. The thought ripped across her brain. Her husband was standing in the yard, staring at his lover, his back to his wife. *Bastard.* She gunned the engine, but still he didn't look back. Slamming her foot on the gas, Kenya slammed her car into Christopher's and the driver side door buckled like plastic.

She backed up and rammed into the car again and again. *Yeah, you're looking over here now.*

Christopher was running again, tearing back across the yard, trying to stop her. He was running alongside the car, his arms reaching in through the window to grab at her, and then yanking them out as she slammed into the car again and again. As she backed up for another strike, a car came down the street. Its headlights temporarily blinded her and caused her to snap out of her daze. Kenya sped off in the direction Terrence had run.

Kenya had to find Terrence. He would need her.

Chapter Forty Nine

"What in the hell is going on here?" Dee climbed from the newly arrived car and stared at Christopher and his severely damaged vehicle. "Do you hear me? Who are you and what the hell is going on here?"

Christopher stared at the dark brown petite woman in front of him. Her eyes looked familiar. He turned back to his car. Kenya had demolished it. Lani stood in the doorway with a gun.

A gun? What is she doing with a gun? What had he been thinking? If Kenya filed for divorce, she could use this against him. He could lose physical custody over his son and have to resort to visitation and child support payments. *My baby. My baby boy.* Christopher's heart felt like it was falling through his chest, exploding into bits. He had thrown it all away. For sex. For an easy release, he might lose his son.

Clarity slapped him across the face like a wet towel. *I need to get home.*

The tiny woman in front of him spoke again, as if he couldn't hear her. "Ricky, I think he is in shock. Come over here, will you?" She led Christopher by the elbow to the curb, and tugged him until he sat down. Then she stood in front of him and bent down, staring into his eyes.

"Ricky!!"

"Dee, I am right here. I hear you, babe."

Christopher watched as the powerful force packed within the barely five foot frame drew itself in. The tiny woman changed the tone of her voice and seemed oddly demure. "I'm sorry boo, I didn't see you."

"Who are you?" she asked again, more slowly. Christopher wanted to laugh.

"Christopher. I'm not in shock, it's just that I ...," he swallowed and took a deep breath. "Who are you?"

"Deidra," she answered and stood up straight. He noticed that she pronounced the first "I" in her name, the one that most seem to skip over. He could tell she was detail oriented. Probably immaculate. It was odd, the things people thought of during the most random of times.

"Are you Lani's sister?"

"Yep. What is going on here and how do you know Lani?"

"I am Kenya's husband."

Dee's eyes became big as saucers. She looked at his car, back at him, then at her husband.

"I guess that was Kenya, then, that pulled off, driving like she was trying to light the road on fire?"

Christopher nodded.

"Damn ...," she started, but her husband cut her off.

"Dee, babe, go check on Lani. She is standing in the doorway holding heat."

319

Christopher watched Dee turn sharply and focus, squinting, at the doorway.

"Oh shit, I didn't even see her." She ran toward the house.

Ricky lowered his body to the curb like an old man. He and Christopher sat in silence.

"You alright man?" Ricky finally said.

Christopher looked up at the burly man, who wore a mechanic type jumpsuit, Christopher knew that he probably wore his jumpsuit whenever he was relaxed, he seemed like that type.

"Yeah."

"Look, can I take you home or something? You can handle this in the morning."

Home. Kenya isn't going to let me in the house. But I got to try to make things right. I got to get to my baby. "Please ... I would appreciate it."

Ricky nodded his head and took out a cell phone. He quickly texted a message and Christopher had no doubt that the text was sent to Dee. Ricky helped Christopher off of the curb and they quietly got into the car.

Thirty five minutes later, Christopher stood in his yard. Kenya's car wasn't there. He peered into the garage, but it was empty. *She has already left me. Has already taken my son.* Hurt pounded in his gut. He fumbled with his keys and opened the front door.

"I was starting to get worried."

The deep voice startled Christopher and he jumped backward.

"I didn't mean to scare you, son," chuckled Kenya's father. "I've been watching baby boy, here. His momma don't have him on no type of schedule. Right baby boy?"

A sigh of relief passed Christopher's lips and he rushed over to hold his son.

"He has been awake for close to two hours now. Left right when his hard headed momma walked out of here," James stood up and stretched his body, "but I kept him entertained."

"Thanks, Dad. The last few days have been ..."

"Yeah. You don't have to tell me. Doesn't take much common sense to piece together this nonsense going on here."

Christopher bit his lip as he cradled his son. He couldn't discuss this with Kenya's father. He was *her* father; *her* most loyal supporter.

"Look, I'm not going to ask no questions. And I haven't always been the best of husbands. But I hung in there. Me and Connie, we made choices and sacrifices for our family. For our child. And along the way, we found something special that made it all worth it. That's all I want for you and my daughter."

"I know, Dad. I just don't think Kenya and I ..."

"No, I won't hear that. Hold your ground. Whatever you did wrong, let her have her say. Apologize and do whatever it takes to keep it together. On one condition, once it's forgiven, it's over. Don't no person, not you and not her, deserve to have to live with their mistakes constantly being thrown in their face."

Christopher gazed at him, unable to find a response.

James nodded his head. "You hear me? If you stay and make it right, then it's over. What happened, happened; but that's it. That goes for the both of you."

"I hear you."

"You know, this family waited a long time for a boy." James grabbed his hat and jacket off of the sofa. "Connie couldn't conceive any more children after Kenya."

"I know, you told me."

"Yep. The future, it rests on our children. This little boy here, he's blessed. Got two generations of love and solidarity to be handed to him. Tradition. Family. He's blessed."

"Blessed ..." Christopher repeated as he hugged the small body close to him while little Christopher stared into his face, one arm bobbing up and down.

"Well, I'm going to head out. Connie will start calling soon."

Christopher nodded again, unable to look at his father-in-law completely in the face, certain that tears were going to escape his eyes.

"No need to walk me out. Good night, son."

The answer had just been delivered to him. The confirmation was clear. Christopher couldn't risk losing his son, no matter what. Nobody, not even Lani, was worth that. He sat on the couch, rocking his son to sleep. No matter what he had to do or say, he would make things right.

~ New Edition ~

Chapter Fifty

Lani lay quietly on the bed, watching Dee pace back and forth. Dee's mouth moved, but Lani didn't hear a thing. It was over. Her marriage was over. A crushing weight pressed against her chest, a pain throbbed in her core. It reminded her of something, something nostalgic. Yeah, the pound felt like Poochie's cheap shots to the stomach, when they used to wrestle and fight in the basement of her Aunt Marie's house. Lani snorted out loud. Poochie would laugh at her for being a punk and acting like she had.

Dee stopped walking and faced Lani. Her mouth moved and her arms waved frantically in the air. She looked worried. Dee would make a plan and make it all better. If she could. Dee was always the problem solver. But Lani knew deep down that even Dee couldn't fix this. Somehow, Terrence had become nestled into the pit of her essence. She didn't want to breathe without him. She wanted to see his long frame fill the doorway, wanted to feel his smooth face leaning against her. She hoped he would forget: forget that she had actual launched two small metal missiles at him. Maybe he would know, deep down, that she would never hurt him. Never. Even now, even though he clearly would have crossed the line and probably would have hurt her.

Lani whimpered without realizing it. She didn't want to live this life without him. All of the best of her had been poured into making this relationship work, shaping this life into something similar to what she had seen on television, what she thought black professional life was. Somehow, his leaving didn't seem so bad, his reliance on Kenya was something she could and would handle. The thought of living in the house alone, without him, even in his silence and distance, terrified her.

Where is the strength I felt earlier? I am not this weak. I can do this. I have to do this. I can't keep groveling, can't keep meaning nothing. The practical, intelligent woman in her pleaded for logical thought; attempted to break through the barrier of pity. But the little girl that remained curled into a tight ball within her, who always waited for the anvil to drop, who knew life's loneliness and fear; that little girl called out for Terrence, whispered his name over and over again in her head and made her regret every decision she had made over the past four days.

"Where the hell did Ricky go? You have to get up. We gotta pack. No way am I staying in this mammoth house and have that bourgie idiot burn this mutha down." Dee slammed across the room, mumbling cuss words and throwing back the windows, looking into the night. "You shot at him! You shot at your husband! What the hell were you thinking?" Dee's voice broke into Lani's turmoil.

Lani made herself focus on the short brown figure in front of, eyebrows furrowed together and one hand on her hip.

Lani shrugged.

325

"Lani, what the fuck? You don't shoot at your husband. That gun wasn't for him, it was for protection. You could beat his ass if you had to, you didn't have to get raw. Damn, punch him in the nuts and run for it, if you have to."

"Dee, what do you want me to say? You didn't see him. You don't know."

"I know his ass had been looking for you for damn near two days. I know that he has always been up under you, taking you wherever his pretty ass went. Shit, he didn't violate the major rules—he didn't cheat, he ain't no pervert and he didn't beat your ass."

"He was going to."

"Hell no he wasn't …"

"You didn't see him."

"Lani, were you with her man?"

Lani didn't answer.

"You heard me. Were you with her man?"

Lani stared at the wall just behind Dee.

"Alright then, did you push him to a limit? Was his back against a wall?"

Lani's lips trembled around the lie. "No."

"Bullshit. This brother drives up and down the damn East Coast and when you come home he flips the hell out. You know how this goes; you've seen it over and over again. Oh what, because your mamma and aunts got their freak on in back rooms, they different from you? Hell no."

"Dee, don't even go …"

"No. Damn that. You know a man's limits, Lani. I taught you. Ma taught you. Life taught you. Then you take his spoiled ass, stretch him past all understanding and now you got to take out a gun to protect yourself."

"It's not *my* fault."

"Fault? What the hell are you talking about?" Dee dragged her words slowly, rolling her head in the process, while her arms flailed in the air. "We are women! This is real life, not soap opera drama. Not that college bullshit. Don't buy in. The truth is the truth whether it is PC or not."

Lani sighed and rolled onto her stomach. She wanted Dee to stop yelling at her, to take her side, to comfort her. She didn't want to hear this.

Dee kept lecturing. "You know your man. You know how to deal with men. And you know how to torment them. You took him there. You punished and you dealt that shit out past what he could take, Lani. You know it."

"He took me past what I could take, Dee. He took me past what I would do for love. I just wanted him to love me."

"That's the problem, girl. He does love your ass. If you all would just be married without the damn infatuation love-hate bullshit, we wouldn't be in this mess now."

Lani buried her head in a pillow.

"Where is the gun?" Dee demanded.

"Why?

"I am taking that shit back, that's why! I damn sure ain't leaving it with you. You think I would pull out a gun on Ricky? On the man who pays my bills, raises my daughters and heads my house. Hell no. I don't care what his ass did."

"Never say never, Dee."

"Never." Dee began throwing Lani's things on the bed. "I can say that shit, because I wouldn't pull no weekend disappearing act in the first damn place."

"Dee, damnit, stop judging me. I don't want to hear this shit."

"Lani, I am being real with you." Dee disappeared into the closet and her voice sounded slightly muffled. "I am telling you how I see it. There are deal breakers and he didn't come close to any of them. So, his little bratty ass walked out pissed off. And? You knew he was coming back. You knew you had him like that."

"Whatever ..."

"You *knew* it! You never for a second thought that Kenya could take him from you." Dee returned with a few jogging suits and threw them on the bed. "Shit. I taught you better than that. So, why did you take him all the way there? You had to make his ass pay, huh?"

"I needed to escape Dee, damn. You don't know what its like, how he treats me, what I have been through. I shouldn't have to be in the street looking for my damn husband. Shouldn't have to always scrape him out of Kenya's ass. Fuck him."

"Fuck him she says, through tears and snot." Dee snorted and went back into the closet as Lani covered her head with a pillow again. She didn't want to hear

328

anymore. No one would understand that she and Christopher were still the victims, and had helped each other. No one would hear her point.

Dee returned. Lani wished she had tape to put over her mouth. Dee met her eyes. "Baby girl, you won the battle, no doubt. Stuck that sword right through his heart. Taught him not to mess with you. But the learning may not be worth it, if your sword kills his soul in the process. Shit, the war is just about to begin now …"

Lani began rocking back and forth. Dee was always right. Lani had won the battle, had indulged herself and had taught him the lesson of leaving. She hadn't consciously thought of it that way, but the truth was that giving herself to Christopher freed her in a way that could only destroy Terrence. He needed to know, needed to see that she was worth more. But, on the other hand, it had spun out of control. She had lost control of the situation. Christopher hadn't been a revenge thing, it had been a comfort. And fighting Terrence had been terrible.

Nothing made sense. Her spirit was so confused in one second she felt vindicated, glad that Terrence was hurting. Alone. Angry and remorseful. He should feel what she had been feeling for years. But the other part of her with pure love hurt for them both, for the shabby state of disrepair their marriage was in. The truth was there was no recovery.

Dee marched back into the room with more clothes. "This should cover you for a little while."

"Dee, I am not leaving."

"I'll be damned if I sleep in this big ass house with a pissed off spoiled ass man on the loose, looking for revenge. And you know I ain't leaving you here."

"I can't go."

"A hotel then?"

Lani shook her head. "I'll change the security code. We'll know if he crosses any of the zones. I need to be here."

Dee walked back to the window, ignoring Lani. "Where in the hell is Ricky."

Chapter Fifty One

Kenya pulled her car slowly into the yard. Her mind focused on one mission: she would pack up little Christopher and go. *His daddy wants to play games? I got plenty of games for him.* She walked slowly to the front door, sighed deeply and prepared to smile and front for her father. Her father would never understand; would never really hear her side. Smoothing her face with her hands, she took a deep breath before unlocking the door. Opening the door, Kenya's eyes fell on Christopher's large frame resting on the sofa, holding little Christopher on his chest. His eyes were closed, but she knew he wasn't asleep. *How did he get here?*

She shut door.

"Your dad left," whispered Christopher. He opened both eyes and studied her. She looked at his watery bloodshot eyes. He had been crying. She had never seen him cry. Never. The tear tracks stained his cheekbones and his nose looked red. He had tear tracks down his face.

His ass should cry. He is about to lose everything over that bitch. She wanted to demand that he put her son down, but she never played that game with him. She knew better.

"So, you decided to come home, huh? Your bitch must be alright, must not need your aid?" Kenya crossed her arms and stared at him.

He stood and walked past her, his arm brushing hers. He climbed the steps and carried little Christopher to bed.

Kenya walked into the kitchen and slammed her purse on the counter. *He has some nerve. He doesn't get to just walk in here like this, to just return to family.* He had chosen Lani, a woman she despised, and he had chosen her instead of his wife. She heard him walking down the stairs. His footsteps tracked across the family room and then sounded muffled on the carpet in front of the couch. *How the hell do I get him out of here? How am I going to get the baby out of here without fighting him?* Kenya eyed the heavy Emeril pans hanging from the narrow rack. Her eyes traveled to the knives. *How could he do this, how could he have embarrassed me like this?*

"Kenya."

She didn't answer, staring at the knife block.

"Kenya, we need to talk."

"There is nothing left to say, is there. You got a little girlfriend and a new life, huh? That's what you chose?" Kenya stood in the doorway of the family room and stared at him in what she hoped was her most intimidating evil glare.

"No. I chose this life when I married you. But *you* never chose to do this with me. You never cut Terrence back and treated your husband as the number one man in your life." He sighed, his elbows rested on his knees and his eyes focused on the floor.

"And I didn't even know it was missing anything until now."

"What, did Lani tell you that?" She stepped into the room. "Now you're quoting your tramp?"

Christopher winced. It pissed Kenya off. There was no telling what Lani had called her and had said about her. She bet that they had sat around and discussed her for hours.

Christopher sat forward with his eyes locked into Kenya's. "Kenya, you want a fight. I am not going to fight with you. I am here. I am here."

"So what? You are here and what? You were with her. Then you left again and went to her. While her man was being shot at, you were running toward her. Where am I in this picture?" Her voice increased until she heard herself screeching and her voice cracking. "Where am I? Where does your wife fit, while you have a girlfriend? Tell me that."

"Kenya, this is where I am at. Do you understand? I am here."

"What? I am supposed to be honored because you brought your arrogant ass home."

"No. You are supposed to understand that we both made mistakes. We both messed up. And we both came home."

"I came home to get my son and—"

"Our son."

"—leave." She shouted and headed toward the stairs.

"My son has a home. He is staying in it. Don't test me on this, Kenya."

She kept walking toward the stairs with her head held high. But her heart began to pound frantically. She didn't want to test what he would do if she tried to take little Christopher. She knew, instinctively, that little Christopher was the real reason he had returned, the real reason he chose home. If she tested him on that, she might lose the only standing she had.

Stopping at the bottom of the staircase, Kenya turned around. Christopher was only a few inches behind her. She hadn't heard him, forgot how fast he could move. She hesitated, her eyes wide and he took a step back.

"Kenya. We have to move forward. What's past it passed."

"Whatever," she whispered as she watched him. Kenya breathed heavily. She needed to remember how she felt when she spotted him stroking Lani and hugging Lani. She needed that feeling to keep her head clear.

"I need you to forgive me and I will forgive you."

"Forgive me? I am not the one who slept with another person."

"There is no real way for me to know that, is there?" The words slid out, Kenya could tell he hadn't meant to say it. He immediately looked at the floor, the wall, the ceiling. He pressed his palms flat against his eyes and rubbed them furiously.

"You know it, because I said I didn't."

"You ran out. In the middle of the night. You ran out after Terrence. You left us and ran out of this house."

"I went to talk to my friend. I talk to my friend all the time and it never bothered you before."

"You never lied before. You never manipulated before. And it felt different."

"It wasn't."

"It was." He looked into her eyes and Kenya felt a chill go through her. She felt exposed. "He told me and I believe him."

Kenya's heart dropped. She had decided to forget about the details of her kiss with Terrence. She had to forget how her body had immediately responded to him, how ready she had been to feel him inside of her. It was a longing she had never experienced before, a desire she had never known experienced. It wouldn't have mattered if it had been good or not, she knew she would have been satisfied by any piece of Terrence. Desperate. She had been desperate to have Terrence. Just once. And Christopher knew.

"I sat here like an ass. Worrying about you. Looking for you. Trying to convince her that my wife wouldn't run out with her husband. Praying to God that you weren't dead. My peace ended because my wife ran out to try to jam her hands down Terrence's pants."

She shook her head. She wanted to explain but there weren't any words.

"What am I supposed to do with that Kenya? What am I supposed to say?"

"What did you do with Lani?"

He paused, took another step back, sat back on the sofa, stared into her eyes. It was a question he would never answer. Meaning he still held Lani close. Still cared. And there was nothing she could do. He wasn't offering her all of him. He wasn't expressing regret. He was simply calling a truce. An uneasy, uncomfortable, 'life moves forward', truce. And she realized that a truce was all she would get.

Chapter Fifty Two

Christopher stared at his wife. He wouldn't talk to her about Lani. That was between him and Lani and would be tucked in his heart, in the deepest recesses of himself. He wouldn't let Kenya ruin it by trying to explain himself; divulging information that would only make her want more information, only make her obsess over details that she didn't need to know.

What would he say? "I felt a deeper attraction with Lani that I ever felt with you. I wish you knew how to release yourself and enjoy me like Lani does?" No. So it was best for him to say nothing at all.

Kenya crossed her arms. "You won't answer questions about Lani?"

"No."

"Why not?"

Christopher shrugged.

"She has ruined my life and you—"

"Kenya stop. Okay, I apologized and you should do the same. Then we can move on."

"Apologized? You apologized? Where was I when that happened? I never heard an apology."

337

Christopher sighed again, starting to fold his arms across his chests and then decided against it. He held his arms awkwardly at his side. He focused on his wife and watched her lips move around words that weren't important. Christopher hadn't really looked at her in the past few days. Her chocolate skin seemed ashen; the neat bun at the nape of her neck seemed frazzled. Her long eyelashes batted furiously as she spoke. He liked her narrow lips, narrow face and thin hips. They were wider than before his son was born, at least. She was statuesque. Wifey. His wifey. A queen, prepared and perfectly coifed for a life different from what he was. An ice queen. Rigid. Sometimes frigid. Sometimes. Her current meltdown was more emotion from her than he had ever witnessed before.

Although venom seemed to pour out of her mouth right now, her eyes contained panic. Pure panic. And Christopher knew that Kenya knew; that she realized that she was just as wrong as him. He sighed, thankful that he had picked up on that truth. This situation wasn't out of his control. Not at all. If Kenya was afraid, then she knew she was just as responsible as him, if not more so. But he knew her well. She wasn't going anywhere. If she had wanted to leave, she would have left already. A tear tumbled from her face and he watched it land soundlessly on the rug. Others followed, a river flowing from her depths.

"I'm sorry," Kenya mumbled. "Damnit, I'm sorry."

Christopher reached for her. But she took a step backward and wrapped her arms tightly around herself.

"I'm sorry too, baby. I swear I am."

"Are you done with her?" Kenya's question was valid, although Christopher didn't want to answer it. "Is it over?"

"I'm here. I'm home. This is where I am."

"Answer me, Christopher." She looked into his eyes deeply. "Is it over?"

His heart fell. He knew he couldn't have his cake and eat it, too, but he had hoped not to deal with this situation head on to eliminate making a promise he didn't want to keep. But Kenya pushed, giving Christopher no choice.

"It's over." He took another step toward her, and this time she didn't walk away. Kissing her forehead, Christopher wrapped his arms around his wife. He had almost lost his family. He could never let that happen again. "I love you Kenya."

She didn't reply.

Lifting her chin, Christopher stared into her eyes. "Did you hear me?"

"I heard you, but I know the truth. I know."

"Can we start over?"Christopher closed his eyes and waited for her answer.

"We can try," she whispered, shaking her head. "I don't want to lose what we have, but I know that you don't love me. Not like that."

"I do, Kenya." Christopher said the words that he felt he needed to say. "You will see that I do." Within the vortex of pain and confusion, he saw a glimpse of acceptance shining through. That is what he would have to focus on to strengthen his family. That is what he would have to rely upon to solidify his relationship with his wife. But for now, his heart opened and poured a thankful prayer to the heavens. At least he still had his family.

Chapter Fifty Three

Terrence kicked the rocks in front of him as he sat on the curb in front of the restaurant. He had to move, they would call the police on him soon. He didn't want to go back to jail. He wouldn't go back to jail. He should've strangled Lani, though. The way she had disrespected him in his house. He should've strangled her and then hit Christopher across his round head with a damn shovel. He could have put a quick end to all the bullshit that way. Terrence laughed loudly, then realized that any humor he found in the situation was a sign that he was still out of his mind.

Where should he go? *Shit, Kenya's is out.* Terrence laughed again, shaking his head. He could call a frat brother but he hadn't needed a favor like this in years, and most of his boys were married, anyway. The last thing he wanted was everyone in his business. How could he talk about it without letting it out that Lani had cheated and was cozied up with the man in *his* house.

Terrence wondered whether Kenya had made it home alright. He felt drained: worried about Kenya, mad at Kenya, wanting Kenya and hating Kenya. So much had happened that he had never considered before. More emotions dealing with Kenya in the last

341

few days than the past twenty years. He wanted to go home. To have Lani draw him a bath, scent the water for him and wash him with her ocean sponge. Maybe it could all go away. Maybe they could make it right.

No. I am not a damn punk. He stood quickly and walked down the main route. He wouldn't go to his parents; they didn't need to get involved. Not yet. His mother would have plenty to say and his father would shake his head and ask how he had let that fine daughter-in-law of his escape. He wouldn't tell them everything that Lani had done. They didn't need to know. He wouldn't tell them everything that he had done either. His mother would find his behavior inexcusable.

There were a few female friends that he kept in touch with and flirted with by email every now and then. But another woman right now was definitely not the solution. He wanted to be alone, and intruding their personal space would come with a price tag of indulging them or entertaining them. He wanted to go home.

Maybe I should check into a hotel. Chill for a few days, take vacation, and work things out. Can I forgive her anything? Shit. How can a man overcome this? There is no reason to stay; I can never trust her ass again. Maybe I could stay, but do my own thing. But then what is the point of staying. Because I miss her. Even now, even after she shot at me, I miss her. But, I have to have some self respect. Shit, she wouldn't want me now, if I came back groveling after all this. Plus, that bitch fired a gun at me.

A gun. Where had she gotten a gun? How long had he lived in a house with an irrational woman who had a gun hidden in the house? Had she considered using it before? Had his life been in question before and he didn't know it? Would she have actually shot him? In one night two things happened that were deal breakers. He had gone to jail and she had fired a gun at him. *No way in hell I am going home.*

There was a Comfort Inn up the street, a thirty minute drive, an hour walk. He patted his back pocket. He didn't have a wallet. He had left his personal belongings in the driveway, where they slipped out of his hands as he watched Christopher caress his wife. No hotel for him.

"SHIT!" He screamed into the thick night air. "SHIT, SHIT!"

Terrence punched the air in front of him, swinging with all of his might. Helplessness settled into his heart. He had nothing: no home, no money, no identification, no marriage, and no love. The sinking empty pain surrounded his mind and a destitute feeling overwhelmed him.

It was his entire fault. Lani had loved him. Completely. He had managed to let her slip away. For a quick, inexplicable moment, it occurred to him that he could easily end all this pain. He could simply attempt to cross the street of this major route and choose not to look right or left. At night, the cars raced through this area at least 20 miles over the speed limit. It could be over. The confusion, the hurt and the helplessness could all be over. He could easily be done with it. He turned around and glanced into oncoming traffic. It could be so simple ...

Terrence stepped slowly over the yellow line and his foot eased into the first lane. "God, forgive me."

It could be over. It could be over. Then they wouldn't know how he had failed, how he had ruined everything. No one would ever have to know. His mother wouldn't find out about jail, his father wouldn't shake his head in disappointment. Kenya would remember the good, and forget all the harsh words, all the blame. She would forget how helping him had caused her to lose her husband, her family. Lani would forget all the years of pain she had been suffering, staring at that computer screen, wondering about him, while he worked desperately to ignore her. It could all be erased. He took another step. This one felt more steady and direct. He would do it. This was right. It was the correct choice, the best way to rewind four days of turmoil, four days of hell. Maybe his godson would grow up and know about him. But then again, he wouldn't. They wouldn't want to tell him about his godfather's suicide. No one spoke about that. It was for the best.

Terrence hoped it wouldn't hurt too bad. He didn't want to be dragged or mutilated, yet left alive. "I give up." he whispered, his eyes staring at the ground as tears poured out of them.

He would miss seeing little Christopher grow up most of all. That was a privilege that he had lost this weekend, without a doubt. His godson, who would receive all he had, would never know him. The third step seemed more difficult to take.

Just do it. You won't get to see him anymore anyway. Kenya will never let you back in his world. And how many of your kids did you let Lani kill? You don't deserve any better anyway.

With the fourth step, he was completely off of the shoulder and was only a few steps from standing in the center of the first lane. He wondered if he would make it across all three lanes going in that direction before someone clocked him on the other side, in one of the three lanes going in the opposite direction.

"I'm tired," Terrence whispered. Horns were honking and he could hear the cars buzzing by, slamming on their horns and warning him not to cross. Terrence ignored them. Another step. A car slowed down with the horn blasting. The person slammed on the brakes, other cars swerved to avoid him, going around the car and Terrence. The bright lights shocked him. The window rolled down.

"What the fuck? Get your ass in this car."

Terrence stared at the cars swerving around him in shock. He couldn't move, certainly he was going to be killed in any moment. He didn't want to die. What the hell *was* he thinking?

"Get in the car before I get hit, then Imma be mad as hell." The voice had a Brooklyn accent. Terrence peered across the open window to the brown face sitting behind the wheel. He sighed with relief and then dread filled his heart. If Ricky was here, so was Dee.

Chapter Fifty Four

"Negro, damn, what were you thinking?"

Terrence stared straight ahead. He didn't know what he had been thinking, but Terrence certainly wasn't going to discuss his moment of weakness with Dee's man.

"Yo, are you in shock or something? You got me needing a damn drink. You scared the shit outta me. I saw you when I was passing on the other side, did a U-turn at the light. Didn't know if I was going to make it back in time."

"Where are we going?"

"I told you. I need a drink. Damn, you need one, too. You can't let no woman get in your head like this, especially them women we got." Ricky laughed.

"Had." Terrence stared straight ahead.

"No, got." Ricky steered the car into the parking lot of the restaurant Terrence had left. He turned off the engine and removed the key. "Come on, partna. Let's get something warm in us."

Terrence looked at him for the first time since he had climbed into the car. He didn't want to have to hear about this for the rest of his life. He just needed to dull the aching pain. Terrence dropped his head into his hands.

Ricky nodded. "Listen man, I know, alright? More of us go there than they talk about. It ain't anything new; they just don't report it when we do it. Alright? I ain't judging you. Let's get some food in ya."

He climbed out of the car and Terrence followed. Ricky walked around to Terrence and put his arm around his shoulder, patting him lightly on the back.

The waitress smiled pleasantly. "How many?"

"Two." Ricky looked around, twirling the tooth pick in his mouth. He watched the television screen for a little while taking in the sports highlights.

"Right this way, gentleman." Her blonde ponytail bounced as she walked and her blue eyes focused on Terrence. He tried not to look at her. She didn't stand a chance with him on a good day. Besides a few high school "experiments," Terrence didn't mess white girls. There was no option of taking them around his mother. He appreciated her interest, as she purposely leaned across him to move his silverware in place.

"Your server will be here in a moment. Is there anything I can do for you?" She smiled pointedly at Terrence.

He smiled back. She was way too young to be flirting with a grown ass man. He had to chuckle. "No, thanks, but I'm good."

"Yes." She grinned widely and turned around, while maintaining eye contact. "I am sure you are."

Terrence laughed out loud as she walked away.

"Damn, she didn't ask me shit." Ricky laughed, leaning back in the booth.

"Ricky, I didn't even know you talked this much."

Ricky shrugged, "I guess we never had much to say to each other, huh?"

Terrence glanced at the table and then the television. After an awkward pause, he met Ricky's eyes. "Man, I don't even know how to begin."

"It's alright. We are from different walks of life, no doubt."

Terrence nodded. "I have messed some shit up, that's for real."

"Yeah, ya'll have been on some dramatic shit the past coupla days. Messin' my home life all up. Got me on the road when I could be getting taken care of, you know?"

Terrence nodded. "I sure wish I was with my wife right now."

Another thin white girl approached the table, a more practical type. She took their orders, delivered chips and walked away.

"Boy, what the hell has been going on?" Ricky leaned forward with his elbows on the table. "You had Dee ready to tune your ass up."

"I bet," he laughed. "She never liked my 'pretty ass' anyway."

"Naw, that ain't true. She likes you. She just thinks you take her baby sister for granted. And after she sacrificed her life for that girl, Dee takes it personal, you know."

"I am starting to figure out."

"Yeah, if she didn't like you, she woulda sent them wild ass cousins of theirs down here days ago."

Terrence shook his head, chuckling. It hadn't been funny before. Before, he thought they were ignorant and ghetto. Now, he saw it differently. Saw Lani as being a diamond and her family a protective hedge. *They had to protect her from me?* "I probably deserve that ass whipping, man."

"Don't no one deserve that foolishness. Them fools tried me one time—" Ricky put up one finger for emphasis, "—trust me, they won't never step my way again."

They sat in silence. Ricky slid the salt shaker back and forth between his hands across the smooth surface of the table.

"You know what I don't get about you? Since we are being real?" The words came out of nowhere. Terrence looked at him, waiting for the worse.

"If you ain't like who Lani was, why'd you get with her?"

"What do you mean?" Terrence asked.

"I mean, we ain't your type of people. You made that obvious. And Lani never lied about who she was."

Terrence shrugged. "No, it wasn't like that. I never thought about it like that. I just, I just didn't fit in with her family."

Ricky sat back and stared at the television over Terrence's head. Their drinks arrived. Terrence stuffed the lime into his Corona, while Ricky grabbed a

Budweiser. They both picked up a chicken wing and bit into it. The hostess walked past and winked at him as she led another couple to a table. Terrence almost choked and looked away.

Ricky held his bottle up. "Well man, to us—the men in love with these crazy ass women."

Terrence laughed, wiped the sauces from his hand and lifted his bottle and tapped Ricky's. They ate and drank in comfortable silence, Terrence was thankful to have a warm body next to him, someone who knew without him telling, and didn't hate him. Ricky finished his second beer and slammed it onto the table with emphasis.

"No more for me."

"Yeah man, you're driving."

"You ready?"

The uneasiness that had trapped Terrence earlier began to return. "I just need a hotel room, somewhere to lay low."

"By yourself? Hell no. You got too much on your mind, that's for damn sure. I'm taking your ass home."

"Man, I can't." Terrence met Ricky's eyes. "I think we are finished. She won't leave. I know she ... cheated."

"What?"

"Yep, my best friend's husband."

"Aw damn." They sat in silence again. "I don't have any words for that one."

Terrence understood. He didn't have any more words either.

"Listen. I got some repairs to your front window, front yard, garage door. I ain't doing them by myself. Your ass is coming home. They will just have to deal with it."

"She shot at me."

"Aw damn." This time Terrence laughed out loud at Ricky. "What did you do to get shot at?"

"I lost my mind."

"Yeah," Ricky winked, "I could see that."

Ricky rubbed his head and motioned to the waitress for the bill. "Dee is blowing me up. I have been trying to ignore her, but it's getting worse. We gotta go."

"Will you take me to the hotel?"

"Damn, man. I guess I don't have a choice. If she shot at you ..." Sighing, he snapped open the vibrating phone.

"Yeah, Dee, I got him right here, we just finished eating. He's alright. He ain't bleeding or nothing. Yeah, I know. What? Hell no. No, we are not driving back to New York tonight. Women, I am tired as all hell." Ricky looked over at Terrence while he nodded and listened to his wife.

The restaurant was too loud for Terrence to hear anything. The waitress returned with bill and Ricky tucked money into the bill carrier while listening carefully to the instructions streaming out of Dee. Terrence watched quietly, aware that his fate was being decided without his input.

"Alright babe. Alright. Naw, I'm good, just had a couple. Alright babe. That can wait. Alright, in a few." He snapped the phone together, chuckling and shaking his head slightly. "When you find a good woman, you got to hang on to her."

"What did she say?"

"I got to take you home, man. If you want to go to the hotel after that, I got you. But, I don't wanna have to argue with my wife on this one. Ain't worth it man."

"I understand." Terrence felt like he was going to execution. How would he be heard between Lani and her sister?

"Don't worry though, my man," Ricky said slowly, watching his expression. "Dee is trying to find a way to make this right."

Chapter Fifty Five

The front door was unlocked. Miles hated when she did that, when she left the doors open as if pleading for him to return. What if some stranger just happened to try the door and walked in on his wife? What would he do if something unforgivable occurred because he was out and his wife wanted him to return? Almost sabotage.

Like setting up something bad to happen so it could be my fault. But Miles knew better. Jackie was simply too practical to place herself in harm's way. She didn't want him to wake her, fumbling around for his key in the middle of the night, ringing the door bell when his patience finally wore thin. He knew that was the reason. But Miles also hoped that she unlocked the door to let him know that he would always be welcome home, the door would always be open. He hoped. Right now, he honestly didn't know what Jackie thought.

Miles stood in the doorway for several minutes. He needed to clear his mind before he entered. They led a peaceful life for this very reason; both composed themselves before dealing with the other. But now this very method made Miles convinced that they were just going through the motions, living polite but disentangled. Sighing, he opened the door.

"Hey babe," came Jackie's warm voice, causing a flood of emotion to surge through his body. He felt himself rise to attention and shifted his pants in an attempt to cover himself. Just the sound of her voice could mess him up.

Miles put his keys on the sofa table. "What you doing up?"

"Couldn't sleep," she answered. He followed the sound of her voice around the corner of the foyer, into the informal dining room. Pictures lay all over the crème table cloth, along with scrapbooks, colored paper and little colorful items. Turning his head, Miles examined one of the photos.

"I decided to print out the pictures I took this weekend. With C.J." she said lightly.

"C.J.?"

"What I call him when he's here. Since Kenya won't let us use nicknames." She shook her head and chuckled. "As if little Christopher is better. At least C.J. doesn't throw in a hip hop moniker."

Miles turned slightly. He didn't want to see the pictures and he didn't want to think about the baby. It was alright for her to want a baby and yearn for it, but his longing had to be bottled up. The last thing he needed, with his alcohol content hindering on extremely drunk, was to talk about the baby.

Miles bumped into the doorway as he walked back to the kitchen. "Why do this now? Don't you need to get some rest?"

"It's alright. Look—here is when you were feeding him. I thought you were going to drop him for a second."

"Yeah, so did I." Miles chuckled. He moved closer to her, kissing her softly on the cheek. She moved and leaned her face away. She must smell the alcohol. But she didn't ask. And he knew she wouldn't.

Straightening her back, Jackie continued rearranging pictures, observing them and placing them on the colored sheets.

I guess I am dismissed. He chuckled again, taking a step back. The shorty at the bar with the bountiful boobs didn't seem like such a bad option after all. *I could have had her from every direction, and still I wouldn't have even had to answer for it.* Shaking his head, he headed back to the foyer to hang up his jacket.

"Did you eat?"

"Huh?" Miles stumbled backward.

"I said did you eat something? If not, I can warm up some dinner."

"You cooked?" He sounded slurred. It must be bad if even he noticed it.

"Yeah. I came down to apologize and fix you some dinner, but you were gone." Her voice trailed off wistfully. It was the closest she would come to letting him know she was upset, that she didn't appreciate him leaving, that she had decided to apologize and cook, only to find him gone. He understood her well and knew that this was her way.

"I'll take a taste of what you cooked." The least he could do was eat. And it would get her away from those damn pictures and thoughts of babies.

Miles heard her chair slide back as she moved away from the table. He walked toward the kitchen again, following behind her. She wore a simple robe that zipped up the front; her hair was pulled back into a simple ponytail. He still thought her beautiful. Before he could think, he reached out and rested his hand on the curve of her hips.

Jackie stopped walking. She didn't resist and didn't turn away. He took it as a good sign. Holding her by her hips he pulled her backward into him and pressed her firmly against his hips, he slid his hands to rest against her thighs.

"Are you alright?" Miles whispered.

"I'm better, now."

"Why now."

"Because you're home."

"I needed some fresh air."

"Don't explain." Jackie shook her head a little. "I never doubt you."

Damn. He knew that those were words millions of men would wait a lifetime and still never hear. This was why Jackie was the wife for him, the woman he loved. He turned her around gently. "You don't ever doubt me?"

"No. Never." She didn't blink, looking directly into his eyes. "I know you love me. That's all I need."

"Are you sure?" Miles breathed. "It doesn't feel like I am enough for you. Not when …"

"Miles, I want a baby. That has nothing to do with us. It's just not fair. I, I …" she shook her head, closed her eyes and leaned it to his chest.

No. It isn't fair. But it isn't fair to me either. I could have a child with any woman. I am choosing to be childless for my wife. For my love of her. And what acknowledgement do I get for my sacrifice in the name of love? But he would never utter those words.

"I'm sorry for burdening you, though. I know how much you are giving up for me." Jackie leaned back and looked into his eyes. "Believe me, I know. And I don't know if it's right to ask so much …"

Guilt flooded his mind. She knew. She knew what he had been thinking. And she felt bad about it. The last thing he needed to do was add to her misery. She deserved so much more.

Miles kissed the tip of her nose. "I haven't lost anything. You are everything I will ever need." He kissed her forehead, her cheek, and her soft full lips and put all his painful thoughts behind him.

Chapter Fifty Six

When Ricky pulled into the yard, Terrence felt his breath catch in his throat. His house looked like a battlefield. Christopher's wrecked car sat awkwardly at the edge of the driveway, the rear tire on the passenger's side was hiked up on the curve, the driver's side smashed beyond repair and glass sprinkled the ground like drops of rain. His front window was also shattered. A golf club jutted from the bushes and the grass appeared trampled in various spots.

"Damn," he muttered.

"Yeah, damn." Ricky agreed. "I never wanted to see this place like this. We gonna have to call a tow truck in the morning and get that car out of here. Then we got to repair that front window, do something with the yard. You see what I mean ..."

Terrence pointed to the trampled grass spots and sighed. "Come on man, let's get this over with."

Feeling like he was marching to his doom, Terrence followed Ricky to the front door and waited as Ricky rang the bell. The door opened immediately.

"Ricky...I was just passing the door," she said. Her smooth voice caught him by surprise. He hadn't prepared to see Lani just yet. Lani smiled faintly at Ricky, a 'relieved to see you' sort of smile. Obviously, no one had informed her that Terrence was with him, because her warm face immediately turned to stone when she caught sight of him.

Lani looked back and forth between Ricky and Terrence, stunned. "How, how ... how did he wind up with ..."

Ricky took a step forward. "Lani, Dee thought he should come over."

She shook her head slightly and then stepped back into the foyer. Ricky followed her and walked right past her, disappearing around the corner and walking faster than Terrence had ever seen him move. Terrence stepped into the foyer and observed Lani. She stared back at him.

"Well, you didn't hit me. With the bullets anyway," he said quietly.

"I can see that."

"You don't sound too remorseful."

"I didn't aim to harm you."

That shut him up. He hadn't even known she had a gun, now he was learning that she actually knew how to use it. The whole thing was disconcerting. What else was Lani capable of, what other "skills" did she possess?

Terrence leaned back against the wall. She would be gorgeous no matter what. Despite the swollen eyes and the red nose, he still thought she looked incredible. *I love her. This isn't even love, what I feel, it's something more. There is no word for more than love, but that's what I feel. I can get past this. I can forgive her. I know that I would never have thought it possible, that I would scoff at anyone I know who stayed with a woman who put them through this much shit. But I could stay. I could forgive her. I could forgive her anything.* "So now what?"

Lani shrugged, closing the front door. She leaned against the front door, standing side by side with Terrence.

"We really fucked up." Terrance waited for her to answer, wondered if she would answer with animosity on her tongue.

"Yep. We did."

"I can forgive you. Can we work past it?" There, he had said it. He let her know that he wanted to stay and try. He had put the unthinkable on the table. He wondered if she would feel relieved.

"I don't know."

Terrence snorted. "I think, under the circumstances, that you have a little more to be sorry for than me." He shouldn't have said that. He realized it as soon as the words departed his lips.

"I have more to be sorry about? How do you figure? Did I ignore you and treat you like shit for years? Did I run in after my married best friend like a damn puppy? Did you spend our entire marriage being the third wheel to any man that took priority in my life? Hell no. You don't want me. Haven't for years—"

"That's not true—"

"Yes it is. When was the last time you made love to me? You don't even know. Fucking me in between telephone conversations with your damn girlfriend.

Everything with me has to be rushed because you and Kenya got so many plans."

"Lani, no! That's not true! You were with Christopher. I saw you! You were with him for an entire weekend. I saw you, damnit. Don't deny it ..."

"I was with him for a weekend. You've been with her our entire relationship. How can you even compare the two?"

"But ..." This was going the wrong way, he was fading fast. His position of power felt like it was slipping. How had she done that—flipped the script so that her weekend of cheating seemed less scandalous than his friendship. *This is insane. I'm not apologizing. She's in the wrong, not me!* He stared at her, his neck strained to focus on her standing next to him, her back flat against the wall.

"YOU WALKED OUT!!" she screamed, her eyes bugged out. She wasn't looking at him, but straight ahead. "You know what that means. That means that, in your heart and mind, this marriage was over. So what I did after you told me to go to hell and left me is not worth apologizing for. You know why? Because I was husbandless at that point ..."

Terrence sputtered "Lani, you can't just decide to be husbandless. What are you talking about? We had an argument, I left to calm down, and when I came back you were playing games."

"Bullshit. I said your name and you said ..."

"I know what I said. I didn't say I wasn't coming back—"

"Oh my God. I'm not doing this...I am not going over every word for you to give them a different meaning." She still refused to look at him, tears pouring down her face. "You left..."

"I didn't leave. As usual, you got to make shit more dramatic than...."

"Terrence, THIS MARRIAGE IS OVER!" Lani turned and looked him dead in the eye, her breathing heavy and ragged; her chest rising and falling. She threw herself back against the wall, as if using it to support herself.

He stood there stunned, his head shaking his mouth opening and closing. *She can't declare the marriage over. She's lucky to have me. Who the hell does she think she is?* She had missed the point and didn't understand that he was willing to forgive her, willing to let her stay. Maybe he had said it wrong. Didn't she understand how much of his pride he was destroying by taking her back? Wasn't that pure proof of his love to her?

Terrence forced out a response. "No, I'm telling you, despite what you did, I am willing to stay."

She grinned but the grin was sad and confused. He kept talking, hoping he could clarify his intent. "I am saying that although *you* violated us, we can work it out. We can get counseling or something, but we can work it out."

Tears tumbled down her eyes, falling over that sad little grin which was pissing him off. "Terrence, you don't understand. I don't want to be married to you anymore."

Terrence stared at her.

Lani kept talking, filling the silence with finality. "I can't do this anymore. Isn't that what you said to me? That's how it all started, right, me begging and you realizing that you couldn't be in this relationship anymore. So now I am agreeing with you. This is something we both need to walk away from. You did it first and I tried to hold on. I should have walked away then. But I am doing it now."

"So, what, you don't want me. *You? You* are walking away from *me?*" Terrence couldn't believe it. How could she possibly be leaving him?

"No." She spoke slowly, as if he were hard of hearing. "You left. I am finally letting go."

"I get it." Terrence walked to the steps. "Back to the tit for tat shit, right. Still these high school games—you have to have the last word, you have to make sure that *I* hurt as much as I made you hurt. Alright, Lani, I get it."

"Terrence, I am not keeping score. And I damn sure am not playing games."

"The hell you aren't." Terrence sat down to balance his body and keep from falling over from the blood rushing his head. "Has it ever occurred to you that I could have had enough? Enough of you. Enough of Kenya. Enough of being treated like shit and being second in your life. I have had enough, too."

"You need to think about this. Think about what you're saying. I am not easily replaced; you won't get this lucky twice."

"Wow." Lani shook her head and slid to the floor. "Lucky, huh? Damn, Terrence, how about letting me know what you really think."

"Lani, you know what I mean."

"Yeah, I do. And that's the problem. You think you're better than me. Years of listening to you judge me. Feeling your judgment. I *was* your wife, but you judge me."

"You are my wife."

"Not anymore, Terrence. I won't do this anymore."

Placing his knees on his elbows, Terrence leaned over and hung his head. She didn't want him anymore. It had never occurred to him that she had a choice or that she wouldn't choose him. He suddenly felt lost, like one little person in the huge mass and confusion of the world.

"I don't want to be without you, Lani," he whispered.

"We aren't a partnership. I can't worry about what you do or don't want." There was no emotion in her voice.

His head snapped up. That was such a cold answer from her, so blatant and matter of fact. He hadn't heard her talk like this since the beginning of the relationship when they first met. "I don't mean anything to you then."

Lani sighed. "You mean everything to me. But my everything just isn't good enough for you. And I accept that."

"What happens next?"

"I don't know."

They sat in silence for a long time. He wanted to hug her, to hold her, to cry and beg and tell her how he couldn't imagine life without her. But her tone held finality to it that Terrence knew was impenetrable. He had pushed too far, stretched out this relationship cord and lost the elasticity to reel her back in.

"What about our home? Our life?" Terrence looked around the huge foyer.

"We should sell everything and start over."

Lani wants to purge herself of anything related to us, huh? Terrence grasped at his head, his fingers running through his spongy soft hair. "So that's it?"

"Yep, that's it."

"And you're sure?"

Lani nodded. "You can stay until we get this straightened out."

"You won't feel the same way tomorrow."

Lani stared at him, "Believe me, this is one decision I'm sticking to."

Terrence had to ask for clarity. "So, you don't love me."

"I adore you-it's more than love. You know that, Terrence. But I gotta love me more."

Terrence stared at the ceiling of the high foyer. He felt at a loss, unable to understand Lani's logic. *If she loves me, how can she let me go?* He leaned over, his head between his knees and his fingers clasped on the back of his neck. He needed to contain his composure, to keep from crying right here. He glanced up and noticed that Lani looked like a rag doll, sitting limply on the floor, her legs now crossed and her elbows planted on her thighs.

"So, you love me, but it's over."

She sighed, tears pouring down her face and dropping on the marble floor. "Yes."

Lani stood and walked out of the room. Terrence slumped against the wall and focused his attention on the dense hollow feeling taking over his chest. He had lost her. And this time he knew it was for real.

Epilogue

Dear Sophie,

I am sure you heard. My life has flipped upside down. I can only imagine Dee filling you in on all the drama that went down. But I am doing alright.

I owe you an apology. A lifetime of apologies. I am sorry for having judged you, for letting so much time go between visiting you or sending you something to know that you are loved and thought about.

The night that Tommy died, my life changed. The unstable existence that we had, with Dee and I trying to protect ourselves while you were out working, living and trying to make it, seemed to just evaporate into thin air. I am sure things were rough for you time, probably much worse than for us. But, as a little girl, I went from feeling safe to living every moment waiting for the tight rope holding my life together to snap.

I wish we could have that time back. I wish that Dee and I were enough for you to stay home with, to spend time with. I wish that we had been enough so that men like Tommy wouldn't have to be in our lives. And I guess I hated you, because we weren't enough and your search brought in so many horrible men.

How can a little girl understand that? Only now, as a grown woman, do I understand the need for partnership, the search for love in a man.

Aunt Marie tried hard to fill in the gap for you. She loved us. She and Aunt Sharon formed a wall of protection around us, as best they could. But Dee and I also watched love decimate them one by one. They were no different from you, me, every other woman in search of fulfillment through men.

When Aunt Lela's husband left her for a younger woman, she never quite got over it. She cleans up when she comes to see you, but I am sure you know she is normally in a drunken stupor, like an incoherent ghost of her previous self. Then Auntie Marie found her second husband Mark (do you remember him?) trying to climb in her daughter Lela's bed. I know she never told you about that. She tried to pretend like it didn't happen, until Dee told Uncle Lonzo. They stomped his ass something terrible. I don't know if they ever found him. But it didn't matter, Lela never really recovered from that and now she claims she can't stand men. Dee is always telling her that no one can stand them, that has nothing to do with keeping one. Dee is forever optimistic, who would think that after all this she would be the one who still believes in love.

Life is weird that way, I guess.

But in the end, I finally realize that you paid the ultimate price. Mommy, I hate that you are in that place, that you have to breathe a second behind those bars. The thought breaks my heart, that's the real reason I don't visit or write. It's selfish of me, I know, but visiting and writing makes me think about you in there, and I feel so helpless and scared that it swallows me.

I'm not like Dee. She can come up there with her daughters and everything, like nothing is wrong. But I can't. God knows I have tried. Do you have any idea how many times I just wanted to be near you, even if I had nothing to say? But I can't take it. I try to imagine how you sleep, eat, shower ... stay sane. I would have lost it a long time ago.

But those are all my excuses, all my selfish reasons. And they made sense before, when I was angry at you. They were sufficient justification, then. But I recently stood in your shoes. And I finally learned how closely related love and hate actually are.

The thin border between love and hate literally disappeared. I can't let myself ever get that close to the invisible border again. If I do, then everything you fought for and all of Dee's sacrifices for me will have been for nothing. And I owe you both more. Much more.

Terrence had the ability to make me lose myself in hate or worse: self pity and anguish. I have to remove myself from the chaos. The way I have been behaving, like a femme fatale version of Dr. Jekyll and Mr. Hyde, is ridiculous. I have been doing everything in my power to get this husband of mine to love me. What is wrong with me? I guess you're right—when will I start loving me? Tell me, Mommy, when does that happen?

I allowed him to embarrass me, manipulate me and humiliate me for years. I have lost my babies and destroyed my idea of my life, to do whatever he needs and wants. And I can't forgive myself. I can't release the idea of my children, I can't let go of the belief of the family that I signed on for. And the only way I can let go and move on is to walk away. Mommy, I am walking away from it all.

You told me that I was worthy of love once, years ago. Those words have played over and over again in my mind over the past several months. I am worthy of love and Christopher showed me that. I am worthy of love and Dee reminded me of that. I am worthy of love and Kenya and Terrence reminded me of that. You paid a price for my success. You made a choice for me to have a future when you had to kill instead of be killed, instead of leaving us to the mercy of a madman.

Dee paid for my life through her sweat and tears, working to send me money for college and to make sure that I had what everyone else had, while she lived in the projects and made by on next to nothing. And I sold you both out when I didn't demand more. I dismissed you both when I allowed myself to be the butt of every inside joke, the unspoken cause of every eye roll among Terrence's inner circle. I sold out the sacrifice of all my aunties who held my family together and gave me a sense of self, despite my wanting to hide that you were in jail.

So, the marriage is over. Terrence and I lived together for another few months, in separate bedrooms, until we could sell the house. I avoided him and spent weekends in New York reconnecting with "us," with my real family. During the week, I worked long hours at the firm and did everything in my power not to see Terrence's face or give into his demands.

In the beginning, he didn't believe I was finished. He waited for me to change my mind, for us to fall into our normal routine. But he soon noticed that I wasn't engaging in any relationship things. I had the lawyer draw up the separation papers. When I handed them to him he shredded them. I left copies for him every day until, in a fit of anger, he signed them. That time he stomped around the house yelling and screaming. I wondered whether he recognized the behavior and finally understood the frustration that caused it. The repercussions of all that frustration that would make a person act like a maniac.

So, the house sold. I have my own apartment. I didn't argue over the disbursement of the proceeds. Terrence is furious and being nasty, so I got nothing. But I will get what is rightfully mine during the divorce proceedings. If I demand it. And I don't care. I feel free. I feel whole. I feel as if I am worth something again, even if it is just me, myself and I. I don't need the money or any of the superficial stuff anyway.

I haven't seen Christopher. Terrence made a point of telling me that Christopher and Kenya stayed together. He said it tauntingly, as if he were stating that Kenya was the winner in all this. And she is. Because she has Christopher. I feel sorry for him, sorry that he is trapped in a marriage that doesn't give him the type of love he deserves. But I am also proud of him. He is an honest and good person. He sacrificed his life and what it could be to stay in a marriage for his son. What more could a person want in an individual, in a husband?

Kenya sent a note of apology to our house soon after the big blow up. Typical. So polite and perfunctory. She is still a bitch. She apologized to our "household" for her "unsavory display" and hoped that everyone would be "mature" enough to move on.

I ain't. I still hate her ass. I still hate that she hides behind that stiff, superficial bullshit. She didn't owe my household an apology, she owed me an apology. And by not acknowledging that, by not admitting that she was a contributor in the years of nonsense that I put up with between her and my husband, her little empty note pissed me off even more.

I wondered if she sent the note because of Christopher, more of a demonstration to him of her maturity, than any real caring for us. Either way, I poured ketchup and mustard on it, put it in the toaster oven for a few minutes, sprayed a dollop of whip cream on it, with one cherry, and left it on the counter on my finest china for her little boyfriend, my husband. She and Terrence belong together.

I miss Christopher, but I love him too much to mess with his life in any way. I don't want to cause him any more pain or hurt. And his son deserves the family that he is trying to provide for him. He deserves that security. Christopher sent a text message. Just one, in all this time. The message was perfect, "I heard. I am sorry. Will always B here 4 u. When u r ready."

Sometimes I miss Terrence. Not the current him, but the Terrence I fell in love with. I miss those days when we spent hours wrapped in each other, only separating because of some necessary thing. I miss how he used to adore me, used to watch me in awe and tell me he had never met anyone like me. I miss the scent of pure love. I should have paid attention, though, and noticed when that smell turned stale. I won't ever linger and inhale stale love again.

So, Mommy, I finally get it. If you choose to live this life, then you will experience pain, hurt and shame, along with beauty, love, glory. There will be a down to many ups. But, the test is, do you have the courage to keep pressing forward, to keep living life despite the painful valleys? For a while, I guess, I stopped living. I existed without contributing. What was it that you said—that I had lost my color? You were right. I ran around in an endless trap of despair, hiding from life, hoping to force my dream into a reality, into a barrier to protect me. But the dream never manifested and I accepted misery as a constant.

Now, I have decided to live. To step out in front and take what life throws my way, without cover or comfort. And, for the first time in years, I feel good about myself. Relieved that I am engaging, living and surviving this thing called life. I hope that you will one day find a reason to be proud of me. Until that time, I am working on being proud of myself.

Love,

Lani

www.guaranteedpaperpublishing.com
www.facebook.com/guaranteedpaper
www.twitter.com/guaranteedpp

Guaranteed to bring you the hottest!!!

~ New Edition ~

GUARANTEED PAPER PUBLISHING PRESENTS

OLO SHIVERS

A SEXY COLLECTION OF EROTIC SHORT STORIES BY

WILSON

COMING SOON